Blood on the Arch

Also by Robert J. Randisi

Murder Is the Deal of the Day
In the Shadow of the Arch
Alone with the Dead

Blood on the Arch

A Joe Keough Mystery

Robert J. Randisi

Thomas Dunne Books
St. Martin's Minotaur ❧ New York

THOMAS DUNNE BOOKS.
An imprint of St. Martin's Press.

BLOOD ON THE ARCH. Copyright © 2000 by Robert J. Randisi. All rights reserved. Printed in the United States of America. No part of this book may be used or reproduced in any manner whatsoever without written permission except in the case of brief quotations embodied in critical articles or reviews. For information, address St. Martin's Press, 175 Fifth Avenue, New York, N.Y. 10010.

www.minotaurbooks.com

ISBN 0-312-24179-8

First Edition: May 2000

10 9 8 7 6 5 4 3 2 1

Blood on the Arch

Prologue

THE BLOOD SHONE wetly on the silvery reflective surface of the Arch.

It's a messy thing to batter a man to death. The killer stared for a moment. It looked more black than red in the moonlight. He decided not to try and clean it off but rather to leave it as a beacon. After all, the body was going to have to be found sooner or later.

He grabbed the dead man by his ankles and dragged him down the ramp toward the entrance of the Arch Museum—which also led to the Arch itself. The dead man's head left a bloody trail of brain and bone behind. The killer had a key, so getting inside was no problem.

The museum was dark and quiet. Earlier in the week he had paced off his route so he wouldn't need any lights. He knew the schedule kept by security. He had time to finish.

He dragged the dead man right to the tram without missing a step.

One

THE SKY WAS filled with kites of all sizes, shapes, and colors. It was the Forest Park Festival of Kites, the first one Keough had attended since moving to St. Louis a little over nine months ago.

Valerie Speck was standing next to him, watching the display with wide-eyed fascination.

"How do you manage to keep them from getting tangled with each other?" she asked.

"You have to have the touch," he said, "the magic t—"

"Luck?"

He laughed. "A lot of that."

"I had no idea there were so many varieties," she said, shading her eyes from the sun with her right hand. It was difficult to look up into the bright sky, even with sunglasses on. "Why is yours so . . . plain?"

"I like plain," he said. "Besides, I hate having to reel them back in. It'd be foolish of me to buy expensive kites."

Although they'd been seeing each other for just over six months—having met during his very first case in St. Louis— she had never been kite flying with him. She understood it was a private thing, a respite from the rigors of his job, and she respected that. What she didn't know was that he also used the time to think, to solve problems, whether they were private or business related. He would never be able to do that if someone were with him.

This day was different, though. There were thousands of people and hundreds of kites, but no time to think or be alone.

The irony here was that Keough *wanted* to be alone with her, especially today. He had some things he wanted to discuss with her, but that would have to come later. . . .

A beeper went off.

"Yours or mine?" she asked.

"Mine."

He looked down at the instrument clipped to the right side of his belt. He kept his holster on the left. The display was his office number. It was either Captain McGwire or his partner, Detective Al Steinbach. His money was on the captain.

Somebody was dead. He'd never quite thought of it that way before, but they only called him when somebody was dead.

"Joe?"

He looked at Valerie but decided not to let her in on his thoughts. Instead, he scanned the crowd.

"What are you looking for?" she asked.

He held up one finger, then smiled, and beckoned her to follow him.

They approached a small boy of about five or six who was watching the kites in awe.

"Hello," Keough said, crouching down.

The boy wiped his nose on his arm and said, "I'm not supposed to talk to strangers, mister."

"Is that what your mommy told you?"

"Yes."

"Well, that shows how smart she is," Keough said, "but you see," and he took out his badge, "I'm a policeman."

"A really real policeman?"

"A really real one."

The boy looked at Valerie and asked, "For true?"

She had been watching Keough with the little boy, thinking how good he was with children—thinking it *again*, since it had been a child's plight that had brought them together. When the boy spoke to her, she smiled reassuringly.

"Yes, he really is."

"Do you have a kite?" Keough asked.

"No."

"Would you like one?"

The boy looked at the string in Keough's hand and then followed it up.

"Which one is it?"

"The red one, right up there," Keough said, pointing. "It's my favorite color. What's yours?"

"Blue."

"Oh."

"But I like red, too," the boy was quick to point out.

"Well, good," Keough said. "It's yours, then."

The child started to reach out, then pulled his hand back, and said in a conspiratorial whisper, "I better ask my mom, first."

"Why don't you take us to her," Keough suggested, "and we can ask her together?"

The boy thought this was a great idea, then tugged on Keough's windbreaker, and led the way.

"Whatta we got?" Keough said into the pay phone.

"A bad one," Captain McGwire answered. "Your partner's down there, but I need you there, too."

"It's my day off, Cap."

"I need you, Joe," McGwire said.

Keough had spent his time in St. Louis becoming the city's number-one homicide man. A lot of cops held it against him, but most realized he'd reached that point based on his abilities—abilities he'd honed working for the New York City Police Department for the better part of a dozen years. He liked being judged on his talents, he liked being needed, and he enjoyed being number one—even if it did occasionally interfere with his private life.

"All right, give me the address."

"That's easy. It's under the Arch."

"*Under* the Arch?"

"Right under it."

"Okay, I'm on my way."

He hung up and turned away from the phone to face Valerie, who had heard his end of the conversation.

"Who's under the Arch?" she asked.

"I don't know," he said. "I'll find out when I get there."

"When *we* get there, you mean."

"No," he said, "you're going home."

"Can't. We came in one car . . . yours."

She had a point. Her car was parked in front of his house in the Central West End, which actually wasn't that far from where they now stood.

"I can take you back—"

"I think you told your captain you'd be right there," she said. "I'll come with you."

"Valerie—"

"You won't even know I'm there."

"Val—"

"You're wasting time, Joe."

He ground his teeth hard enough to make a muscle in his cheek jump, then he took her arm and said, "Okay, let's go."

Two

KEOUGH HAD ONLY seen the Arch close-up twice since moving to St. Louis. He decided to park on the top level of the municipal lot because he didn't know any other way to get there.

Valerie got out of the car with him and together they walked to the landmark. There was a group congregating on one side of the southernmost base, yellow crime-scene tape had been strung about. Several patrolmen were trying to hold the onlookers back.

Keough spotted his partner, Steinbach, among the group just as Steinbach saw him and waved him over.

"Stay here," he told Valerie, touching her arm. "I'll be back as soon as I can."

"I'll be fine, Joe. Just do your job."

Before getting out of the car, he had taken from the glove compartment a line of elastic that had a metal clip on each end. He was dressed casually in a T-shirt and light windbreaker, with no pocket from which to hang his shield case as ID. He clipped the case to the elastic and hung it around his neck.

Keough knew very little about the Arch and, in truth, didn't care how high it was, how wide it was at the base, or how long it took to build. He'd felt the same way about the Statue of Liberty and the Empire State Building when he lived in New York. They were there. He enjoyed looking at them but had never been up in any of them. Right now he was more concerned with the blood on the southern base of the Arch and the bloody trail leading from it.

"Where's this go?" he asked Steinbach.

"To the elevator," Steinbach said, "only it's not an elevator."

"What is it?"

"It's a tram, or a trainlike thing. There are two, south and north—"

"Okay, explain to me what it is later, Al. For now, tell me what we've got . . . or need I ask?"

"A body, Joe, in one of the trams. We can go down and have a look in a minute. We're still waiting for a captain to show up."

"None of us can go anywhere until he does," the ME said.

The medical examiner's name was Donaldson, a generally cheerful man who enjoyed his job immensely; however, he exhibited few of the clichés one expected from a man in his position. He did not eat while happily dipping his hands into some poor corpse's intestines; he did not make jokes about cadavers at the crime scene, and he did not delight in causing young detectives to faint at their first autopsy. He was a thoroughly professional man who could not help but smile day in and day out, no matter how many bodies came into the morgue. And it was because he smiled so much his nickname was "Smiley," not because he was a dour man.

Keough genuinely liked the man.

"We'll get through as fast as possible, Doc."

"That's okay," Donaldson said. "I'll wait. I wouldn't want you to be anything but your usual anal self, Detective."

Keough looked at Steinbach. "Okay, what have we got?"

"Security came by and saw the blood on the structure and on the ground."

"When was this?"

"This morning. He only saw it in the daylight, never noticed it during the night."

"And did he follow the trail?"

"He did. It goes down the ramp and inside the museum, right to the Arch tram."

Keough frowned. "How did the killer get inside?"

Steinbach shrugged. "No sign of forced entry, and the alarm never went off. I guess he had a key."

"Sounds pretty stupid to me," the ME said.

"What does, Doc?" Keough asked.

"Letting you fellas know he had a key. Stupid."

"Or arrogant."

"How so?" the doctor asked.

"He's letting us know he has a key because he doesn't care if we know," Keough said. "He's telling us we're not smart enough to catch him."

"Hmm," Donaldson said, "I never thought of that."

"What about all these people?" Keough asked. "Any witnesses?"

"No," Steinbach said, "apparently not. They started to gather only after we got here."

"Have someone talk to them."

"I'll get on it. You ready to go down?"

"Let me have a look here first."

Keough took in the scene quickly. The blood had spattered when the blows were struck. The blood on the ground was obviously from the wound. The killer had dragged the body by its feet, leaving the trail behind it. Keough quickly looked around in every direction.

"I've had uniforms searching the grounds," Steinbach said.

"Mmm, good," Keough said. His own cursory examination of the area had turned up nothing. "How far are they looking?"

"Starting here up to and including the Arch park across the

street. Every inch of the grounds. If the killer dropped something, or left anything, they'll find it."

Keough stared doubtfully at the crowd, which by now
could have trampled a small but important piece of evidence.
There was nothing to be done about it now, though.

"Ready?" Steinbach asked again.

"Yeah, but I'd better give Valerie my car. Give me a ride
home later?"

"Sure."

"Okay, give me a minute."

Keough walked back to where Valerie was standing and
handed her his keys.

"What—?"

"Take the car and go home," he said. "I'm going to be here
awhile. I'll get a ride from Al."

"I'll go," she said, closing her hand over the keys, "to your
home and fix dinner. It'll be waiting for you when you get
there."

"I don't know how late I'll be."

"I'll wait."

"The house key is there, too," he said, pointing to her
hand. "I'll see you later."

He kissed her shortly, once, not wanting to put on a display
for the crowd.

"I'm sorry as hell about this," he said.

"I'm sorry, too. This was your day off."

"There'll be other days to fly kites." And to talk to her
about what was bothering him. She turned and walked away,
and he watched until Steinbach came up beside him.

"Ready?"

"Yeah," Keough said, "let's go."

Three

"WHAT'S GOIN' ON with you two?" Steinbach asked, as they went down the ramp. Keough waved to Donaldson to join them, which he did.

"I've got something on my mind," Keough said.

"Want to talk about it?"

"Yeah, I do," Keough said, "but later."

"Okay. Let me lay this out for you, then. There's a south and a north tram. Our man is in the south."

As they approached the door to the Arch Museum, a uniformed man opened it for them. There was a security patch on the sleeve of his shirt.

"This is Security Officer Brooks," Steinbach said. "This is my partner, Detective Keough, and the medical examiner, Dr. Donaldson."

"Good to meet you both," Brooks said. He was a well-fed forty or so, and from the looks of his Sam Brown belt had been letting it out a notch or two at a time recently.

"You found the body?" Keough asked.

"Yes, sir. Saw the blood and followed it down here. I opened the door with my keys, kept my gun out, and found the body in one of the south trams."

"One of them?"

"Each tram has eight cars. The body is in one of the cars."

"How does this thing work?"

"There are tracks inside the arch. The tram travels along the tracks. Each tram has eight barrel-shaped cars, joined together like a train."

"And the tram runs up and down the legs of the Arch?" Keough asked.

"Right," Steinbach said, taking up the verbal tour. "There's a device inside to keep the passengers level until they arrive at the top."

"Is the elevator—the tram—locked up at night?" Keough asked the security man.

"Yes, sir."

"And was it locked when you found him?"

"No, sir."

"So somebody had a key for the entrance and a key for the elevator?" He wasn't going to be able to avoid calling it an elevator, so he stopped trying.

"That's how it looks."

"Who would have those keys?"

"Any number of people who work here," Brooks said, "starting with the superintendent of the Arch."

"Okay," Keough said, looking down at the floor. "I guess we can pretty much follow this trail to the elevator, right?"

"They're gonna want to wash this before they open to the public today," the guard said.

"No way," Keough said firmly. "This place is shut down as of now, pending my investigation."

"Jesus," the guard said, "they're not gonna like that."

"Tough," Keough said. "Nobody comes in here, Officer, without my okay. If you can't handle that, say so now and I'll get someone else."

The man stiffened. "I can handle it."

"Good," Keough said. "I'll be counting on you." He looked at Steinbach. "Is one of our guys at the elevator?"

"Yep. I posted a man there right away."

"Okay." He looked at Brooks again. "Thanks for your help." He started away, then turned back. "Are you supposed to be off now?"

"Yes, sir," the man said. "Shift ended two hours ago."

"You want some overtime?"

"Sure, why not?"

"Thanks. I'll get back to you."

Keough and Steinbach followed the path of the stain, which continued down a ramp and around a barricade where people would line up to wait their turn in the elevator. It was obvious that the trail led from the Arch to the elevator and not the other way around. Also, the blood had spattered the Arch as the blows were struck. The murder scene was, without question, the southern base of the Arch.

When they reached the tram, a uniformed police officer stepped aside, and Keough saw the body for the first time.

It was lying on its stomach in the center of one of the tram cars. Keough walked back and forth, counted eight cars, as the guard had said, with enough room inside each for about five people. He could see that the back of the head had been caved in.

"What's at the top?" Keough asked.

"An observation deck," Steinbach said. Keough looked at him. "I've been up there with my kids."

"Have we had anybody up there?"

"Not yet. We can send someone in the second tram."

"Good," Keough said. "Have him look for blood up there."

"I'll take care of it before we leave."

"What's the cause of death, Doc?" Keough asked the ME, as a matter of formality.

"Near as I can tell without an autopsy," Donaldson said, "somebody hit him with a heavy object more than once."

"I guess there's no point in putting gloves on," Keough said aloud, though speaking primarily to himself. "He wasn't killed here, and there must be hundreds of people a day in and out."

"More than that," Donaldson said.

"Same goes for the Arch itself," Steinbach said. "The smooth silvery surface is great for prints, but there must be thousands."

"Ah, well," Keough said, "a crime scene with no usable prints. What else is new?"

Keough stepped into the car to have a look, carefully avoiding the bloody trail, even though it appeared dry.

"Eight or nine hours, Doc?"

"Close to it. How'd you know? You didn't even touch the body yet."

"The blood's dry on the floor," Keough explained, "but still looks tacky. It's not crusted or flaking yet." He looked at Steinbach. "Al, let's have the techs check for footprints in the path. Maybe our man got careless."

"Right."

Donaldson looked at Steinbach, who nodded and said, "He's good."

"That must be why he gets—" Donaldson started, but Keough cut him off.

"Don't you dare say 'the big bucks,'" he warned. "That's reserved for you honchos with medical diplomas."

"If I wanted the big bucks," Donaldson said, "I would have become an orthodontist."

"Or a plastic surgeon," Steinbach offered.

"Nah," Donaldson said, "then I'd have to live in California."

"What's wrong with that?" Steinbach asked.

"I *hate* California."

While the two bantered, Keough avoided the body and walked to each end of the tram, examining the walls and floors.

"Are these cleaned at night?" he asked Steinbach.

"I'll check."

"Looks like it."

He returned to the body and bent over to it, moving it only enough to get a look at the man's face. When he did, his stomach went cold. He backed up quickly out of the tram car, stumbling and staggering as he fought for his balance.

"Joe? What's the matter?" Steinbach asked.

Keough turned, his face devoid of color. He looked like a man who had been struck in the stomach.

"Do we have an ID?" Keough asked.

"Yeah," Steinbach said, "I have his wallet." He took it out of his pocket, but Keough didn't reach for it.

"Remember the fella I told you got me the interview with the police here? Helped me find a place to stay?"

"Oh, yeah," Steinbach said, "you mentioned him a few times. What was his name?"

Keough swallowed and said, "Meet Mark Drucker, Al."

Four

KEOUGH TOOK THE wallet from his friend and studied the contents. Sure enough, all the ID bore the name MARK DRUCKER.

"I guess the killer didn't mind helping out with ID," Donaldson said.

"This looks like a message killing," Keough said.

"A what?"

"The killer is sending someone a message," Keough said. "Did nothing to hide the body or the ID, or the fact that he has keys to the place."

"Joe—" Steinbach said.

"I'm all right, Al."

"Were you good friends?" Donaldson asked.

"Not as good as we should have been—as I should have been—considering how much of a help he was to me."

"Where did you meet?"

"In New York, when I was still with the department there. He was in town for some political convention, and I was assigned for security. We just sort of got talking one day and exchanged addresses. When I had to leave New York, I called him to see what my options might be. In short order he'd made a few appointments for me to interview here."

"So you got the job. . . . and then what?"

"And then we hardly saw each other. He was always busy
. . . or I was always busy."

"Hey," Donaldson said, "that happens to people. You've
got your own life to lead, you know."

"Yeah," Keough said, "I do . . . but he doesn't anymore."

Keough assigned men to search the museum and the Arch
grounds for anything that might be helpful. At the same time
some of the uniforms continued to question onlookers and
search for witnesses. Steinbach had a man ride to the top in
the other tram—when they got someone who could run it—
and he found bloody handprints by one of the windows in
the observation deck.

"The sonofabitch went up for a look after he killed him,"
Keough said, shaking his head. "Ballsy bastard."

He'd allowed Donaldson to remove the body once the captain arrived on the scene. Even when the body was gone,
however, he was reluctant to leave the scene himself.

Truth be told, Keough *had* thought of Drucker from time
to time, considered calling him for dinner or a drink, but just
never seemed to follow through. Now he'd never get the
chance, and the man had gone out of his way for Keough
when nobody else would.

"Uh-oh," Steinbach said.

"What?" Keough asked, looking at his partner.

"I see that look on your face."

"What look?"

"The look that says you 'owe' Mark Drucker something."

"Well, I do."

Steinbach didn't say anything. In the relatively short time
they'd been partners, he had come to respect Keough's abilities and the way he comported himself during investiga-

tions—but he *had* seen him take things too personally from time to time.

Obviously, this was going to be one of those times.

"What about the family?" Steinbach asked.

"There's a wife—or there *was* a wife."

"Ex-wife?"

"Well," Keough said, "it sounded like they were headed that way, at one time."

"Kids?"

"No."

"Have you ever met the, uh, wife?"

"No," Keough said, "but I'll be the one to tell her."

"What about his job?"

"What about it?"

"Do you know what it was?"

Keough hesitated.

"Joe?"

"I'm thinking," he said. "I know he was involved with politics but . . . no, I don't know exactly what his job was."

"So we don't know if he had a partner or coworkers."

"No," Keough said. "We'll have to find out from the wife."

"Detectives?"

They both turned to see a uniformed officer looking at them.

"Yes?" Keough said.

"There's a man here says he's the superintendent of the Arch."

Keough looked at Steinbach. "Good, at least we don't have to go searching for him." He looked at the cop. "Where is he?"

"He's outside," the cop said. "We haven't let him in."

"Okay," Keough said, "we'll talk to him there."

They walked back through the museum to get to the front door. They could see officers searching the museum floor, behind displays, *inside* some displays—a covered wagon, then a tipi. The museum beneath the Arch was all about the exploration of the West, to which the Arch itself was considered the "Gateway." There was also a bookstore, which was also searched.

When they reached the front doors, there was a man waiting impatiently with a young woman at his side.

"Detectives Keough and Steinbach," the guard, Brooks, said, "this is Mr. George Eastmont, Superintendent of the Arch. The young lady is Miss Morgan, his secretary."

"Assistant," the young lady said.

"Sorry," Brooks said, "his assistant."

"Mr. Eastmont, Miss Morg—"

"What do you mean telling my security guard not to let me into my own museum?" Eastmont demanded. Eastmont's tone was officious, which went with his appearance. Every white hair on top of his head and in his beard and mustache had been perfectly trimmed. The cut of his suit was flawless. He would have been impressive but for the fact that he was barely five and a half feet tall. The best you could say for him was that he was "dapper." He appeared to be twice his twenty-something assistant's age.

"Mr. Eastmont," Keough said, in a reasonable tone, "I'm afraid I'm going to have to insist on asking the questions at this time. There's been a murder here, which puts me in charge. No one goes in or out without my say-so."

Eastmont firmed his jaw and said, "May I at least ask when we will be allowed to open?"

"Not today, I'm afraid."

"What? That's . . . that's impossible! We simply cannot—"

"Sir," Keough said, his tone still reasonable but firm, "the longer it takes for me to get answers to my questions, the longer you'll be shut down."

Eastmont narrowed his eyes.

"I'm willing to bow to your authority for the moment, Detective, but I must register my strong protest and tell you that I will be taking this matter up with the chief and the mayor."

"That's fine, sir," Keough said. "Your protest is noted."

"Very well," Eastmont said, squaring his shoulders, "I suppose we can proceed. What can I do to help?"

"We'd like to know who has access to the keys to your facility, other than yourself," Keough said.

"Well, certainly no one outside of my office."

"And how many people would that include?"

"Well, myself, of course," Eastmont said, frowning as he concentrated, "my secretary . . ."

Keough looked at Miss Morgan, who seemed as if she were going to protest again, but she did not.

". . . my assistant, his secretary—"

"I'm sorry, Mr. Eastmont," Keough said, "but I thought Miss Morgan was your assistant."

Eastmont sighed, annoyed at having his concentration interfered with.

"Yes, well, she is my administrative assistant," he said. "I was referring to the assistant superintendent and his secretary."

"He doesn't have an assistant?"

"No," Eastmont said, "he has a secretary."

"I see," Keough said. "All right, go on, please."

"Where was I, then? . . ."

"What about the head of security? Does he have access to the keys?"

"Well, yes, of course."

"And the security guard on duty at night?"

"They don't have their own keys," the superintendent said, "but they have access to them at night, yes."

"Does anyone ever take the keys home with them?"

"No."

"Not even you?"

The man smiled condescendingly. "I would have little use for the keys at home, Detective."

"I'm going to ask you to go inside with an officer and see if all your keys are accounted for," Keough said. "You'll have to come right out again."

"Yes, well, very well." Eastmont seemed fatigued by it all.

"Tell me, sir," Keough said, "if someone were to have taken a key, made an impression of it in clay, and then returned it to its place, you'd never know, would you?"

Eastmont's face contorted into an annoyed frown. "No, I suppose I wouldn't."

"I tell you what, sir," Keough said. "Why don't we all go to your office, after all. We're going to need a list of all your employees, their addresses and phone numbers. . . . Would you be able to give that to us?"

"Well . . . it would take some time to make copies. . . ."

"Miss Morgan?" Keough asked. "Would it be possible?"

She looked at her boss, who passed her no obvious signal, and then said, "I suppose I could. . . ."

"Good," Keough said, "then let's get started, shall we? The sooner we do, the sooner we can finish.

They left two hours later with Xerox copies of the employee records of everyone who worked at the Arch. There had been a brief moment there when the superintendent brought up the subject of a warrant, but Keough assured him that while one could be obtained with no problem—since they were in such close proximity to the courthouses downtown—he was sure that Eastmont would simply rather cooperate. In the end, the very efficient Miss Morgan put everything together for them with no trouble at all.

When Keough and Steinbach left the Arch, they had Eastmont and Miss Morgan escorted from the premises as well. The Arch files were under Steinbach's arm. Keough promised to let Eastmont know when the Arch could reopen, and the superintendent promised to talk to the mayor.

The search of the Arch Museum and grounds had turned up nothing. All they had were the bloody handprints at the top, of which they took photos and prints.

"I can't believe this killer would leave his prints at the scene," Steinbach said.

"I know," Keough said. "Something's going on here."

Keough released most of the extra officers who had been commandeered for the search but left two behind to protect the crime scene.

They walked to Steinbach's car, which was parked down the long flight of steps from the Arch, almost in front of the President Casino on the Admiral. ("The President" is the name of the casino, and "The Admiral" is the name of the boat. The Admiral has been in St. Louis forever, in several incarnations of which this casino is the latest. Why they didn't just call it "The Admiral Casino" is anyone's guess.) In the car, in an effort to get his partner's mind off the Drucker case for a few moments, Steinbach asked a personal question.

"Something going on between you and Valerie?"

"Maybe," Keough said, "I don't know."

"What's that mean?"

"There's something going on with me personally," Keough said, "and it might affect me and Val."

"Wait a minute," Steinbach said. "Were you gonna tell her before me?"

"Don't get territorial on me, Al," Keough said. "I've been meaning to talk to you about it."

"Well, I hope so," Steinbach said. "We're only partners."

Keough rubbed his eyes. He already had something on his mind before the Drucker murder, and now *that* was going to be weighing him down, too.

"Let's stop somewhere," he said, "and I'll fill you in."

"Where?"

"There's a new Einstein's Bagels in the West End, on Laclede and Euclid. Let's go there, get some coffee, and talk."

"Fine by me," Steinbach said, "I could use a bagel and some strawberry cream cheese about now."

Keough's stomach lurched at the sound of his partner's favorite bagel topping, but he kept quiet. There was enough other crap on his mind.

Five

WHEN THEY WERE seated at Einstein's—Steinbach with his coffee and bagel, Keough with just coffee—Keough told his partner a story. . . .

Keough didn't know many of his neighbors where he lived. After all, he was just house-sitting and not a home owner. Some people seemed to take that as a personal affront, which was okay with Keough. He wasn't the type to become very friendly with his neighbors. There was, however, one man he had become acquainted with, an older man who lived right across the street. He was a widower named Jack Roswell. Jack was about sixty-three and usually alone except when his daughter came to take him to her house for dinner.

"She's a lovely girl," he'd tell Keough, "but her husband's a putz, and the two kids—my grandchildren—are monsters."

Looking back, Keough wasn't even sure how he and Jack had become friends. They ran into each other occasionally on the street, when Jack was taking a walk and Keough was either leaving for work or returning home. One day the conversation turned to chess, and they started playing a couple of times a week. Sometimes they'd meet at Dressel's Pub and play there; sometimes they'd play at Jack's house or at Keough's.

Over the course of a few months, they gradually began to play more and more at Jack's. When they did, Keough noticed Jack had acquired a limp. He'd also noticed it a few times when Jack was taking his walks—and then the walks stopped.

So one night, while they were playing, he brought it up, and Jack admitted there was a problem.

"Diabetes."

"What?"

"I've got diabetes," Jack said.

"How long?"

"Years," Jack admitted, "but I never really took care of myself. Now, I guess I'm paying for it."

"How?"

Jack was having problems with his feet. He had open sores that wouldn't heal. He could take his walks, but he had to wrap his feet in bandages every day.

"See," Jack said, "the sores and cuts won't heal, and they leak during the day. . . . Ah, you don't wanna hear this crap."

Actually, Keough didn't, but he felt an obligation to the older man.

"What about your daughter? Does she know?"

"Sure she does. That's about the only good thing about this. I don't have to go to her house so much anymore. I tell her my feet hurt, and she leaves me alone. She yells at me on the phone about why I didn't take better care of myself, but then she leaves me alone."

"Well," Keough said, for want of something better, "that sucks."

"Sure does," Jack said, and then, "Checkmate."

While they were setting up for another game, Jack said, "You know, you bein' a cop an' all, there is somethin' you could help me with . . . if you would."

"You don't have a car, so it's not parking tickets."

"Naw," Jack said, "that's another thing about the diabetes.

Started to affect my eyes, so I can't drive no more."

"Well then, what can I do for you, Jack?"

"It's my doctor."

"What about him."

"He's this diabetes specialist I started goin' to, an' I don't trust him so much."

"Why not?"

Jack leaned across the board and said, "He does research."

"So?"

"I get the feeling maybe he's givin' me like, ya know, experimental drugs."

"Don't you have to sign a waiver for that?"

"He says I didn't qualify for his research program, or I coulda got some of my treatment for free, but what if he's just tellin' me that, ya know? And experimentin' on me?"

"What do you want me to do, Jack?"

"Maybe you could go in and talk to him, see what you think?"

"Jack, I can't officially question—"

"I figured that out."

"You did?"

"Sure," Jack said. "You could go in as a patient. Ya know, undercover? Tell him I recommended him?"

"Jack—"

"It's just that I don't know what to do, Joe," Jack said mournfully. "The guy's expensive, and if he's gonna help me, I can afford it . . . somehow. But if he's just takin' my money—ya know, I'd rather just die and leave it all to my daughter and grandkids."

"Jack," Keough said, "you're not going to die—"

"Then you'll do it?"

Keough had never noticed before how washed out Jack's eyes were, and somehow the man had acquired an . . . an odor, a sickly odor. Right now, Jack's washed-out blue eyes looked real hopeful.

"Okay, Jack," he said, "I'll go see him. . . ."

"And this is what's bothering you?" Steinbach asked.

"No," Keough said, "it's what happened when I went to see this doctor."

"And what was that?"

"He examined me."

"And is he on the level?"

"I checked him out, and he seems to be a very respected research specialist in the field of diabetes. He's written books, does fund-raising. . . . He looks clean."

"So? What's the problem?"

"The problem is," Keough said, "I went to him as a patient, you know? He examined me, took blood, urine, the whole works. . . ."

"And?"

Keough pushed his coffee away and looked at his partner.

"He told me I've got it, Al," Keough said.

Six

"OKAY, WAIT," STEINBACH said. "I admit I don't know much about diabetes. Is this serious?"

"This doctor says that, normally, your sugar should measure between seventy and one fifty."

"And what was yours?"

"Three twenty-six."

"Wow! How could you not know that? I mean . . . you didn't feel anything?"

"That's what he wanted to know," Keough said. "Was I thirsty all the time? Was I urinating a lot?"

"You drink about as much stuff—coffee, pop, beer—as I do. If you got it, maybe I do, too."

"I don't know what to tell you, Al," Keough said, "but this has been bothering me—"

"Wait a minute. How long have you known?"

"A couple of weeks."

"And you didn't say anything?"

"I don't know," Keough said. "Maybe I was in denial."

"Is this why I haven't seen you have a beer lately? Or a donut?"

"Look," Keough said, "I don't know what to do. This doctor says I should be eating a certain amount of carbohydrates a day. If I stick to that, my sugar should come down."

"That's all?"

"No," Keough said, putting his hand in his pocket. He took out two plastic vials of pills.

"What's that?"

"This one I'm supposed to take twice a day, once in the morning and one at night."

"And that other one?"

Keough picked up the larger container. "This one I should take once a day. Al, if I didn't have the department's medical coverage, this would be break me."

"What you said about this guy being in research. Are you— is he using you—?"

"I haven't agreed to anything, yet," Keough said, "but I've done some research on my own."

"And found out what?"

"This stuff," Keough said, indicating the pill he was to take once a day, "has killed thirty-four people."

"What? Out of how many?"

"Thousands."

Steinbach sat back. "I still don't like the odds."

"I know," Keough said.

"You been takin' this stuff?"

"Not yet."

"Why'd you get it?"

"I thought about taking it, then I decided to wait."

"So what are you gonna do, Joe?"

"I don't know."

"What about the department? Have you let them know?"

"No, not yet."

" 'Cause they'll want you to go to a department doctor."

"I know," Keough said, putting his pills away. "I don't know what I want to do yet. I don't know how this will impact my job, my life. . . . I just know one thing."

"What's that?"

"I don't want to have to wrap my feet every day and have somebody drive me around . . . but I don't want to be checking my blood all the time and be eating bland foods. . . ."

"You need somebody to tell you what to do, Joe," Steinbach said, "educate you, and you don't seem to be trusting this research guy any more than your friend Jack does."

"I know."

"What did you tell Jack?"

"Nothing yet. I . . . I guess I'm avoiding him. It's painful to watch him . . . you know?"

"That doesn't have to happen to you, Joe," Steinbach said. "You're young, you're . . . I mean, nothing, uh, irreversible has happened yet, has it?"

"This doctor told me there's some indication that my kidneys might be involved," Keough said, "but no, he didn't say it was irreversible."

"And what are you gonna tell Valerie? Are you afraid she won't be able to handle this?"

"We eat out a lot, Al," Keough said. "It's something we enjoy together, you know? Trying different foods. What happens when I tell her that has to change? And maybe some other things?"

"Like what?"

"Well . . . the medication could affect my sexual performance."

"Has it?"

"I'm not sure," Keough said. "I mean . . . I haven't felt like it much, lately, but . . . that might just be because I don't know how I'll . . . do, you know?"

"Joe . . . jeez, I don't know what to say . . . but I do know one thing."

"What?"

"I'm going to my doctor tomorrow."

* * *

Steinbach drove Keough the five or six blocks to his house and stopped right in front. The view reminded Keough again about Mark Drucker.

"Is she inside?" Steinbach asked.

"Yeah, she said she'd make dinner."

"Jesus, what if she's makin' something bad for you?"

"I'll eat it."

"Are you gonna tell her, Joe?"

"I should," he said. "I want to. . . ."

"We got enough shit goin' on without this."

"Tell me about it."

"Tell her, Joe," Steinbach said, "if just to get it over with."

Keough nodded. "That's good advice, Al. Thanks for listening."

"Hey," Steinbach said, "that's what partners are for."

Keough opened the door and stepped out. Steinbach leaned across the seat so he could see Keough through the open passenger window.

"Good luck."

"Thanks," Keough said, "I think I'll need it."

Seven

VALERIE HAD PREPARED dinner for him a few times over the past six months, but it was usually at her place. He had to admit, coming in the door and smelling her cooking was not a bad thing.

"Anybody home?" he called out.

"Kitchen," she shouted back. "And you call yourself a detective?"

Keough was still wearing the jeans, T-shirt, and windbreaker he had donned that morning for what he thought would be a leisurely day of kite flying. He took off the jacket and tossed it on a chair.

He walked into the kitchen. Valerie was standing at the stove with her back to it. He admired—as he often had—her hair. It was long and brownish, but "brown" didn't quite describe it. "Chestnut" seemed a better word. It always had a sheen and a clean smell, even after they'd been out for the day. He also admired the fact that she had not rushed home to change her clothes. She was also wearing what she'd had on the last time he saw her, a pair of khaki walking shorts— she said they called them "walk" shorts now—a purple T-shirt, and a pair of Top-Siders. Her pale legs were bare. At the moment, her shoes were somewhere else, and she was barefoot.

"Have a nice day, dear?" she asked, looking at him over her shoulder.

"It was nasty," he said, kissing her forehead.

"I'm sorry. Why don't you have a beer?"

He almost said yes, then remembered how bad it was supposed to be for him. If he was going to take this diabetes thing seriously, he'd have to stop stocking it.

"Just a Coke," he said, and then realized that was bad for him, too. He should probably be drinking diet soda but did not have any of that in his refrigerator right now.

"I'd like a glass of White Zin, please."

"Coming up."

He grabbed the bottle of wine from the refrigerator and poured her a glass. Was alcohol bad for him, too? He didn't know, so he didn't have any.

"What's for dinner?" he asked, setting the wineglass down where she could get at it. "It smells great."

"Étouffée." She picked up her glass and sampled the wine. "I thought you were having something?"

"Water," he said, "I'll have water." He put some ice in a glass and filled it from the tap. "Have you made that before?"

"I have," she said, "but not for you. I don't think I've ever seen you just drink water."

"I'm just . . . it'll cut my thirst."

"Can you talk about it?"

"About what?" he asked, misunderstanding.

"Your nasty day."

"Oh, sure. Can we go into the living room? Do you have to . . . stir or something?" he asked.

"I can get away for a few moments." She grabbed her wine and followed him to the living room.

He told her about the body at the Arch, and how it turned out to be someone he knew.

"I'm so sorry," she said. "Have I ever met him?"

"I don't think so," he said. "His name was Mark Drucker."

"I recognize that name," she said, frowning. "What did he do?"

"He was involved in politics."

"Hmm," she said, "maybe I met him at a fund-raiser or something. What did he do, exactly?"

"I can't even tell you," he admitted. "Some friend I was."

"I have lots of friends whose occupations I don't know."

"That's a lie."

"Well, I have . . . some."

"I just don't understand why I never bothered to ask."

"We're all a little self-involved at times," she said. "Don't be so hard on yourself. Maybe you should wonder why he never told you. Dinner's almost ready."

Her glass was empty, and she started back to the kitchen.

"I'll take a quick shower," he said, and ran upstairs.

She knew he'd be true to his word. He was the only man she'd ever known who could get in and out of a shower so fast he hardly had time to get wet at all.

She made their salads, and he was back, tightening the belt on a white terry-cloth robe as she was putting dinner on the table.

"This is wonderful," he said after a few bites, but he was also wondering what it was doing to his sugar.

While in the shower, he'd tried to think of several ways of bringing up his diabetes, and he finally decided just to tell her flat out.

"Val, there's something I need to tell you."

"It's about time."

"What?"

"You've had something on your mind for days—maybe longer."

"You've noticed, huh?"

"It's hard not to. You've been pretty moody lately, Joe. Is this where you say you're tired of me and don't want to see me anymore?"

"No, of course not," he said. "That'd be silly."

"Then what is it? What's been bothering you?"

He put his fork down and leaned his elbows on the table. "Let me tell you about my friend Jack. . . ."

When he was finished, she sat back and stared at him.

"Why has it taken so long for you to tell me this?" she asked finally.

"I don't know, exactly," he replied. "I guess I wasn't sure how you'd take it. Hell, I'm still not sure how I'm taking it."

"Well . . . you're doing what the doctor said, aren't you?"

"Sort of . . ."

"Oh, God," she said, looking at the food on the table, "and I probably made something that's bad for you. I'm sorry, but I don't know that much about diabetes. . . ."

"Neither do I, I'm afraid. I guess I'm going to have to learn, though."

"I guess the first step in doing that is admitting you have it," she said, "but . . ."

"But what?"

"But maybe you should make sure you do, first."

"What do you mean?"

"I mean, see another doctor," she said. "Get a second opinion. Isn't that what people do when . . . when they're told they have a . . . a disease?"

There was that word, the one that really bothered him: "disease." He had a disease. It sounded so . . . final. It made him feel like he had a time bomb ticking away inside of him.

And it scared him.

"I've been thinking about a second opinion, but . . ." he said.

"But what?"

"I guess I . . . just don't want it to be the same, you know?"

"Go and see my doctor, Joe" she said. "He's only a GP, but he could tell you if you have diabetes, I'm sure."

"I guess the fact that the doctor I went to is a researcher made me think he might have his own agenda, so . . . yeah, I will go see your guy, Val. Thanks."

"I'll call my doctor tomorrow and make an appointment for you."

"That'd be great."

"Meanwhile, maybe you should take those pills—"

"Ah, I don't think so. Not after what I heard."

"Who told you one of them killed thirty-four people, anyway?"

"The pharmacist," Keough said. "He said there are safer medications I could take that would accomplish the same thing."

"I think a second opinion is really the way to go," Valerie said.

"So do I," he said.

She reached across and touched his hand.

"Did you think I'd run out the door screaming?"

He gripped her hand and said, "I'm glad you didn't."

"Why don't we finish eating?" she said. "After you've seen my doctor, we can decide what we want to do about your diet."

Keough actually felt better for having discussed it with Valerie. Suddenly, he was hungry.

Eight

KEOUGH MANAGED TO rise the next morning and leave the house without waking Valerie. On his way to work he did something he hadn't done in a couple of weeks. He drove through McDonald's and got himself a sausage McMuffin—with no egg or cheese—hash browns, and a large cup of coffee. He figured if he was going to see another doctor, he might as well enjoy his food before he was cut off.

When he arrived at the office on Fourteenth Street, there were three detectives there, one of them his partner, Steinbach, who was in the act of removing a chocolate-chip bagel from a bag. He froze when Keough entered.

"Oh, sorry, Joe, is this gonna bother—what's that? Is that McDonald's?"

"Yes, it is," Keough said, his tone defensive even before he knew it.

"But I thought—"

Keough sat at his desk and said, "Val and I had a talk last night when I got home." He took his breakfast out and bit into the muffin. "I'm going to hold off on changing my lifestyle until I get a second opinion."

Steinbach frowned at his partner. "Do you think that's smart?"

"I don't know if it is or isn't, Al," Keough admitted. "Val's making an appointment for me with her doctor. If he concurs with the other one, then I'll start thinking about it again. Right now I want to concentrate on this homicide. I think Mark Drucker deserves my undivided attention, don't you?"

"Sure, Joe," Steinbach said, "whatever you say."

The other two detectives present, Hawthorne and Ellis, were partnered up and were among those who thought that Keough's rise to top homicide man was a little premature, experience or not. If they understood Keough and Steinbach's conversation, they did not let on.

"Have we heard from the ME yet?"

"Not yet."

"He's waiting for us to go down there," Keough said. "That's what we'll do, right after breakfast."

"Okay."

"Is the boss in?"

"Not yet."

"Did you get a paper today?"

"Aw, Joe, don't—"

"Read it yet?"

"I read the sports section, yeah."

"Give."

"Joe—"

"Come on, Al," Keough said. "It's all in fun."

"He doesn't think so," Steinbach said, but he handed over the sports section of the *Post-Dispatch*.

Keough accepted the paper and tore the front page of the sports section away from the rest. As was the case more often than not, it showed a photo of Mark McGwire hitting another home run for the St. Louis Cardinals. He went into the captain's office and taped the page to the man's chair, then came back.

"Why do you do that?" Steinbach asked.

"It's fun."

"He hates it."

"That's what makes it fun."

Captain McGwire—whose first name was, amazingly enough, Mark—hated all the attention the baseball Mark McGwire had been getting since he'd signed with the Cardinals. He hated seeing "his" name in the paper every day. When McGwire—the ballplayer—was first traded to St. Louis, McGwire—the captain—took it in stride. He even joked that he was the "first" Mark McGwire in the city. But as coverage of McGwire, the ballplayer, got heavier and heavier, as he got closer and closer to setting a new home run record, Captain McGwire began to get more and more annoyed. He even went so far as to stop reading the newspaper. That was why Keough took every opportunity he could to display the headlines someplace in the man's office.

"If he ever finds out it's you—" Steinbach said.

"Come on, Al, he knows it's me."

"Yeah, well . . . maybe . . ."

The other two detectives called out that they were leaving and waved. Steinbach waved back. Keough asked, "What've they got?"

"A couple of cases from yesterday," Steinbach said. "They're kind of pissed. They were working yesterday when the call came in from the Arch. The captain called you in from your day off instead of signing one of them."

"Not my fault," Keough said. "I can't afford to feel guilty about it. I'm carrying enough guilt around as it is."

"I never said you should feel any guilt."

"Come on," Keough said, tossing his greasy breakfast bag into the trash can next to his desk, "let's get out of here before the boss comes in. He'll want to be briefed, and I want to get down to the ME's office."

"You know," Steinbach said, around the last bite of his bagel, "it amazes me how you don't even care to stay around to see the results of your jokes."

"Hey, if they work, they work," Keough said, "whether I'm here or not."

"I guess so," Steinbach said, following him out the door.

Smiley Donaldson looked up from his desk and grinned at Keough and Steinbach as they entered his office.

"I've been expecting you gentlemen."

Keough had noticed long ago that Donaldson's smile seemed to affect his entire face. His blue eyes twinkled, lines appeared and disappeared on his face with each grin, as opposed to the lines that were permanent and deeply etched, well earned over his fifty years. He was short, solidly built; a man who still got in at least nine holes of golf each morning—when there wasn't a rush on an autopsy.

"Have a seat," Donaldson said, eyes searching his desk. "I've got it here someplace." He shuffled some folders that were spread out across the desk, covering every available inch. "Ah, here it is." He opened a folder. "The cause of death was severe trauma to the back of the head, caused by one or more blows with the proverbial blunt instrument." He looked at them over the top of the folder. "I think the first blow killed him, but someone was either extremely angry or wanted him dead in a very messy way."

"Other injuries?" Keough asked.

"None," Donaldson said, closing the folder. "No sign of any other violence to the body. He'd eaten sometime before—lots of vegetables, if you care—no alcohol in the blood."

"Time of death?"

"You were a bit off on that," Donaldson said, with no apparent satisfaction. "You said six to eight hours. It was more like ten, somewhere around eleven P.M."

"I'll live," Keough said. He turned to Steinbach. "I forgot to ask, did we get anything from the grounds or the crowd?"

"Oh yeah, I got that call this morning," Steinbach said.

"Blood on the Arch and the ground matches the, uh, victim's type."

"That's okay, Al," Keough said. "You can refer to him as the victim. Just because I knew him doesn't make him any less of one."

"Right, right."

"Sorry," Donaldson said, "I forgot that, too."

"No problem, Doc," Keough said, waving away the man's apology. "Is there anything else we need to know?"

"No defensive wounds on the hands or arms, nothing under the nails," Donaldson said. He closed the folder and dropped it on the desk where it blended into the sea of folders there. "He never saw it coming."

"Okay, Doc," Keough said, "thanks." He and Steinbach stood to leave. "Uh, Doc. Do you know much about diabetes?"

"Only that it's nothing to fool around with," Donaldson said. "There are several different kinds, several different treatments. . . . I'm not well versed on the subject. The, uh, victim didn't have it, if that's what you mean."

"No," Keough said, "that's okay. Thanks."

As they left the ME's office, Steinbach said, "Glad you're not giving it much thought until you get your second opinion."

"I may be in denial, Al," Keough said, "but I'm not stupid."

"Glad to hear it, partner."

Nine

WHEN THEY RETURNED to their office, they were immediately called into Captain McGwire's office. Keough noticed the newspaper he'd taped to the man's chair was now in the trash can, crumpled up. Nothing was said about it.

"Brief me," McGwire said.

"I can write my reports—" Keough started.

"After you brief me, you can write your reports," McGwire said. "I've already had calls from the chief and the mayor this morning."

Keough frowned. "About what?"

"About the Drucker murder."

Keough and Steinbach exchanged a puzzled glance. "Cap, we haven't released the victim's name—" Steinbach started.

"He was found in the Arch elevator, Detective," McGwire said. "How long did you expect to keep that quiet?"

"But the mayor? The chief?" Keough said. "Why are they involved?"

"Do you know who Mark Drucker was?"

"Actually, I do, Cap," Keough said, and explained to his superior what a help the dead man had been to him in relocating to St. Louis.

"I didn't know that," McGwire said softly. "I'm sorry you lost a friend, and I'm sorry you had to find out that way . . . but do you *really* know who he was?"

"No," Keough said, "I can't say that I do."

"Well, I don't either," McGwire said with a scowl, "but he was enough of a somebody to have the chief and the mayor up early and on the phone. I don't know what's going on here, boys, but mark my words it's about politics."

Keough made a face. He hated politics. It was a game he had no time for.

"Well, I guess I know now how he was able to get me those interviews," Keough said.

"And a great place to live," Steinbach said.

"That, too."

"So brief me on what you've got."

"Not much . . ." Steinbach started, and Keough sat back and let his partner do the talking. McGwire listened carefully and asked only a minimum of questions until Steinbach had finished. There were a lot of things Keough liked about his boss, and his tendency to listen was one of them.

"Wait a minute," McGwire said, when Keough finished. "This nut took a ride to the top to have a look *after* he killed Drucker?"

"That's the way it seems," Keough said. "The bloody handprints match the blood type of our victim. No fingerprints from the killer, though. He was wearing gloves, probably rubber."

"Well," McGwire said, looking at Keough, "you had a helluva day off."

"Yes, sir, I did . . . and we have to talk about that."

McGwire waved Keough off and said, "We'll make it up to you later, after you clear this case. What about the wife?"

"Ex-wife," Keough said. "We're going to see her today."

"She'll probably already know what happened," McGwire said. "But see what the hell else she knows. The mayor said he's going to call me back this afternoon. Get me something to tell him by then. That's all I ask."

"Right, boss," Keough said.

"Is that all, Cap?" Steinbach asked.

"No, it's not," McGwire said. "The mayor wants to know when the blood can be washed from the base of the Arch, the floor of the museum, and the tram—when they can reopen for business. As long as it's closed, the city is losing revenue."

"I'll talk to the lab," Keough said. "If they have everything they need, I guess it's okay for the crew to wash up tonight and reopen tomorrow." Keough looked at his partner, who nodded. It sounded as if Superintendent Eastmont had made good on his threat to call the mayor.

"Find out for me so I can let him know."

"Yes, sir."

"Is that all?" Steinbach asked.

"That's all for you, Al," McGwire said. "Let me talk to Joe alone for a minute."

Steinbach gave Keough an "I told you so" look, figuring McGwire wanted to talk about his partner's newspaper jokes.

"Sure, boss," he said, standing.

"Thanks, Al," Keough said.

McGwire waited until Steinbach had gone out and closed the door behind him.

"What's up, Cap?"

"Are you okay to work on this, Joe?"

"What do you mean?"

"I mean you're personally involved."

"Oh . . . well, sure, I can work it. I owe the guy—"

"That's what I mean," McGwire said. "You should be working the case based on the facts and because it's your job, not because you figure you owe the victim anything."

"I'll do my job, Cap," Keough said.

"And you're damned good at what you do . . . usually."

"What does that mean?" Keough asked, bristling a bit.

"It means I'm going to get heat on this," McGwire said,

"and you're my extinguisher. You protect me, and I'll protect you, Joe. That's how it works. Understand?"

"Sure, Cap," Keough said, "I understand. It's politics."

"You're damn right it is, and I'm well aware of your feelings about politics," McGwire said. "You're gonna be talking to a lot of important people in this town, no doubt about it. All I'm asking is that you don't ruffle anybody's feathers unnecessarily, because if you do, it's gonna come right back here." He tapped the top of his desk with the tip of one thick index finger. It made a dull noise. "And if it comes back here, you know where I'm going to send it next."

"Don't worry, boss," Keough said. "I'm on it."

"I'm counting on you, Joe."

"I appreciate that. Can I go? I'd like to get to the wife before too many people talk to her."

"Go," McGwire said, sitting back. "Get me something I can tell the mayor."

"I'll try."

McGwire grunted.

"What was that about?" Steinbach asked. "The newspaper?"

"No, not that at all," Keough said. "He's worried about the fallout from this case."

"I didn't know the boss had political ambitions."

"I don't think he does," Keough said, "but he's going to be our buffer against all the politicians who are involved."

"Shit," Steinbach said, "I hate dealing with politicians."

"Well," Keough said, "that's his job. Now all we have to do is ours."

"Find a killer."

"Without getting anyone *too* upset."

"Yeah," Steinbach said, "what are the chances?"

"Slim and none, but I'm not worried. I'm going to do my job no matter who it pisses off."

"So what do we do now?" He had no doubt his partner meant what he said.

Keough looked at Steinbach's desk, where the files from the Arch were stacked. Steinbach followed his look.

"Let's get those files to your computer sweetie, and then go and see the wife."

Ten

"WHAT'S THE ADDRESS?" Steinbach asked.

They were riding in his car on Clayton Road in the affluent area behind the Galleria Mall. The homes were set back from the streets with driveways so long they had been named. Mark Drucker's was One Kennilworth Circle. Keough had been surprised to find that Drucker had lived in this area. He hadn't suspected the man had that much money.

"Jesus, look at these places," Steinbach said, as they searched for Kennilworth. "My wife loves driving around here. She'll shit a brick when she finds out I was in one."

"As attractive a picture as that conjures up, Al," Keough said, "let's keep our eyes open for the street signs."

"That was it, I think," Steinbach said suddenly.

"Where?"

"Back there. We passed it. Wait. I'll turn around."

Steinbach drove into the parking lot of one of the trendy Clayton strip malls, then pulled out and headed back the way they had come.

"There. Doesn't that sign say 'Kennilworth'?"

It did. It was a shingle hanging from a signpost, and not

only did it say ONE KENNILWORTH CIRCLE, it also said, THE DRUCKERS.

"I never could understand why people would announce their names like that," Steinbach said, as they turned into the driveway.

It took them to a large stone house built in old English style, then the road circled around and headed back out. They pulled in front of the house and stopped. Keough thought the house would look right at home in Yorkshire, England, with a castle in the background.

"Why do I get the feeling you could have gotten a lot more help out of this guy?" Steinbach asked, as they got out of the car.

As they walked to the door, Keough commented on the fact that there were no other cars in the driveway.

"I wonder if his is downtown, in the Arch parking lot," Steinbach said.

"We'll get the make and model from the wife—maybe even the plate—and then have someone take a look."

They stopped at the front door and rang the bell.

"How do you want to do this?" Steinbach asked.

"Since I knew him," Keough said, "why don't I start out doing the talking?"

"Fine with me," Steinbach said. "I hate talking to the victims' families. Plays hell with my appetite."

Keough had never noticed that, but he didn't say anything.

They were ready to speak to a maid or a butler, but instead the door was opened by a handsome woman in her late thirties, tall, solidly built, perfectly made up. She had long dark hair, was dressed in jeans and a white T-shirt which showed off her well-toned arms and torso.

"Yes?" she asked, eyeing them curiously. "May I help you?"

"Mrs. Drucker?" Keough asked.

"That's right. Who are you, please?"

"Ma'am, my name is Detective Joe Keough." He showed

her his shield, as did his partner. "This is Detective Steinbach. We're here about your husband."

"He's dead," she said. "I heard—and he's my ex-husband."

"I see. We'd still like to come in and talk to you about him, if that's all right?" Keough asked.

"Sure, come ahead," she said, stepping aside to allow them to enter, "but I don't know what I'll be able to tell you. I didn't know his business when we lived together, and I sure don't know anything about it now. This way, please. We might as well be comfortable."

She led them to an expensively furnished living room and invited them to sit. Steinbach chose an overstuffed chair, Keough one that was a bit more solid. Mrs. Drucker sat on the sofa, knees together and hands in her lap.

"I'm sorry," she said, "I should have offered you something—"

"That's all right, ma'am," Keough said. "We don't need anything."

"You said your name is Keough?"

"That's right."

"Why do I know—oh, you're that detective who came here from New York last year."

"Yes, ma'am."

"You caught that nut who was grabbing women from mall parking lots."

"That's right," Keough said, "my partner and I did, with some help from the FBI—"

"Mark was very impressed with you then. He was supposed to call and congratulate you. Did he?"

"No, ma'am, he didn't."

"He was always saying he was going to do something, and then—well, you're not here to hear my complaints. Do you have some questions?"

"Were you still together last year, at that time?"

"Yes," she said, "we didn't split until six months ago."

"When did he move out?"

"Six months ago."

"Have you had much contact with him since then?"

"Only through our divorce attorneys."

"So you'd have no idea what he was doing down by the Arch last night?"

"Not a clue."

"Or who'd have a reason to kill him?"

She smiled wanly. "My husband—sorry, soon to be ex-husband—was involved in politics, Detective. Lots of people wanted to kill him, I'm sure."

"Mrs. Drucker—"

"Could you call me Marcy?" she asked. "I'd prefer that. I'm petitioning to get my maiden name back."

"All right, Marcy. . . . What exactly did your husband do for a living?"

"You're not going to believe this," she said, "but I don't know. I never knew."

"How long were you married?"

"Eleven years."

"And in all that time—?"

"He never discussed his business with me," she said, cutting him off. "I went to parties with him, political rallies, and functions. People came up to him, shook his hand, made appointments, and asked for favors . . . but as to what he did *exactly?* You'll have to ask somebody else about that."

"Like who?" Steinbach asked, speaking for the first time.

"His lawyer, I suppose."

"And who would that be?" Keough asked.

"Well, that would depend," she said. "He's got a divorce lawyer, a personal lawyer, a corporate lawyer—"

"Would any of these lawyers also be friends of his?"

"Oh, sure, his personal lawyer, Ken Ryan. They've been friends for a long time. Ken could answer your questions better than I could."

"Can you give us an address on Mr. Ryan?"

"Yes," she said. "In fact, I'll go you one better. I'll call him for you."

"We might have you do that, ma'am, after we've asked a few more questions."

"Marcy, please," she said. " 'Ma'am' is almost as bad as 'Mrs. Drucker.' "

"All right, Marcy. I'm sorry. I'll remember. You said he was your soon-to-be ex-husband?"

"That's right."

"When were you going to be divorced?"

"As soon as my lawyers figured out how to break our prenup. You see, this was a second marriage for both of us, and I'm afraid this was the one where I married for money."

"And you signed a prenup?"

"I thought I could get him to change it after we were married," she said with a fatalistic shrug.

"And?"

"No chance."

"Why would you divorce, then?"

"Because we'd both had enough, Detective," she said. "It was time."

"And given the conditions of the prenup, how would you have done?"

"Well," she said, "but not well enough to continue to live like this. Oh, wait a minute." She put her hand to her mouth. "I've gone and made myself a suspect, haven't I?"

"You're his wife, Marcy," Keough said truthfully. "You were a suspect even before we walked in here."

"Well then," she said, "before I call his lawyer for you, maybe I'd better call my own."

"You're certainly entitled to do that, Marcy," Keough said.

"If you gentlemen will excuse me," she said, standing up. "I'll be back in a few moments."

Eleven

KEOUGH AND STEINBACH could hear Marcy Drucker's voice coming from another part of the house as she spoke—they presumed—to her lawyer on the phone.

"What do you think?" Steinbach asked.

"I think she was doing fine until she put her foot in her mouth," Keough said. "We probably won't get anything else out of her now."

Steinbach made a face. "I hate lawyers, and this sounds like we're going to have to deal with a lot of them."

"I tell you what," Keough said, "one of us will handle the lawyers and the other the politicians. Which do you want?"

Steinbach blew out a disgusted breath and said, "Some choice."

They fell silent as they became aware of Marcy Drucker's voice coming closer and closer, leading them to conclude that she must be on a cordless phone.

As she entered the room she was saying, ". . . can let you talk to one of them, if you like."

Steinbach gave Keough a look that said he had just made his choice.

"I'll speak to him if you like, Marcy," Keough said.

"Thank you," she said. "Here's one of the detectives." She handed him the cordless phone.

"Hello?" Keough said.

"To whom am I speaking, please?" a man asked.

"This is Detective Joseph Keough. What is your name, sir?"

"I am L. J. Fowler, Detective, Mrs. Drucker's attorney."

"Her divorce attorney?"

"That's right," Fowler said, "and I do not appreciate having my client questioned about her husband's m-m-death while I am not p-p-present. I have advised her n-n-not to answer any f-f-further questions."

Keough wondered if the man stuttered, or if his stammering was simply a result of nerves. He was, after all, a divorce attorney.

"With all due respect, Mr. Fowler, do you think you should be advising Mrs. Drucker on a criminal matter?"

"Until she directs me otherwise, D-D-Detective, I am her only attorney. P-p-please don't ask her any more questions until I get there."

"There's no need for you to hurry over, Counselor," Keough said. "We're finished with our questions. All we'll need from Mrs. Drucker at this point are the names of her late husband's attorneys and the address of each office. Would it be all right for her to give us that information?"

"I d-d-don't see why n-n-not."

"Good," Keough said, "then I'll put her back on the phone. We can make arrangements for you to be present some other time, if we feel we need to question Mrs. Drucker again. Good day, sir."

"G-g-good day, Detective."

Keough smiled at Marcy Drucker and handed her the phone.

"Lee? Yes . . . yes, I see. All right, I'll do that. Thank you."

She broke the connection and set the cordless down on a table.

"He says I can give you the information you need."

"Good."

"I'll write it all down. Would you come with me, Detective? There's a writing desk in the other room."

Keough looked at Steinbach, who shrugged and stood up. "I'll wait in the car," he said. "Good day, Mrs. Drucker."

"Good-bye, Detective."

They walked out into the foyer together and there separated. Steinbach went out the door, and Keough followed Marcy Drucker down a hallway to a room lined with empty bookshelves and a writing desk that seemed out of place.

"This was my husband's office, but as you can see he moved all of his things out. Now I use it."

"Do you have need of an office?"

"Not yet," she said. "I only come in here to write checks for bills . . . and information for handsome detectives."

Keough ignored the remark. If Marcy Drucker was coming on to him, he didn't want to encourage it, even though he found her very attractive.

She sat down at her desk and opened a phone book. She turned to a page, made a note, turned to another, and a third, then closed it. She stood up and handed Keough the piece of paper.

"The first is—was—Mark's lawyer, who I told you about. Ken Ryan."

"Yes, you also offered to call him for me?"

"I will. I'll tell him to expect you. The other names and address were his, uh, business attorneys, Shepp, Anson, and Associates.

"In what business?"

"You'd have to take that up with them, I'm afraid."

"And could you call ahead to them, also?"

"I don't think so," she said. "I'm really not on speaking terms with them."

"And your husband's office?"

"I'm afraid I don't know where that is, Detective. His lawyers should, though. Don't you think?"

"I'm sure they will. Thank you for the information, Marcy. I'm sorry we had to bother you.

"It was no bother, actually," she said. "I rather enjoyed your company." He assumed she meant his specifically. "In fact, don't worry about checking with my lawyer before you come back. Just call me, and we'll make some arrangements."

"Marcy," he said, "if I were you, I wouldn't depend on Mr. Fowler too heavily in this matter."

"Are you telling me I need to retain a criminal attorney?"

"You were the one who felt the need to call an attorney," he pointed out. "All I'm saying is call one who can be helpful. Mr. Fowler sounded a bit . . . nervous to me."

"That was just his stammer," she said. "It's usually not that bad . . . but I see your point, Detective. I'll look into it. Thanks for the advice."

"No charge," he said, smiling.

Keough found Steinbach outside, lounging against the side of the car.

"I checked around back," Steinbach said. "There's a garage. I was able to look through a window and saw one car inside, a Lexus."

"Shit," Keough said, "we forgot to ask about Mark's car."

"I'll check with motor vehicles," Steinbach said. "No point in going back inside. What did she say after I left?"

Keough took out the addresses Marcy had written and handed them to his partner.

"She gave me the names of two law firms."

"There are three numbers on here," Steinbach said.

"What?"

Steinbach handed it back. "No address with the last number," he said. "What do you want to bet it's her number?"

Keough folded the piece of paper and tucked it away.

"Did she come on to you?"

Keough walked around to the passenger side of the car and got in. Steinbach got behind the wheel.

"Did she?" he prodded.

"Something might have been said," Keough replied. "Maybe I misinterpreted her meaning."

"I don't think so," Steinbach said. "She was looking you up and down like you were a corn dog on a stick."

"A what?" Keough asked. "Couldn't you come up with a better analogy than that?"

Marcy Drucker watched from a window until the two detectives drove away, then looked down at the cordless phone in her hand and dialed a number from memory. When it was answered, she said, "Mr. Shepp, please. Tell him it's Marcy Drucker."

Twelve

THEY DECIDED TO go and see the attorneys for Mark Drucker rather than return to Fourteenth Street.

"The captain's probably gotten some more pressure by now," Keough said, "and I don't want to hear about it."

Steinbach agreed.

"Which attorney first? The personal one, or the business?"

"Where are they located?"

"Read me the addresses."

Steinbach was still the one who could pinpoint locations just from the address. Keough was not that familiar with his adopted city yet.

He read the two addresses to his partner, who said, "The second one is in Clayton, in the business district. Let's check it out first."

"Okay," Keough said. "Where's the other one?"

"I'm not sure, but I think it's off of Page. It sounds real familiar."

Keough looked at his watch. "Anyplace in Clayton you'd want to stop for lunch?" he asked Steinbach.

"Tons."

"Why did I ask?"

Steinbach picked The Fatted Calf for lunch. He was of the opinion that they served the best hamburger in the city. Keough told him to go in and order, and he stayed outside to call the lawyer from a pay phone.

"Ken Ryn," a man's voice said.

Keough was surprised. He had expected a secretary—but then, maybe that was what he'd gotten.

"I'd like to speak to Mr. Ryan, please?"

"That's Ryn," the man said, and then spelled it. Keough quickly pulled out the piece of paper to double-check, and there it was, "Ryn." It had just sounded like she was saying "Ryan."

"I'm sorry, Mr. Ryn. This is Detective Keough. Did Marcy Drucker call you about me?"

"Oh, Detective. No need to apologize. That mistake is made all the time, and yes, she did call. You want to talk about Mark Drucker?"

"Yes, is today convenient?"

"It's very convenient, as a matter of fact. I have no court dates, and I'll be in all day. In fact, I'll be eating my lunch at my desk. When would you like to stop up?"

"In about half an hour or so?" Keough said.

"Very well," Ryn said. "That would make it about one-thirty?"

"One-thirty, sir. See you then."

Keough hung up and went inside. He was surprised at the long line that stretched out ahead of him, but then he saw Steinbach already seated at a table with two bottles of Coke, and went to join him.

"I tinned my way to the front," Steinbach said proudly. Keough hated using his "tin," his "badge," to get special treatment. "I got you one with onions and lettuce. I know you don't like any fancy stuff like cheese."

"Thanks. We've got a meeting with the attorney, Ryn, at one-thirty."

"Ryn?"

Keough explained about the pronunciation of the man's name. By the time he was done, a woman with a white apron came over and plopped down their burgers and fries in front of them.

"Thanks, hon," Steinbach said.

She left without a word. Keough looked around and noticed that the people in line were staring at them.

"Ignore them," Steinbach said. "Eat."

"I feel like I ran over an Ethiopian kid," Keough said. "I hate using my shield to get ahead of people."

"You said our meeting was one-thirty, right?"

"Right."

"Well, start eating. We barely have time to make it."

Keough tried to ignore the angry stares while he ate.

The conversation was meandering as they ate, meant to pass the time more than anything else, until Steinbach said, "I just thought of something."

"What?"

"Drucker got you your house, right?"

"That's right."

"A sublet?"

"No, I'm house-sitting."

"For who?"

"The owners."

"Do you know who they are?"

"No—I mean, I know their last name, but that's about it."

"You mean you're a detective, and you haven't bothered to find out who these people are? Looked in those closed-up rooms?"

"I'm a detective, Al, not a snoop."

Those "other rooms" Steinbach was talking about were

ones with furniture covered with sheets, and Keough was telling the truth. He hadn't gone snooping. Maybe it made him
boring when he was away from work, but he reserved his
curiosity for the cases he was working on.

"Well, what happens now?" Steinbach asked.

"What do you mean?"

"Drucker's dead; you don't know the owners. Where are
they? When are they coming back? Will his death mean you
have to move out? Where will you live?"

"Jesus, Al," Keough said, staring at his friend incredulously,
"as if I didn't have enough on my mind!"

Thirteen

THE CITY OF Clayton was home to many municipal buildings and courthouses, as well as a brand-new prison. There were also banks, insurance companies, stockbrokers, travel agents, one of the largest independent bookstores in the country, art galleries, and a host of fine- and fast-food restaurants. It was also the location of an annual food fair and an art show.

Like most business areas, it was busy between the hours of nine A.M. and five P.M. Steinbach had been able to find a parking spot around the corner from The Fatted Calf, right on Forsythe, in front of an art gallery. As coincidence would have it, Ryn's law offices were in a building right across the street.

They entered the lobby and found a listing for the lawyer on the directory. KENNETH RYN, ATTORNEY-AT-LAW, Suite 401.

On the outskirts of the Clayton business district was its residential area, made up of affluent homes and condos. As they entered the elevator, Keough wondered if Ryn lived nearby.

They got off the elevator at the fourth floor and found Ryn's suite. There was a waiting room and a receptionist's desk, but no receptionist. From another room they could hear a humming sound, probably from a computer.

"Hello?" Keough called out.

"Detective Keough?"

"Yes."

"Come on in."

Keough walked past the desk and through the door into what he now assumed was Ryn's office. Steinbach followed.

"I know you," Steinbach said, as soon as he saw Ryn standing behind his desk.

The man was stocky, with gray hair and a gray-black beard. His long shirtsleeves were rolled up to expose thick forearms, and he had no tie on. He was standing in front of a computer terminal. The walls around him were lined with bookshelves containing thick green, red, and blue tomes with gold lettering on the spines.

"You watch television," Ryn said.

"That's it," Steinbach said, looking at Keough. "He stars in his own commercials."

The man shrugged, looked embarrassed, and asked, "Know anything about computers? My receptionist is the expert, but she's out today."

"Mr. Ryn," Keough said, "I'm Keough. This is my partner, Detective Steinbach."

The men all shook hands.

Steinbach asked, "What's the problem?"

"Well, I was on-line and suddenly I lost my watchamacallit, the arrow thing."

"The cursor?"

"That's it," Ryn said. "The cursor disappeared."

Steinbach moved around behind the desk to stand beside the man. "That happens sometimes. Let me see if I can get it back."

"Have a seat, Detective," Ryn said, "both of you. I can't offer you anything. I make terrible coffee. We could go across the street to the bagel place, if you like—"

"That's okay," Keough said. "To tell you the truth, we just had lunch."

"Okay, then," Ryn said. "What can I do for you while your partner tries to fix my computer?"

"What was your relationship with Mark Drucker?"

"On one level, client-attorney."

"And on another?"

"We were friends," Ryn said.

"For how long?"

"Some years—six or seven, I think. He helped me get set up in my own practice, threw some work my way. He had a big firm handling most of his business, but he let me work on some smaller things, like wills, grants—"

"Divorce?"

"Yeah, I'm handling that, too . . . or I was. Guess it's not real necessary now, huh?"

"I suppose you'll be probating the will?"

"Mmm, yes."

"How well do you know his wife?"

"Not well at all. In fact, we've never met."

This was all beginning to sound very familiar.

"How often would you see each other?"

Now Ryn seemed uncomfortable.

"Actually, not that often. I, uh, found Mark to be a really loyal friend but, uh, I have to admit that we didn't, um, keep in contact outside of business. . . ."

"I think we have something in common, Mr. Ryn," Keough said, and then explained his relationship with Mark Drucker. "I see a pattern here."

"Apparently he was a helpful, loyal friend, but he didn't keep in close contact with people," Ryn said. "Here I was feeling guilty after I heard he was dead."

"Me, too," Keough said. "I wonder if he had any close friends?"

"I don't know."

"What do you know about Shepp, Anson, and Associates?"

"They're a very big law firm in town," Ryn said. "Very active in the political arena. Why?"

"Apparently, they were representing Mark in some capacity. Tell me, do you know exactly what business he was in?"

Ryn hesitated, then said, "Well, now that you mention it, I don't."

"I didn't, either," Keough said. "We were hoping you could help us with that."

"Seems like we're in the same boat, Detective," Ryn said. "At least you know more than I do."

"Do I?"

"You know what's in his will."

"Well . . ."

"Got it," Steinbach said. "There you go."

"Hey, you did it," Ken Ryn said. "I got my cursor back."

"Mr. Ryn, when will you be reading the will?"

"Hmm? Oh, at Mrs. Drucker's earliest convenience."

"Does she inherit anything?"

"Looking for a motive?"

"I'm afraid so."

"Well, I'm afraid you'll have to wait to find out until after the will is read."

"Do you know anything about Drucker's office?"

"Probably as much as you do."

"How about kids? I didn't think he had any."

"He didn't."

"All right," Keough said, taking out one of his business cards. "After you've read the will to Mrs. Drucker, would you call me and let me know what was in it?"

"Sure . . ."

"Thanks."

". . . with her permission, of course."

"Of course."

Keough and Steinbach left after Ryn thanked Steinbach profusely for getting his cursor back.

"Well, that should make you feel better," Steinbach said, as they crossed the street to the car.

"What should?"

"You weren't such a bad friend, after all," Steinbach said. "It looks like this Drucker was just a hard guy to know."

"Yeah, but why was he so helpful to me?" Keough asked. "And why throw somebody like Ken Ryn some business when you've got Shepp, Anson, and Associates representing you?"

"Maybe," Steinbach said, unlocking his door, "we should ask Shepp, Anson, and Associates that question."

"My thoughts exactly."

Fourteen

THE OFFICES OF Shepp, Anson, and Associates were in one of two buildings that could be seen from Highway 270, just before the exit for Page Avenue. The two buildings were twins, mirror images of each other, identical in every way.

Steinbach got off the highway at the Page exit, found his way to Craig, and then to the mirror-image buildings. Which building Shepp, Anson was in was no problem. There was a directory for each building very visible from the highway.

Steinbach parked, and they got out.

Steinbach checked his watch.

"Guess we should have called ahead."

"A big firm like Shepp, Anson is not going to shut down during lunch," Keough said. "Somebody will be there."

Somebody was. A very attractive, professional-looking brunette in her forties was sitting at a desk in a reception area; she smiled as the two detectives entered.

"May I help you gentlemen?" she asked.

Both men displayed their identification.

"I'm Detective Keough; this is Detective Steinbach. We'd like to see Mr. Shepp or Mr. Anson, if they're available."

"I'm afraid they're both out right now."

Keough asked. "When will they be back?"

"I'm not sure I can say," she answered. "You see, they're away on business."

"Out of town?"

"No, I mean, they're in court," she said. "I can let you talk to Miss Henry, our office manager."

"Is that the best we can hope for right now?"

She gave them an apologetic look and said, "I'm afraid so."

"Then I guess we'll settle for Miss Henry."

"I'll tell her you're here." She picked up a phone, dialed three digits, and spoke into the receiver. "There are two police detectives here to see Mr. Shepp or Mr. Anson. Yes, I told them that. Yes, all right, I'll tell them." She hung up. "Miss Henry will be right out, gentlemen. You can wait over there."

She pointed to a green leather sofa, in front of which was an expensive-looking coffee table covered with a variety of magazines.

"Thank you," Keough said. He and Steinbach walked over to the sofa but remained standing.

"Think they're really out?" Steinbach asked. "Maybe somebody warned them we were coming."

"Like who?"

"Mrs. Drucker? Or the other attorney, Ryn?"

"Why would they warn them? And why would they leave if they had been warned?"

"Maybe they don't care who killed Drucker."

Before Keough could reply, another professional-looking woman appeared and walked toward them. This one appeared to be in her late thirties, wearing a severely cut jacket and skirt that did little to hide her figure. Her hair was cut short, in what Keough thought might still be called "a wedge"—the Dorothy Hamill look. Her most arresting features were very big, bright gray eyes that she now trained on both of them with an expectant look.

"Gentlemen? I understand you're from the police?"

"Yes, ma'am," Keough said, once again showing his badge. Steinbach reached for his, and she stopped him.

"No need," she assured him. "Would you like to come back to my office? We can talk there. Perhaps I can offer you some coffee?"

"No thank you," Keough said, "but we'll accept the invitation to your office."

"Come this way, then."

As she led them back through a maze of corridors, they passed offices and cubicles, all of which seemed to be occupied.

"There certainly are a lot of people here," Keough remarked.

"We employ one hundred and ten people full time," she said, "as well as some part-time law clerks."

Keough was impressed, but said, "I meant, a lot of people for lunchtime."

"Oh, well, many of our employees take their lunch in their offices," she said. "We have a man with a cart who comes in selling sandwiches and donuts and coffee."

"Do Mr. Shepp or Mr. Anson eat in?"

"Rarely," she said. "In fact, our partners are very often out of the office."

"How many partners are there?"

"Just the two," she said. "This is not the sort of office that keeps adding partners until the name of the firm becomes unwieldy."

"Like Merrill, Lynch, Pierce . . . uh, whoever?" Steinbach asked.

"Exactly."

They passed rows of bookshelves covered with the same multicolored law books Keough had seen in Ryn's office. These were a staple in all the law offices he had ever been in. Finally they reached her office. On the wall outside her office were two paintings. Under one a plaque said Franklin Anson and under the other Dexter Shepp. She allowed them to precede her, then entered, and rounded her desk to sit. Out the window behind her they could see Highway 270.

"Please, gentlemen," she said. "Have a seat."

She sat down and unbuttoned her jacket. Beneath she wore a silk fuchsia blouse with pearl buttons.

"What can I do for you, please?"

"We're here about Mark Drucker."

"He's a client," she said. "What about him?"

"I'm afraid he's dead."

The color drained from her face immediately, and for a moment Keough was afraid she might topple over. In fact, she grabbed her desk for support.

"I'm sorry," he said. "I thought you might have been called—"

"No," she said, then cleared her throat, and said again, "no, no one called. That's . . . quite a shock."

"I assume you knew him?"

"Well . . . we have a lot of clients I'm not acquainted with, but he was fairly . . . prominent so, yes, I knew him."

"Was his business handled by one of the partners, then?"

"Yes," she said, "he usually met with Mr. Anson. This will be quite a shock to both men."

"Are you all right?" Keough's tone was solicitous.

"I'm fine," she said, releasing the hold she had on the edge of her desk. "I'm sorry, it was just . . . a shock. I'm not . . . used to hearing about the violent death of people I know."

"We didn't say his death was violent," Steinbach pointed out.

She looked at him, the color coming back into her face, but her big gray eyes were still slightly glazed.

"No, you didn't," she said. "I'm sorry, I assumed since you were policemen that his death would have been . . . violent. Was I wrong?"

"As a matter of fact, no," Keough said.

"Too bad," she said. "I wish I had been wrong. How did he . . . uh . . . die?"

"He was bludgeoned to death."

"My God. Where? How?"

"At the Arch," Keough said. "We don't know what with, exactly, just a heavy object. He was struck repeatedly—"

He stopped when she held up her hand, and he watched as it took an effort for her to compose herself.

"Is there someone else we could talk to?" he asked. "Someone you could call?"

"No," she said, "it's all right. . . ."

"Don't the partners carry cellular phones?"

"Yes, they do, but I couldn't call them right now. They're either in court or a meeting. Please, tell me how I can help you."

"We're trying to find someone who can give us some information about Mr. Drucker. What he was working on, where his office is. We tried his home. But we didn't know about the separation."

"Did you try his divorce attorney?"

"Do you know that he had one?" Steinbach asked.

"We don't handle divorce work," she said directly to Steinbach. "I assumed he'd have one. . . . Are you trying to . . . catch me in something, Detective?"

"Ma'am," Steinbach said, "I'm just asking routine questions."

He sat back and allowed Keough to resume.

"Do you know where his office is, Miss? . . . I'm sorry, is it Miss? . . . "

"Yes," she said, "Miss Henry . . . Eileen Henry."

"Miss Henry . . . would you know anything about his office?"

"I'm afraid I wouldn't."

"Would you be able to check that file?"

"I'm afraid not."

"Can't . . . or won't?" Steinbach asked.

"You ask all the unpleasant questions, don't you?" she said

to Steinbach. "Is this good cop–bad cop, then? Am I suspected of anything? I'm only trying to be helpful, but you seem to think—"

Her professional veneer was on the verge of cracking. Keough wondered if there was something else going on; if she'd had some sort of relationship with Drucker other than a professional one.

"I'm sorry if you feel put upon, Miss Henry," Keough said. "We ask whatever questions come to mind during a homicide investigation. We can't afford to pick and choose."

"No," she said, "of course not. I'm sorry."

Keough and Steinbach exchanged a glance and then Keough looked back at Eileen Henry.

"Miss Henry, we really need to talk to Mr. Anson about Mark Drucker," he said. He removed one of his business cards from his pocket and set it down on the woman's desk. "Please have him call me and make an appointment."

"Yes, of course," she said, leaving the card where it was. "I'll certainly do that, Detective."

"Today or tomorrow," Keough said, standing up. "It's important that we don't let too much time go by."

"I understand." She started to rise. "I'll see you out."

"That's okay," Keough said. "We can retrace our steps. Thanks for your cooperation."

"Of course," she said. "We'll cooperate in any way we can."

Keough looked at Steinbach, who nodded, and both men went out the door.

Eileen Henry waited a few moments until she was sure they would have reached the lobby, then she got up and closed her door. Next she picked up the phone and dialed three digits.

"Yes, sir," she said, "they just left. Yes, sir, I'll be right in."

She left her office, walked down a hallway until she came to a door with the name Franklin Anson on it, and knocked.

*   *   *

Keough and Steinbach didn't speak again until they were outside the building, walking to the car.

"Good-looking woman," Steinbach said.

"Yep."

"Bad liar, though."

"Oh, yeah."

Fifteen

THEY REACHED THEIR office at about four o'clock, which surprised Keough. They'd covered a lot of ground that day, but then they'd gotten an early start. The office was empty, which was unusual, but there was a written message from Captain McGwire on Keough's desk.

"The boss wants me to call him at home," Keough said, reading the message.

"He say what about?"

"No," Keough said, "it just says to call him as soon as we get in."

Steinbach sat behind his desk, leaned back in his chair, and took a deep breath. His wife had been telling him to cut down on the donuts and bagels. He felt badly winded from a day's worth of running around.

"You gonna call him?"

Keough stared at the message, just two lines in the captain's very neat handwriting.

"I guess so," he said finally.

"You could always say we went straight home and didn't see it until the morning," Steinbach suggested. "Maybe it's about the newspaper business."

"If he was going to yell at me about that, he would have done it by now," Keough said.

"Can't be good news," his partner said. "Not if he *wants* to be called at home."

"Might as well get it over with."

Keough sat at his desk and dialed his superior's home phone. A woman answered.

"Mrs. McGwire?"

"Yes? Who's this?"

"It's Detective Keough, ma'am," he said. "The captain asked me to call him when I got in."

"All right," she said, not sounding happy. "Just a minute."

He heard her put the phone down and walk away, then heard the angry tones of an exchange. Heavier footsteps then approached, and the phone was picked up.

"I don't know what the hell you and your partner did today, Joe, but the mayor wants to see you in his office tomorrow morning."

"The mayor? What for?"

"How do I know? Whose toes did you step on today?"

"Nobody's," Keough said. "We talked to the wife and to Drucker's divorce attorney. We tried to see his other attorneys, but they weren't in."

"Who are they?"

"Shepp, Anson, and—"

"Crap!"

"Close enough," Keough said.

"That's a big firm, Joe, with their fingers in lots of pies— political and otherwise."

"So? Are we supposed to leave them out of our investigation?"

"You know what?" McGwire said. "Don't ask me, ask the mayor. You're supposed to be there at nine sharp."

"Great."

"After that, come straight back to the office. I want to hear what's going on."

"Does he want both of us, or just me?"

"It's your case," McGwire said. "Don't bother bringing Al. Just tell him to be at the office by ten."

"He'll be there."

"Fine. I've got to get back to my dinner."

"Sorry to start trouble, but your message said to call as soon as we got in."

"It's fine," McGwire said sourly. "The trouble started long before you called. That's what I get for coming home early. I'll see you tomorrow."

"I'll be here," Keough said, and hung up.

"What about the mayor?" Steinbach asked.

"He wants to see me."

"About this case?"

"I suppose."

"Not me?"

"No, but the boss said he wants to see us both at ten."

"Somebody bitched to the mayor," Steinbach said. "Who do you think it was?"

"Somebody," Keough said, "who was lying to us."

"Gee," Steinbach said, "and that's always such a small list. Whose dirty little secrets do you think we stepped into this time?"

"I don't know," Keough said thoughtfully. "Maybe the mayor will."

Sixteen

BEFORE THEY LEFT the office to go home, Keough and Steinbach decided that everyone they had talked to that day lied to them. This was not, however, unusual for a homicide investigation.

"That lady at Shepp, Anson," Steinbach said, still sitting back in his chair, "she was the worst. You see her face drain when you told her Drucker was dead? Something was going on there."

"Maybe," Keough said.

"You don't think so?"

"He just never struck me as a ladies' man."

"No? Pretty good-looking wife for a guy who wasn't a ladies' man."

"She explained that," Keough said. "She married him for his money."

"I wonder if she's getting any."

"We'll have to wait to find out."

"Like we have to wait to see his office," Steinbach said. "You know what? I can find his office on the computer."

"How?"

"Utilities," Steinbach said. "It wouldn't be hard. I'll start tomorrow morning while you see the mayor. Once I find it we won't need anybody to let us in. All we'll need is a court order."

"That's a good idea," Keough said. "You do some real work while I have to go and hold the mayor's hand."

"Hey," Steinbach said, "that's why you're the lead man."

"Well," Keough said, "one way or another we better get into Mark Drucker's office tomorrow."

"Don't worry, partner," Steinbach said. "We will."

Harry Brooks wasn't used to having a midweek day off, but because of the murder at the Arch there had been no need for him to go to work. Also, he'd put in enough overtime the morning before that he deserved a day off.

He'd slept late, letting his wife take the kids to school. This was usually his job, one he did when he got home from work, most days. He didn't turn in until both kids were safe in school, one in grammar, the other in junior high.

On this day, however, after his wife drove them, she was going to spend the day with her mother. He'd have to get his own dinner, and she'd be home after that.

The killer didn't know any of this, but it all worked in his favor. He watched the house, saw the wife leave with the kids. When she didn't return right away, he thought perhaps he'd have time to get it done earlier than he'd thought.

He sat in a car across the street from the house in the Sunset Hills neighborhood where the Arch security guard lived. The streets were empty at that time of day. Still, he knew he wouldn't be able to stay there indefinitely without someone paying attention.

Finally, Brooks got up, had his breakfast, and decided to do yardwork he would normally have done on the weekend. Dressed in old jeans and a T-shirt, he entered the garage through a door from the kitchen. He brought a rake and a hoe outside, left them on the lawn, then went back in search of several other items.

The killer saw his chance, left his car, and crossed the street.

That morning Keough presented himself at nine A.M. at the mayor's office in City Hall on Market Street. It was a beautiful old building but looked a minute or two away from being condemned. Keough had too much on his mind, however, to admire it.

When he'd arrived home, he'd found a message on his machine that disturbed him. It was from Valerie. She said she couldn't see him that night, but had made an appointment with her doctor for him for that next afternoon. Great, he thought, first the mayor, then the captain, and then another doctor. He decided to keep the appointment, though. After all, he *did* want to find out for sure if he was diabetic.

That wasn't what bothered him, though. It was Valerie's pronouncement she couldn't see him, with no explanation offered. When he called her at home, her machine picked up. She either wasn't home, or she was and just didn't want to answer the phone.

As he waited for the mayor to call him into his presence, he was still wondering which one it was.

What Keough didn't know was that he was waiting for the mayor's assistant, Kenneth Goddard, to finish a telephone conversation.

"I understand what's at stake here, Franklin," Goddard said, checking his watch for the fourth time in the past five minutes.

"I don't think you do, Kenneth," Franklin Anson said. "I don't think you understand the *complexity* of our position—*my* position—"

"Franklin," Goddard said, "I have to go. Detective Keough is waiting outside."

"Let him wait!"

"That's not a good idea, Franklin," Goddard said. "Look, I'll talk to you when I've finished with him."

"Kenneth," Anson said, "we *have* to get into Drucker's office before the police do. We *have* to."

"I'll call you back," Goddard said, and hung up on the sputtering attorney.

Goddard stood up, removed his jacket from the back of his chair, and put it on. He smoothed his hair down, shot his cuffs, and then went out to meet with Detective Joe Keough.

When Keough saw the man approaching, he knew he wasn't going to get to see the mayor. This man was too young, and he was white.

"Detective Keough?"

"That's right."

The man approached with his hand out. He appeared to be in thirties, well dressed, neatly trimmed, everything the bright, young, ambitious politician should be.

"You're not the mayor." Keough hesitated only a moment before accepting the man's hand.

"No, I'm not," the other man said, smiling. His handshake was firm, and he pressed Keough's hand between both of his.

"I was told the mayor wanted to see me."

"Actually, it was I who wanted to see you, Detective," the man said, "on behalf of the mayor." He finally released Keough's hand. "I'm Kenneth Goddard, the mayor's assistant."

"Is he too busy this morning?" Keough asked. "I could come back."

"That won't be necessary, Detective," Goddard said. "If you come with me to my office, I'm sure we can wrap this up quickly."

"Wrap what up?"

Goddard smiled and said, "We'd be better off discussing this in my office . . . if you would follow me?"

"Sure," Keough said, after a moment, "why not? After all, I'm already here."

"Excellent," Goddard said. "This way, please . . ."

Seventeen

"IF YOU'LL EXCUSE me for asking, Mr. Goddard," Keough said, once they were in the man's office, "what is your title?"

"I'm the mayor's executive assistant."

"That's not an elected position, is it?"

"No, sir," Goddard said, "I was hired by the mayor on the basis of my experience and merits."

Goddard seemed to Keough to be several years younger than himself. He wondered where the man's experience had come from but wasn't curious enough to ask. He had other questions on his mind.

"Why am I here, Mr. Goddard?"

"The mayor is concerned about the Drucker murder."

"How much does he know about it?"

"Well, he's—wait, do you mean about the case or about the murder itself?" Goddard asked.

"You tell me."

"Well, he knows nothing about the murder. I mean—"

"Did he know Mark Drucker personally?"

"Well, of course," Goddard said, "Mr. Drucker was prominent at political functions; he sat on many committees—"

"Which committees?"

"Well, off the top of my head I couldn't say—"

"Could you find out for me?"

"I'm sure I could have my secretary work up a list—"

"Good," Keough said. "Could you do that as soon as possible?"

"Well, yes, but—look here, I asked to talk to you, not be questioned," Goddard said.

"So talk, Mr. Goddard."

"The mayor is very concerned about Mr. Drucker's murder and would like it solved as soon as possible—"

"That makes two of us."

"—but doesn't want it done with a lot of waves."

"Waves?"

"Well, he'd like you to tread softly where some people are concerned—"

That was enough for Keough.

"Mr. Goddard," he said, "I don't play political games—especially not when I'm conducting a homicide investigation. My job is to find out who killed Mark Drucker, and I would like to do that as soon as possible."

"The mayor recognizes that fact, Detective Keough," Goddard said. "He is very much aware of your accomplishments since your arrival in St. Louis—"

"I'm not Mark McGwire, Mr. Goddard. I don't need my accomplishments tabulated by anyone."

"I didn't mean—"

"By the way," Keough said, cutting him off once again because he doubted the man had anything to say that would interest him, "how well did you know Mark Drucker, Mr. Goddard?"

"Me?"

"You must have met him at some political function."

"Well, of course," Goddard said, "I'm familiar with most of the people in town who are involved in politics—"

"So how familiar were you with Drucker?"

"We met in passing, I'm sure, but I didn't know the man

very well," Goddard said. "Say, why are you asking me—?"

"I really have to be going," Keough said, backing toward the door. "Why don't you have your secretary draw two lists up for me?"

"Two lists?"

"Yes," Keough said, "the one we spoke about earlier—committees that Mark Drucker sat on—and a list of names of people the mayor would like me to tread lightly around, and I'll see what I can do."

He was out the door before an outraged Kenneth Goddard could say another word.

Keough knew he'd be hearing about this later.

Goddard was incensed. How dare the man dismiss him that way! Keough barely gave him time to speak, questioned him as if he were a suspect, then brushed him off and breezed out the door. Two lists, indeed! He wouldn't have acted that way if he'd been talking to the mayor.

He could have chased the man down the hall and dragged him back into his office, but that wouldn't have looked classy—and Kenneth Goddard was always aware of appearances. He was going to have to figure out another way to handle this Detective Keough. He didn't care how much of a hero the man was for catching that maniac who'd been grabbing women from malls last year. Nobody shrugged off Ken Goddard that way and got away with it.

He stared at the phone, then remembered that he was supposed to call the attorney, Anson, back. He certainly couldn't tell Franklin Anson the way this meeting had actually gone. He decided to wait before calling the man back. Maybe he could still salvage something by calling Keough's supervisor.

Detective Joe Keough was going to find himself playing a lot of political games before Ken Goddard was through with him . . . and he was going to discover who the master of political games was in this town.

Eighteen

WHEN KEOUGH ARRIVED at his office just after ten, Steinbach was seated at his desk, speaking into the phone. He held up a hand in greeting as Keough walked to his own desk.

"No coffee?" Steinbach asked, as he hung up.

"Didn't have time after my meeting at the mayor's office."

"What did the great man have to say?"

"Beats me," Keough said. "Apparently it was some pissant assistant who wanted to talk to me."

"Assistant? Who?"

"Somebody named Goddard."

"Kenneth Goddard?"

"You know him?"

"I just know that he's some boy wonder the mayor hired last year, supposed to help him improve—what was it?—improve the profile of his administration? Something like that."

"Well, that boy wonder is supposed to be sending us a couple of lists."

"Lists of what?"

"Names," Keough said. "Committees that Drucker sat on, and the names of some people the mayor wants us to pussyfoot around."

"The mayor? Or Goddard?"

"Most likely Goddard."

"I hesitate to ask this," Steinbach said, "knowing how you feel about politics, but what did you tell Mr. Goddard we'd do with his lists?"

"I was on my best behavior, Al," Keough said. "I told him we'd see what we could do."

Steinbach looked surprised.

"Is the boss in?"

Steinbach shook his head. "Called to say he'd be about half an hour late. I heard his old lady yellin' at him in the background."

Keough checked his watch, saw that it was almost ten-thirty.

"You're not thinking about ducking out before he gets here, are you?" his partner asked. "He wanted us here at ten."

"And we were here."

"Joe—"

Whether they'd stay or run out became a moot point when Captain McGwire came striding into the office, red-faced and obviously in a foul mood.

"In my office, you two," he said, as he passed their desks.

As they both stood to follow, Keough was glad he had not taped a sports page to his superior's desk this morning.

"Close the door," McGwire commanded, as he sat heavily behind his desk. "Joe, talk to me about the mayor. Did you leave him happy?"

"I didn't see the mayor, boss."

"Why not?"

"I saw some twit named Goddard—"

"That twit is the mayor's executive assistant," McGwire said. "Talking to that twist is like talking to the mayor. Jesus, am I gonna get some more calls from the mayor?"

"Excuse me, boss," Keough said, "but did those calls come

from the mayor himself, or from the tw—from his office?"

"I spoke to His Honor himself, Keough," McGwire said, "or rather, I listened to him."

"Well," Keough said, "I certainly would have been . . . respectful as all hell if I'd gotten to speak to the mayor himself."

"Christ," McGwire said, "I don't need this."

"Other problems, Cap?" Steinbach asked.

"You're married, Al," McGwire said. "There are always other problems."

"I hear you."

"All right," McGwire said, "give me a verbal on what you got yesterday."

"Not much," Keough said, and then went through the day for his boss, who, as usual, listened closely and rarely interrupted.

"Shepp, Anson's a big firm in this town," he said, when Keough had finished.

"I know that," Keough said, "but we need to get a look inside the dead man's office, Cap . . . before somebody else does."

"I know that," McGwire said. "When you get the address, I'll get you a court order forbidding anything to be removed. I'll try to get it named an extension of the crime scene."

"Thanks, boss."

"Okay," McGwire said, "type up what you just told me when you get a chance and stay on it."

"Right." Keough and Steinbach both got up.

"Joe, when those lists arrive from the mayor's office, I want to see them," McGwire called out, as they exited the office.

"You got it, boss."

"Oh," McGwire called out, "one more thing. I've got a present for each of you."

They both stopped at the door, turned, and came back to the desk. McGwire opened the top drawer, took out two black things that looked like TV remote controls, and handed them each one. Each man looked down into his hand at a cellular phone.

"Aw, no, Cap," Keough said, "don't do this to us—"

"Cap, I can't carry this—"

"Carry 'em," McGwire said, "and use 'em. Stay in touch."

"Boss, I hate these things," Keough said.

"They go off in movies, restaurants," Steinbach complained. "Every asshole carries one—"

"And now you carry one, too," McGwire said. "The both of you. That's all."

"Cap—" Keough tried one more time.

"That's all!"

"Yes, sir," they both said, and left the office.

"What now?" Steinbach asked.

"We need to get inside Mark Drucker's apartment and office."

"Did we find his car?"

"Yes," Steinbach said, "officers found it in the Adam's Mark parking lot, across the street from the Arch."

"When did we find that out?"

"This morning."

"Why do I have to keep asking for this stuff?"

Steinbach sighed and said, "My life is full."

"What was the address on his car registration?"

"The Clayton address."

"Okay, so we don't know where he went from there."

"Not yet."

"And we can't get into his office."

"Not yet."

"Okay . . ."

Keough checked his notebook, then picked up his phone and dialed.

"Mr. Anson, please," he said, when the phone was answered.

"Who is calling?" the woman on the phone asked.

"The mayor's office."

"One minute."

There were some clicks, and then a man said, "Hello? Goddard?"

"I'd like to speak to Franklin Anson, please."

"This is he. Who is this, please?"

"Mr. Anson, this is Detective Keough, St. Louis Police."

"Oh, Detective Keough," Anson said, sounding puzzled. "I was sure the girl said it was the mayor's office."

"Really? I can't imagine why she would have said that. Anyway, sir, I'm really glad I caught you in. We need to talk."

"About Mark Drucker, yes. I wanted to make sure that we made contact today. I'm so sorry I wasn't here yesterday when you came in."

"When can we get together, sir? I have a few questions for you."

"Of course, I want to help in any way I can," the man said. "Mark's death was such a shock to us all. I'm, uh, in my office now if you'd care to come over."

"That's very kind of you, Mr. Anson," Keough said. "My partner and I will be right over."

"I'll be waiting."

Keough hung up and looked at Steinbach, who gave him some mock applause.

"That was very good."

"It gets better," Keough said. "When he picked up the phone, he thought I was Goddard."

"The whiz kid, not the mayor?"

"That's right."

"We better get over there before he decides to skip on it."

"Right. I'll tell the boss."

A look at Captain McGwire's office door told him that his superior was inside. That was the only time the door was closed. He walked to it and knocked, then opened and stuck his head in.

"... want a fuckin' divorce just say so—What is it,

Keough?" McGwire pulled the phone away from his ear and covered it with his hand.

"Uh, sorry, Cap, didn't mean to intrude," Keough said. "We're heading out to talk to Franklin Anson on the Drucker murder. I just spoke to him, and he's waiting for us."

"Fine," McGwire said, "just keep me informed."

"Yes, sir."

Keough closed the door and looked at his partner.

"Ready to go?" Steinbach asked.

Keough hesitated a moment, then said, "Let's do it."

Nineteen

WHEN THEY ARRIVED at Shepp, Anson, and Associates, their worst fears were realized.

"I'm sorry, gentlemen," the comely Miss Eileen Henry apologized. "There was just no way around it. He was called away right after he spoke to you. He was *very* distressed about it, but there was nothing he could do."

"When will he be back?" Keough asked.

"Not today, I'm afraid," she said. "You see, he was called away . . . to Kansas City."

"Kansas City?" Keough asked.

"Yes, you see, we have an office there, and an emergency came up—"

"All right, then, Miss Henry," Keough said, "we'll talk to Mr. Shepp."

Eileen Henry looked around the lobby for just a moment before she said, "I'm sorry, but Mr. Shepp is in court and will be for most of the day. He's our chief litigator."

"But he'll be back when the court adjourns for the day, right?" Steinbach asked.

"I'm afraid he'll go home from there."

"That's fine," Steinbach said. "We'll go there and see him. All we need is his address."

She spread her hands in a helpless gesture, one that was echoed by the wide-eyed look accompanying it, and said, "If I gave you that, Detective, I could lose my job."

"If you don't give it to us, Miss Henry," Keough said, "you could face an obstructing charge."

"I'm afraid you'd have to adequately prove that my not giving you an address obstructed your investigation beyond repair, Detective," Eileen Henry said, like a lawyer. "Do you think you could do that?"

"I don't know, Miss Henry," Keough said, "but I'd sure like to try."

"If you were to return with a court order instructing me to give you Mr. Shepp's address," she said, "I'd be happy to do so."

"Why do I have the feeling, Miss Henry," Keough asked, "that by the time we got back here with a court order you would have been called away on an emergency?"

Her eyes got wider, and she asked, "Why, whatever do you mean by that, Detective?"

When they left the law office, both men were incensed.

"We're getting the runaround," Steinbach said, "and I don't like it."

"Neither do I, Al," Keough said.

"So what do we do? We can't let them get away with this. What can they hope to gain?"

"All I can think of," Keough said, "is that there's some reason they don't want us in Mark Drucker's office."

"There's something there they don't want us to see?"

"Probably," Keough said, "but since this is politics we're dealing with here, there's no way to tell if whatever they're hiding has anything to do with the murder. It could be something else entirely."

"Evidence of something dirty they don't want to us to see."

"Right," Keough said. "There's got to be someplace else we can get Mark's office address from."

"Well, there is," Steinbach said, as if it were obvious.

"Where?"

"The computer."

"So what are we waiting for? Why didn't you suggest that before?"

Steinbach shrugged and said, "I had no reason to believe the lawyers wouldn't give us the address."

"They're lawyers, Al," Keough said, "and on top of that, politicians. What were you thinking?"

"I guess I lost my head," Steinbach said. "I was assuming they'd want to help find out who killed him."

"They probably will," Keough said, "as soon as they find what they're looking for."

"That shouldn't take long," Steinbach said. "After all, *they* know where his office is."

"Maybe," Keough said, "they just don't know where to look *in* the office, and they're trying to keep us away long enough for them to find it."

"Well, let's get to the computer," Steinbach said, "and maybe we can catch them in the act."

After Keough and Steinbach left, Eileen Henry walked to Franklin Anson's office. She knocked and entered. The gray-haired man behind the desk looked up and focused his pale eyes on her.

"Are they gone?"

"Yes, sir, but . . ."

"But what, Eileen?"

"How long do you think you can keep this up, sir? I mean, avoiding the police? They are investigating a murder."

"We just need enough time to go through Mark's office and find what we're looking for."

"And what if it's not in his office?"

"Then we'll let the police look around," Anson said, "while we search his home. We simply have to stay one step ahead of them." He ran his hand over his impressive mane of gray hair, leaving each hair perfectly in place. "You do see that, don't you, Eileen?"

"Yes, sir," she said, "I just . . ."

"Speak up, Miss Henry. It's just what?"

"I don't like lying to the police."

"Well, Eileen," Anson said, "I believe this firm pays you well enough to lie to *anyone* we tell you to lie to. . . . Don't you?"

She knew what the right answer to that question was, but she didn't give it. Instead she said, "Yes, sir."

"Good," he said, "Now see to it that the girl who put the detective's phony call through to me this morning is out of here by day's end. That's all."

"Yes, sir."

"No, that's not all," he said abruptly, arresting her movement toward the door.

"Sir?"

"You were fairly close to Mark Drucker at one time, Eileen, weren't you?" he asked.

She blushed and said, "You know I was, sir."

"Yes, that's right," he said. "It was my idea, wasn't it? Well, during that time did he ever mention a place, perhaps a secret place—a safe, a safety deposit box—where he kept important items?"

"No, sir," she said. "Mark was notoriously closemouthed about his business."

"Yes, yes," Anson said, "I remember you saying that." It was the reason he had instructed her to terminate the relationship she had *started* at his previous instruction. "All right, that's all."

*   *   *

After Eileen Henry withdrew, Franklin Anson picked up the phone and dialed a number. While it rang, he once again ran his hand lightly over his hair. He swore it was thinning, but no one else saw it—not his partner, not his wife, not even his mistress.

"Darling?" he said, when the woman answered. "We have to talk, tonight."

"What about your wife?"

"I don't want to talk to her," he said. "I want to talk to you."

She sighed. "All right, Franklin, but I'm really starting to hate this."

"I don't like it much either, darling," he said. "I'll see you tonight at the usual place."

Twenty

"BINGO!"

Keough turned and looked over at his partner, who had just gotten off the phone.

"Got it."

"Your computer sweetie came through again?"

Keough did not know this woman's name, or what she looked like, or even where in the department she actually worked. This was his partner's contact; he knew how to get ahold of her, and that was enough.

"You'll never guess where your buddy Drucker's office is."

Keough sat back and eyed his partner for a moment. "From the way you're looking at me," he said, "I'd guess it's in the mirror-image building across from where Shepp, Anson is."

Steinbach's face fell. "How did you know?"

"I didn't," Keough said. "I guessed—and I probably should have guessed sooner. We could have just walked over there and checked the directory in the lobby."

"Well," Steinbach said, shaking off his disappointment, "now that we know where it is all we have to do is get inside."

"We can get a warrant and have the management of the

building let us in," Keough said. He grabbed the phone just as the instrument on his partner's desk rang. By the time he was finished, Steinbach had hung up as well.

"All we have to do is go down to the courthouse—what's wrong?"

"That was the dispatcher from Sunset Hills," Steinbach said. "They need us at the scene of a homicide."

Keough looked around, but there were no other detectives in the room at the moment.

"We can pick up this warrant and be in Drucker's office to-day," he complained. "Let's find somebody else to give it to."

"I don't think you'll want to give this one away, Joe."

"Why not?"

"Because the victim's name is Brooks, Harry Brooks."

Keough stared at his partner for a few seconds and then said, "Yeah?"

"*Security Guard* Brooks?" Steinbach said. "From the Arch?"

Keough's mouth dropped open. When his voice came back, he said, "Maybe we just found our key source without the help of your computer sweetie."

"Exactly what I was thinking."

Keough pushed out of his chair. "Let's go. Maybe we can wrap up the scene in time to pick up the warrant anyway."

"I'm with you, partner," Steinbach said.

They pulled up in front of the house, parking behind de-partment vehicles that were already on the scene—two marked patrol cars and the medical examiner's car, as well as the crime-scene technician's van. There was also an unmarked car they assumed belonged to Sunset Hills police detectives.

With their shields hanging from their pockets, they were admitted to the scene and entered the garage.

"First team's here," Smiley Donaldson said, which drew dirty looks from the two local detectives.

"We could have handled this," one of them said.

"Detectives Keough and Steinbach," Donaldson said, "meet Detectives Fetterman and Budge."

Fetterman—the one who had voiced his displeasure—was in his forties and going to flab. He was the kind of man who always had a portion of his shirt hanging out of his pants and didn't notice. Budge—who wore his feelings on his face—might have been in his late thirties but was scowling too much to make it easy to tell. His sport jacket needed cleaning, as it was peppered with food stains.

"And this is Captain Beltran from Sunset Hills."

Beltran was a big man in his fifties who wore his blues well. He shook hands with both detectives.

"We didn't know what we had here until the doc arrived," he said. "He recognized the victim."

"Once I saw who it was," Donaldson said, "I verified it with the first detectives on the scene and then suggested they call you."

"We can take it from here, Captain," Keough said. The garage had too many people in it.

"You can have it," Beltran said. "Let's go, boys."

"Captain," Fetterman said, "this should be our case—"

"Come with me, Fetterman," Captain Beltran said, "and I'll explain why you don't want it."

The two local detectives followed their superior out of the garage, leaving just Keough, Steinbach, and Donaldson.

"Where is he?" Keough asked.

"Behind the car, and it ain't pretty. The killer used one of those tools for breaking up the earth, you know? Like you see on the commercials? Two handles, a long bar, and then a claw at the end? You dig it in and then turn it? Well, that's what he did."

Keough and Steinbach went to take a look. There was a lot of blood, but it had run under the car and pooled there in the cracked floor of the garage. Brooks was on his back, his arms straight out from his body, the hands clawing at the air. The tool had been buried in his stomach and turning it had released masses of blood and entrails.

"This is even more brutal than the other one," Donaldson said. "A lot of anger there."

"Or we're meant to think that's the case," Keough said. He glanced at a door in the wall to his right. "That lead inside?"

"Right," the ME said.

"Anybody go in yet?"

"Not till you arrived," Donaldson said. "I convinced the captain to call you. The other two detectives wanted this for themselves. I explained to him what the connection might be to the case down by the Arch. I think he's going to talk to his detectives about what the political implications of this case could be."

"Well, that's more than I know," Keough said, looking around. There didn't seem to be any other tools lying around. They were all hanging on hooks on the walls. Keough noticed three empty spaces.

"The claw must have come from there," he said, pointing.

"There's a rake and a hoe outside," Donaldson said, explaining the other two spaces. "Looks like he was going to do some yardwork."

"The killer must have been watching," Steinbach said, "waiting for his chance."

"We'll check for missing items," Keough said, "but I don't think we'll find any. This is another message."

"And what's that?" Donaldson asked.

"The killer is telling us that he got the keys to the Arch from Brooks here, and we're not going to find out who he is—not from Brooks."

"Covering his tracks."

"Very well," Keough said. "Doc, you see any bloody handprints around here?"

"Nope."

"Well, we'll take a look," Keough said. "He left them at the Arch; I'll bet he left a set around here, too."

"Can I have him?" Donaldson asked.

"Give us a minute, Doc."

"Sure," the ME said, "I'll wait outside."

They watched the man leave, and then Steinbach asked, "This has to be connected to the other one, unless we find out that the wife has a boyfriend."

"We'll have to look into that, but I agree. It's too much of a coincidence, him getting killed so soon after Drucker was murdered at the Arch on his watch."

"What if he did Drucker, and now somebody did him?"

"Possible, I guess," Keough said, "but more likely that he made copies of the necessary keys and sold them."

"I wonder if he knew what they were going to be used for?"

"Let's check his bank accounts, see if he made any big deposits. Why don't you get things moving outside, have some of the uniforms hit the neighbors, see if they saw or heard anything. I'll check out the inside of the house."

"And what about him?" Steinbach asked, indicating the dead man on the garage floor.

"Tell Smiley he can have him," Keough said.

"Okay," Steinbach said. "The house is yours."

Keough nodded, waited until his partner had left the garage, and then looked down at the body once more before turning and walking into the house.

Twenty-one

THE HOUSE WAS small, even though it had three bedrooms. He walked through and found it neat and tidy. It appeared the woman of the house did not work at an outside job. Everything was just too clean for that to be the case—unless they had someone come in and clean it. Given the size, however, and the fact that Brooks was a security guard, Keough did not think they were likely to have a cleaning woman.

The biggest rooms were the living room and the master bedroom. All the others were small. Keough walked through it, touching nothing. He was able to estimate the age and sex of the two children by the way their rooms looked.

There were no "extras" in this home, everything seemed very utilitarian. The last room he went entered was the master bedroom, and that's where he found the bloody handprints, right on the vanity mirror in the bathroom. He thought it odd that a home this size would have a master bath. He took just a moment to use his pen to open the vanity and examine its contents. There was only one vial containing a prescription drug, and it had Mrs. Brooks's name on it.

He met Steinbach out front.

"Let's get forensics into the bathroom off the master bedroom," Keough said. "Our guy left his handprints."

"Again? I guess he's decided that's his calling card."

"Find any witnesses?"

"I've got uniforms asking around, but so far nobody saw anything. Kids are all in school, the working spouses are all at their jobs, and some of these people were away this morning. They came back, saw the commotion, and stopped over to have a look."

"Nice, quiet residential neighborhood," Keough said. "Perfect place for a murder."

While Keough had been in the house, Donaldson had removed the body.

"What about the wife?" Keough asked.

"One neighbor said she doesn't work, so she could be back at any time."

"What a thing to walk in on," Keough said. He scowled, scratched his head. "I hate to do this, but we better leave a uniform here to wait for her. I want to see if we can get to Drucker's office this afternoon."

"I'll talk to the captain about leaving someone behind."

"Okay."

Keough turned to take one last look at the house and the garage. The rake and hoe were still just outside the garage door. They looked new. He wondered if Brooks had used the money he'd gotten from selling the Arch keys to buy them.

Steinbach returned. "The captain will leave a man here to wait for the wife. I told him to have his man get an address and phone number from her where she can be reached just in case she doesn't want to stay here."

"Is he leaving one of those detectives, or a uniform?"

"A uniform."

"Good. Come on, let's get over to Drucker's building before something else happens."

* * *

When they reached the mirror-image office buildings, they went into the second one, the one they had not been inside of yet. They checked the directory in the lobby and found Mark Drucker's name listed for a fourth-floor office. All the listing said was DRUCKER ENTERPRISES. At the bottom of the directory was a name and phone number for the management company of the building. They had decided not to take the time to go downtown for a warrant, but rather to see if they could get the management company to let them in. They could always collect the warrant in the morning.

"Why don't you stay down here and try to get them on your cell phone?" Keough suggested. "I'll go up and take a look."

"Uh, I can't."

"Why not?"

"I, uh, don't have my phone."

"Where is it?"

"In my desk drawer."

"We have orders to carry them."

Steinbach gave his partner a baleful stare. "Is this the pot calling the kettle black?"

"Okay, so I bend a rule or two, but I've got my phone." He patted his jacket pocket.

"Fine," Steinbach said, "you call the management company, and I'll go up and take a look."

"Fine."

Steinbach walked to the elevators, and Keough went outside to use his cell phone. He was still inexperienced with it and didn't know how well it would work inside. He dialed the management company number and spoke with a woman who sounded totally intimidated when he identified himself. This, he thought, was good. He told her what he wanted, and she put him on hold. This was bad.

He was listening to Barry Manilow Muzak when the front doors of the building opened, and two men came rushing out. He was standing to the left of the doors. The men came down the steps and turned right. They were wearing windbreakers, one with jeans and one with regular trousers. They had their hands in their jacket pockets. Keough could only assume that the Manilow music had lulled him to sleep because his brain kicked in late.

"Hey!" he shouted. "Hold it!"

Without turning, the two men ran. Keough chased after them, music still coming from his cell phone, which he was holding in his left hand. With his right he drew his gun.

The two men turned the corner, and Keough had to slow down to make sure he didn't run into anything. He inched along, gun held ahead of him, until he was able to peer around the corner. The two men had reached a car and were getting in.

"Hold it! Police!" Keough shouted.

Their hands came out of their pockets holding guns. They fired, and he threw himself to the ground, rolling one way while the cell phone went the other. By the time he came to a stop, up on one knee and ready to return fire, the two men had gotten into the car and were speeding away. It occurred to him only briefly to get into the car and chase them, but two things stopped him. One, he was worried about Stein-bach, and two, his partner had the keys.

"Fuck!" he shouted, and stood up. It was too much to hope that this was a coincidence. He turned and ran for the building, afraid of what he might find when he got upstairs.

As it turned out, he didn't have to wait that long. As he entered the building and headed for the elevators, one of them opened, and Steinbach came staggering out, one hand holding his head.

"Al!" Keough reached him and grabbed to support his part-ner. "Are you all right?"

"I'm okay. . . ."

"What happened?"

"When I got to the office door, it flew open, and two men

came out. We scuffled; one of them slugged me with something hard."

"Must have been a gun," Keough said. "They each had one."

"You saw them?"

"They shot at me."

"Are you okay?"

"I'm fine," Keough said. "I was on the phone and didn't react quick enough. They made it to a car and took off, firing a couple of shots at me. And no, I didn't get a plate."

"Looks like we both goofed," Steinbach said.

"You sure you're okay?"

"I'm fine," Steinbach said, as Keough released him. "I've got a bump, is all. Would you know them again if you saw them?"

"I'm not sure."

"Me neither."

"Fine couple of witnesses we make," Keough said.

"Yeah."

"Fuck," Keough said again.

"Well, one good thing came out of it."

"What's that?"

"When they came out of the office," he said, "they left the door open."

"Okay then," Keough said, "let me get my phone, and we'll go up. I dropped it outside."

On the way out, Steinbach asked, "Were they carrying anything?"

"No," Keough said. "Their hands were in their pockets. When they took them out, they were holding guns."

Keough walked over and retrieved his phone from the ground where he'd dropped it.

"Still working?" Steinbach asked.

Keough listened, then gave his partner a wry look and said, "Still waiting and still playing Barry Manilow."

"What?"

"I'm still on hold."

Twenty-two

OF COURSE, THEY didn't need the management company anymore or a warrant. Because Steinbach had witnessed two men coming out of the dead man's office, they had every right to go in and investigate.

The office consisted of two rooms, an outer office with a desk that was so spotless it couldn't possibly be in use, and then a larger inner office. Steinbach took the outer, Keough the inner.

Steinbach was done first and joined Keough.

"Looks like he doesn't have a secretary," he said. "That desk is empty."

"Well, this one's not," Keough said, "and look." He pointed to the right wall, which was lined with file cabinets.

Steinbach walked over to examine them.

"Couple are ajar," he said. "I don't think our friends found what they were looking for."

"Maybe not," Keough said, "but isn't it odd that they were as neat as they were? Like they didn't want anyone to know they were here?"

"Maybe those were their orders," Steinbach said.

Keough was seated behind the desk with a couple of

drawers open, but he slammed them in exasperation.

"I don't even know what we're looking for."

"A reason for someone to want to kill Drucker."

"I mean a damn business reason. I've looked through his desk, and I still don't know exactly what business he's in."

"Politics."

"For all we know that's a sideline. You saw the house he lived in, and this office isn't cheap. Politicians exist on small salaries and donations when they're running for office."

"And kickbacks."

"Kickbacks and salaries get bigger and better the higher you go," Keough said, "but I don't think Drucker held any important political office."

"Not that we know of."

"What was his angle then?" Keough asked. "What was it he did for a living?"

"Maybe looking through these files will tell us that."

Keough stared at the file cabinets. "I guess we're in for an all-nighter."

"Hey," Steinbach said, "weren't you supposed to see Valerie's doctor today?"

"Jesus," Keough said, looking at his watch, "an hour ago. Well, I guess that's out."

"You could go, Joe," Steinbach said. "I'll stay here awhile."

"You'd never get through these files, Al," Keough said. "In fact, neither one of us will."

"What do you suggest?"

"The place has been burglarized, right? And Drucker is dead? We're got every right to seal this place off and place a man on guard here."

"Two men."

"Right," Keough agreed, "two men. Whoever sent those two guys over here to search the place was trying to find something they don't want us to see. Now that we've got control of this place, I don't aim to let it go. Then we can bring in somebody familiar with politics to go through his desk and files."

"I'll get the locals here," Steinbach said, "and we'll seal it off." As he dialed the phone, he added, "Maybe you can get to that doctor after all."

Keough took out his slightly battered but still operable cell phone and said, "Maybe I can."

The doctor's name was Morgan, with an office in a medical building on Manchester Road in Brentwood. He wasn't a specialist, but for that reason he appealed to Keough. He had decided to simply go in blind for a checkup and see what the doctor had to say.

He called the man, apologized for missing the appointment, and asked if he could still make it. The doctor's nurse said he could. When the local cops arrived, Steinbach chased Keough out of the office, giving him the keys to the car.

"I'll get a ride."

During the ride to the doctor's office, he had a lot to think about. Two murders now, but definitely connected. Then there was the diabetes. Now—thanks to Steinbach—he had to worry about where he was going to live. When the owners of the house heard of Drucker's death, would they ask him to move? And how were they going to hear about it anyway?

Keough had always been able to keep his personal life going smoothly by keeping it simple. Now, suddenly, he was involved in a relationship and had a health problem.

The diabetes was bothering him more than he had realized. Alone in the car, he could admit to himself that he was scared.

Maybe this doctor's finding would be the opposite of the other one's, but then what? He'd just have to go somewhere for a third opinion. It would probably be better if Dr. Morgan concurred with the specialist's opinion, then he could get on with his life. A life devoid of beer, french fries . . . and what else? Somebody was going to have to give him a list of what not to eat, unless they just told him to stay away from everything he liked.

He would have complained that life wasn't fair, but he'd come to that conclusion a long time ago.

This just clinched it.

Twenty-three

"DIABETES," MORGAN SAID. "No doubt."

He was a red-haired man in his forties who wore a perpetually dour look on his face, which would have been youthful for his age if not for the lines. They were sitting in one of his small examination rooms. Keough had been weighed, categorized, his blood pressure and temperature taken and, finally, poked in the finger to have his blood checked.

"Three twenty-six is way too high," the doctor said. "We'll need to do some more tests to see which—if any—of your bodily functions have been affected, but for now I'll put you on some medication to try and get it down. You'll have to change your eating habits, the way you live—what do you do for a living?"

"I'm a police detective."

"Really? How interesting . . ."

The doctor got chatty after that, which Keough put up with. He didn't bother telling the doctor that he already had medication. And, as it turned out, this doctor was putting him on the same thing the other doctor had—Glucatrol.

"A friend of mine mentioned another medication," Keough

said, and then named the other medicine the specialist had put him on.

"I wouldn't take that," Morgan said. "We don't know if you need something like that yet, but even if you do, I'd prescribe an alternative. Why don't we just wait and see, okay?"

"Sure."

Morgan filled out a form and a prescription, and sent Keough out to talk to one of his nurses.

When Keough got in his car, he pulled out the prescription and the vial of pills he already had to compare them. They were the same, dosage and all. Morgan had told him to do some reading on diabetes as well, as far as what to eat and what not to eat. He gave Keough some brochures. Keough had similar ones at home from the other doctor, and he hadn't read those yet.

He was starting the engine when his battered cell phone buzzed. He fished it out of his pocket and keyed it.

"Yeah." He decided to answer it that way because anyone dialing the number knew who they were getting. If it was a wrong number, tough.

"Did you go to the doctor?" Steinbach asked.

"You won't use your cell phone, but you'll call me on mine?"

"Never mind. What did he say?"

"I definitely have diabetes. My sugar measured three twenty-six."

"What's it supposed to be?"

"Between seventy and one-fifty, according to him."

"Wow! It's double."

"I can do the math, Al."

"What are you gonna do?"

"He gave me a prescription."

"Just one?"

"Yeah, one of the same ones the other guy gave me. He doesn't like the other stuff."

"Did you tell him about the other guy?"

"No."

"Why not?"

"Are you still at Drucker's office?"

"Yes."

"What did you find out?"

"He sure sat on a lot of panels."

"Like what?"

"He's on the panel for 2004."

"Okay, I know what that is. . . . What is it?"

"It's all these businessmen and politicians who think they're going to turn St. Louis into a major city in time for the one hundredth anniversary of the world's fair."

"There's money involved, isn't there?"

"You bet. Anytime somebody mentions a 'program' somebody stands to make money."

"What else?"

"The casinos. He's involved with all those problems. The boats in the moats, the open-boarding question—"

"Open boarding?"

"Right now the casinos have boarding times, which they call 'cruises,' only they don't cruise anywhere."

"They don't?"

"Well, St. Charles used to, but Players and Harrah's aren't really boats, and the *President* hasn't cruised in years."

"What about the *Casino Queen?* That cruises."

"That's *East* St. Louis: Illinois's headache."

"I get it. Anything else?"

"Lots. He sat on boards that make decisions about new municipal buildings, new parking lots—he was involved with that whole parking lot thing around the Fox Theater. Joe, he had his fingers in all the pies."

"And what was his title? Or political office?"

"The best I can figure is that he was a political *advisor.*"

"That's it?"

"That seems to be enough."

"So anyone from any of these boards that he was sitting on could be a suspect."

"Right."

"I'll have to get on this mayor's assistant, what's his name . . ."

"Goddard."

"Yeah, the pissant. He's supposed to get us a list of some kind to let us know what Drucker was involved in, politically."

"I think it's going to be a long list."

"Get out of there and go home, Al. Let's deal with this tomorrow."

"Are you going home?"

"Yes," Keough said, "I'm starting my car now, and I'm not going to be one of those people who talks on his cell phone while he's driving."

"Are you okay?"

"I'm fine, Al," Keough said. "I'll see you in the morning."

He keyed the phone off before his partner could say anything else.

On the way home he thought about the murders rather than the diabetes. Obviously, whoever had killed Drucker—or had him killed, since politicians usually hired dirty-work people— had also killed the guard to clean up after himself. It was going to be necessary to speak to the guard's wife to see if she knew anything. It was possible the guard had taken a payoff to look the other way. Maybe she'd know if any large deposits were made in their bank account—unless the man was keeping it from her. Working with cops—especially in New York—Keough had seen many men cash their checks and destroy their pay stubs so their wives wouldn't know how much money they made.

At least he'd never had to hide his money from anyone—

not that he ever had that much. Actually, his bank account was healthier these days than ever, thanks to some money his friend Mike O'Donnell had sent him from that *Kopykat* book. He guessed that the Kopykat-Lover case from New York was going to be part of his life for a long time. He'd caught both men, but the case ended his New York career and sent him here, where—with the help of Mark Drucker—he'd gotten settled.

Round and round and back to that. He owed it to Drucker to find out who the man's killer was. But he was finding out things about the man he never knew, and he doubted the fact-finding was over.

Twenty-four

EILEEN HENRY LOOKED out the window at the policeman stationed in front of the mirror-image building across the way.

"Are they still there?" Franklin Anson asked.

"Yes, sir."

"Damn it."

Eileen let the vertical blinds snap back into place and turned around to face her boss. He'd been looking at her ass while she had been looking out the window. She knew it.

"Where's that damned Shepp?"

"He said he'd be here—"

The door opened abruptly, and Dexter Shepp entered the room. He was a small man, much smaller than his partner, and meek looking. However, it was immediately apparent that he was the dominant figure in the room. It was when she was in the room with both partners that Eileen Henry did *not* feel intimidated by Franklin Anson. And, oddly enough, she respected rather than felt intimidated by Shepp. Maybe it was because she felt sure the man had never looked at her ass the way Anson did.

Shepp, approximately the same age as Franklin, glared at his partner and shook with supressed rage.

"You're fucking this up, Franklin."

"Dexter," Anson said, "it's not my fault—"

"No? Whose, then?"

They were not in either man's office but rather in a meeting room that they had swept weekly for listening devices. All the other lawyers and employees had gone home for the day. It was just Anson, Shepp, and Eileen Henry who were still around.

"Dexter . . . did you see the policemen across the way? We can't get to Drucker's office now."

"We should have gotten into it before, Franklin," Dexter said.

"I had men in there today, but the police detectives interrupted them."

"And what happened?"

Franklin Anson looked at Eileen Henry.

"There was some shooting," she said.

"Oh, great!" Shepp exploded. "Was a cop hurt?"

"No, sir."

"Well, thank God for small favors," Shepp said. "What about the other men? Were they shot?"

"Not shot and not caught," Anson said, as if proud to be delivering the good news.

"Where did you get those idiots, Franklin?"

"They were, uh, recommended."

"I go to Kansas City for a few days . . . Where's Goddard been all this time?" Shepp demanded.

"Keeping a low profile," Anson said, "although he did call the lead detective—uh . . ." he looked at Eileen again.

"Detective Keough."

". . . down to the mayor's office to have a talk."

"Oh, that was a smart idea. What did he do, warn him off?"

"Um, he just told him that the mayor would like him to be, uh, discreet," Anson said.

"Discreet," Shepp said. "Do you know what it means to a detective when you tell him to be discreet?"

Anson, assuming it was a rhetorical question, remained silent.

"It means a cover-up."

"We could buy him off."

"Do you know who this Keough is?" Shepp asked.

"Not really."

"Find out, Franklin," Shepp said. "And I want to see Goddard. I want to see what we're dealing with before we try to buy this detective off. If we can't," Shepp said, looking at Eileen, "then there are other ways."

Eileen Henry had never felt this uncomfortable beneath Dexter Shepp's gaze before.

Al Steinbach let himself out of Mark Drucker's office and nodded to the officer in the hall.

"Have a nice evening, sir," the cop said.

"No one in or out, got it?" Steinbach asked.

"Yes, sir."

"No matter who."

"Yes, sir."

He left the building and had the same short talk with the two cops outside. Before leaving the office, he had called one of his sons to come pick him up. After some hemming and hawing, some bitching and moaning, nineteen-year-old Zack had agreed. Steinbach waited with the two cops, making small talk, until Zack pulled up in his little Mazda.

"Have a good evening, Detective," one of the cops said to Steinbach.

"You, too."

He got into the front seat of the car and pulled the door

closed. His knees were dangerously close to his chest so he eased the seat back.

"Jeez, Dad," Zack said, "Wanda's gonna have a fit. She just got the seat the way she likes it."

"Wanda? I thought your girlfriend's name was Zelda?"

"That was last week."

"Zack and Zelda, and now Zack and Wanda? Don't you know any Bettys, Zack? Or Glorias?"

"Boring names for boring girls, Dad," Zack said. "I'm gonna be late picking Wanda up because of this."

"Don't sweat it, son," Steinbach said. "She'll probably dump you when she finds out I moved the seat."

Zack swore and rammed the clutch into first. Steinbach looked up at the other building and, just for a moment, thought he could see someone looking out through the blinds of one of the windows.

Twenty-five

WHEN KEOUGH WALKED into the house, the red light on his phone machine was blinking. Funny, he'd started thinking of this as *his* house, even though he knew it wasn't. At least, it had become *his* home. Now he wondered if this place was going to suddenly be yanked out from under him.

There was one message, and it was from Valerie.

"It's ten after six, and I'm home. If you want to get something to eat, call me."

He checked his watch. It was five minutes past seven. He picked up the phone and dialed her number.

They met at a place called Zhivago's, in Clayton, a new Russian restaurant that Valerie had been wanting to try. When Keough suggested it, she tried to change his mind because of the diabetes, but he wouldn't allow it.

He wanted to pick her up, but she said she'd have to go straight home, so they each drove and met in front. She kissed his cheek, and they went inside and claimed the reservation she had made.

"You look nice," she said.

He was wearing a maroon silk shirt that she had bought him, khaki pants he'd bought himself.

"Thanks, but I think that's my line."

She was wearing a top that was almost the same color as his, only with a pattern and a border at the bottom. There were a few colors in the border, one of which matched the orange in her skirt.

The waiter came, and she ordered a black Russian, he an iced tea. "Unsweetened," he told the man.

"So my doctor made an impression?" she asked.

"He did."

"What are you going to do?"

"Whatever he tells me, I suppose."

"Him? Not the specialist?"

"Him, for a while," Keough said. "I still can't shake the feeling the specialist had his own agenda."

They studied the menu and discussed the entrées in terms of what he should eat. Finally, he gave up and closed the menu.

"I'll start watching it tomorrow," he said. "Let's make this like the condemned man's last meal."

"Oh, Joe, you're not condemned."

"Condemned to bland foods and unsweetened tea, no chocolate—"

"You don't eat a lot of chocolate."

"Because I didn't want to," he said. "Now I *can't.*"

"It makes a difference?"

"From where I'm sitting it does." She started to say something, but he cut her off with, "Let's order. I'm starving."

While they ate, they talked about the case he was working on rather than the diabetes. Since she was there right at the beginning, she wanted to hear everything about it.

"I know the name Shepp, Anson," she said. "Do you really think they're involved?"

"Involved? Yes, but to what extent I don't know. They *are* avoiding us, though, and that pisses me off."

The only thing he hadn't told her was the part where he had gotten shot at.

"What can you do about them avoiding you?"

"Well, I thought we'd get to see Anson in his office today, but he ducked out on us again. So tomorrow I think Al and I will try to get him at home. But here's what's interesting," he said. "I'm finding out more about Mark Drucker now that he's dead than I ever knew when he was alive."

"Like what?"

"Like I wasn't the only one he tried to help."

"The other lawyer? Ryn?"

"That's right. Why throw the man some work, except to help him out? And yet his own wife didn't like him, and he seemed to be some sort of power broker in politics in this town. We've got a woman in Shepp, Anson who says he was just a client, but if I'm any judge, there was more to it than that. Plus, nobody seems to want to talk about what he did."

"And what did he do?"

"That's just it," Keough said, "we don't know. Apparently, he was some sort of consultant, but he sat on lots of committees. He was involved with the gaming commission, with real estate—"

"What is it?" she asked, as he stopped short. He was looking at something over her shoulder.

Keough thought he was wrong at first. After all, the only likeness he'd seen of the man was a painting—and up until now, he'd had no way of knowing how good a likeness it was.

Now he felt it was pretty damn good.

"Do you know what Franklin Anson looks like?" he asked Valerie.

"No, I don't. Why?"

"Because I think he just walked in. Don't turn around," he added, just in time to arrest the movement.

"Who's he with?"

His jaw fell when he looked at the woman the lawyer had on his arm. He hadn't given her a glance until Valerie asked that question.

"I'll be damned."

"What?"

"It gets curiouser and curiouser."

"What does? Are you going to tell me who he's with or keep me in suspense?"

"Well," Keough said, "I only met her once. She was introduced as Miss Morgan, but her file says she's Hannah Morgan. She's also the administrative assistant to the manager of the Arch."

By the time Valerie turned, Anson and Hannah Morgan were gone.

"Are you sure?" Valerie asked, turning back.

"There's one way to find out," he said, dropping his napkin on the table. "I'll be right back."

"Wha—?" she started, but he was already walking away.

Keough approached the maître d's position and, while the man was talking with another couple who had entered, got a look at the reservation book. There he saw the name FRANKLIN ANSON clear as day.

"Sir? Can I help you? Is your table all right?"

"It's fine," Keough said, "just fine. Thanks. I just... thought I saw a friend."

The maître d' looked around and said, "And did you?"

"No," Keough said, "I most definitely did not."

"Was it him?" Valerie asked, when he returned to his seat.

"It was."

"What are you going to do?"

"Something I *hate* seeing people do in a restaurant."

"What's that?"

Very reluctantly he took out the cell phone Captain McGwire had given him and punched in Steinbach's home number.

Twenty-six

"I CAN'T HEAR you," Steinbach said.

"I'm not going to talk any louder on this thing," Keough said into the cell phone. "I'm in the middle of a goddamned restaurant."

"Go to the men's room," his partner told him.

He looked across at Valerie, who mouthed, "Go to the men's room," at him.

"I'm going to the men's room," he said to both of them.

Once in the men's room, he explained the situation to Steinbach.

"I can't come over there right now," Steinbach said, when he finished. "I'm knee deep in brown water here. Got the toilet all apart. I'd have to get cleaned up, dressed, and by the time I got there he might be gone."

"Okay, partner," Keough said. "I'll go it for both of us. Just wanted to let you know what was happening."

"Uh, Joe?"

"Yeah?"

"You're not going to make a scene in the restaurant, are you?"

"A scene? Me?" Keough asked. "Just because this rich son-ofabitch thinks he can jerk us around . . . no, I'm not going to make a scene. Hell, I can't even talk into a cell phone in a restaurant. . . ."

"Okay," Steinbach said, "just take it easy."

"Oh, by the way," Keough said, "guess who he's here with?"

When he returned to the table, Valerie asked, "Is everything okay? The waiter brought dinner. I didn't know if you wanted me to send it back—"

"No, no," he said, "everything is fine. Eat your dinner."

"But you are going to go over and talk to him, aren't you?"

"You bet I am."

"When? After we finish eating?"

"No," Keough said, "as soon as he starts. . . ."

Keough couldn't see Anson from where they were sitting, so he kept getting up to take a look to see if the man had been served his dinner yet. Meanwhile, Valerie ate hers while his got cold.

Finally, he came back to the table and almost gleefully told her, "Okay, he's been served."

"Good," she said, "because I'm finished, and I'm glad I brought my own car."

"Valerie," he said, hearing the annoyance in her voice, "I'm sorry about this, but this guy has the . . . the *gall* to think he can put me off during a murder investigation—"

She raised her hands to stop him and said, "It's fine, Joe. It's your job. Just go and do it and don't worry about me. I'll talk to you tomorrow."

"Val—" he started, but she stood up and walked out.

Keough realized that his anger had been building ever since Anson had entered the restaurant, to the point where it blocked everything else out. He was going to have to make this up to Valerie, but he couldn't worry about that now. Franklin Anson was about to learn that he wasn't above the law.

He called the waiter over, so he could settle the bill before interrupting the great man's meal.

The woman saw him coming toward the table. He saw her frown, perhaps not recognizing him, but then she placed him and quickly said something to the man. He, in turn, reached across the table to touch her hand and continued to eat with the other one.

When Keough reached the table, he pulled a chair out and sat down.

"Detective Keough, I presume?" Franklin Anson asked.

The words and the smug look on the man's face made Keough dislike him even more than he had already. He resented the man trying to take control of the situation. This was *his* show.

"Hello, Miss Morgan," he said. "Or may I call you Hannah?"

"H-hello, Detective Keough."

"Forgive me for interrupting your meal," Keough said, "but your dinner companion has been avoiding me, and I just couldn't ignore the coincidence that brought us together here."

"Detective," Anson said, "I don't know what you mean when you say I'm avoiding you. We spoke earlier and made an appointment, which I, regretfully, was not able to keep. If you'll call my office and make another one—"

"No," Keough said, "no more appointments, Anson. We're going to talk right here."

Anson gave him a smarmy smile and said, "I don't discuss business while I'm eating."

Keough looked at Anson's barely touched plate, then turned, and waved a busboy over.

"Sir?" the boy asked.

"Mr. Anson has finished eating," Keough said. "Take his plate away."

The busboy looked at the full plate in front of the lawyer, who was not quite as calm as he had been moments before.

"Now, look here—"

"Take it away!" Keough snapped at the busboy, who jumped. His outburst had also attracted the attention of the other diners seated around them, as well as the maître d', who came walking over to the table.

"Is there a problem?" he asked, directing the question to Franklin Anson.

"Yes, I'm afraid there is," Anson said. "This man is interr—"

"There's no problem, here," Keough said quickly. He took out his badge and showed it to the man. "Police business. Let me do mine, and you go back to doing yours."

"But, sir—"

"There's a couple waiting to be seated," Keough said. "Go!"

The maître d' had a look and there was, indeed, a couple waiting impatiently for him. The man looked torn, then turned, and walked back to his station to seat the new arrivals.

Keough looked at the busboy and said, "Now take the plate."

"Yes, sir."

As the boy reached for the plate and lifted it, Anson grabbed for it quickly. Keough reached out to stop him but at the last minute decided to tip the plate, dumping the contents in the lawyer's lap.

"Oh, my . . ." Keough said.

"What the hell—?" Anson snapped.

"I'm sorry, sir—" the busboy said.

"Come on, Franklin," Keough said, grabbing the man by the lapels, "we better go to the men's room and wash that off."

"Hey, wha—?" Anson started, but Keough hauled him to his feet. He began pushing the lawyer across the floor, saying "Excuse me, just an accident," and "My friend is very clumsy, excuse us. . . ." along the way.

When they reached the men's room, he pushed Anson through the door roughly and followed him.

The attorney staggered, righted himself, and said indignantly, "See here—"

"My show, lawyer!" Keough shouted. "You've been avoiding me and, in doing so, impeding a murder investigation. I could lock your ass up for that alone."

"I don't think—"

Keough pushed the man so he banged into one of the sinks. As he reached behind him for support, he pressed one of the faucets, causing it to turn on full blast. Water splashed all over Anson. Keough's vision was impaired by rage, and he knew he was close to losing control. It had happened before, in New York, and he had paid the price. That time it was also in a men's room, when he caught a weeny wagger pulling down a little boy's pants. This time it was a big-shot lawyer, but Keough decided to treat the man like a sex offender. He wanted all of Anson's aplomb to fade away in the moment.

He pushed the rage down so it was at a slow burn in his belly. His vision cleared, and he stepped close to the lawyer as the water ceased to flow.

"A few questions, Counselor," Keough said. "If I like the answers, I won't lock you up."

Anson stared at Keough and seemed to sense the man's controlled rage. There was nothing he could do about this now, but he vowed that the detective would pay for these indignities later.

"W-what do you want to know?" he asked, trying to keep his voice steady.

"How much did you know about Mark Drucker's business?"

"H-he was a client. We knew what we had to know to serve his interests."

"Which were?"

"I—I could answer these questions a lot better in my office, Detective."

"We're not in your office, Mr. Anson," Keough said. "We're in mine."

"I can't—can't do this here, Detective—"

"Do you know who killed Drucker?"

"No."

"Did you have him killed?"

"No!"

"Did you send two men to his office to look for something?"

"I . . . I didn't do any of those things. . . . I . . . I didn't—"

Suddenly Keough decided to let him go. He backed away, giving the man room to move away from the wet sink. As Anson did so, he slipped on a wet patch on the tiled floor and almost fell.

"I tell you what, Mr. Anson," Keough said. "I'm going to let you go back to your dinner companion. Tomorrow morning you're going to meet me and my partner at your office at ten sharp and discuss Mark Drucker's business. Do I make myself clear?"

"Yes, but—"

"If you're not at your office, I'll come to your home." He looked down at the man's left hand and saw a wedding band on his finger. "If you're not there, I'll talk to your wife. Maybe she'd like to know who you were out to dinner with tonight."

"You can't—"

"I can, Anson," Keough said, "and I will. You see, this is a homicide investigation, and I can run it any way I see fit. Do I make myself clear?"

Anson cleared his throat and said, "Yes."

"Fine," Keough said. "Now if I were you, I wouldn't go out there looking like that. I'd get all cleaned up."

He turned to leave, then stopped at the door.

"If your partner, Mr. Shepp, also is there tomorrow, I'll consider that a bonus."

Anson didn't answer. He stood there looking wet, bedraggled, and shaken. Keough knew he hadn't made a friend.

Outside he walked past Hannah Morgan, who was still sitting rigidly at the table, and said, "We'll talk another time, Miss Morgan. Count on it."

As he walked past the maître d', the man said, "Is everything all right . . . sir?"

"Everything's all right with me," Keough said. "The meal was excellent. My compliments to the chef."

"B-but, Mr. Anson—"

"If he's not out of the men's room in a few minutes," Keough said, "I'd go in and check on him if I were you."

Twenty-seven

BY THE TIME Keough got home, he knew he'd made a mistake. How badly he was going to have to pay for it depended on other people. He went to bed and didn't think about it the rest of the night.

When Franklin Anson came out of the men's room, he walked directly to his table and said to Hannah Morgan, "We're leaving."

He barely slowed the car down to let her off in front of her apartment. When he got home, he made a call and was annoyed that his voice shook when he spoke.

"We have to do something about this Detective Keough," he said, "now!"

"Calm down," the voice on the other end said. "Tell me what happened. . . ."

When Keough got to the office the next day, Al Steinbach was already at his desk.

"What happened last night?" he asked. "You were supposed to call me."

Keough told his partner everything that had happened at the restaurant and then said, "I blew it."

"What we don't know is, how bad?" Steinbach asked. "You want to wait for the boss to show up and see if he knows anything? Or you want to head for Anson's office and see if you did any good?"

"Let's go to Anson's office," Keough said. "If he's not there, then he probably made some calls when he got home last night, and I'll hear about it later."

"We'll hear about it," Steinbach said. "We're partners, remember?"

"Not last night, we weren't," Keough said. "Last night was all mine."

In the car, Steinbach, who was driving, asked, "What happened last night, Joe?"

"I told you—"

"No, I mean . . . *what happened?*"

Keough thought a moment before speaking.

"I just lost it, Al," he said finally. "The more I thought about it the madder I got that this guy was jerking us around. I even decided to wait until he was served so I could interfere with his dinner."

"Seems to me there was something else going on, though."

"You mean the diabetes?" Keough asked. "Yeah, you might be right. Might be everything just came to a boil—the diabetes, Drucker's death, wondering if I'm going to have to move, and these lawyers playing us for jerks."

"Was this the kind of thing that used to get you into trouble in Brooklyn?"

"Oh, yeah," Keough said. "I've managed to hold my temper here so far, even with the Mall Rat last year, but last night . . . I don't know. . . ."

"Well," Steinbach said, "we'll just have to wait and see how much damage control we're going to have to do."

"You're a good partner, Al," Joe said. "I'm just glad you'll be able to say honestly you weren't there last night."

"I wish I was."

"Why?"

"I did more damage on my plumbing than good last night," he said. "Today the plumber's coming, and it's going to cost me a fortune!"

When they reached the offices of Anson, Shepp, and Associates, they calmly presented themselves at the reception desk and asked for Mr. Franklin Anson. The receptionist made one call and then said, "Mr. Anson will see you immediately."

Eileen Henry appeared in the reception area moments later and said, "This way, gentlemen."

Keough and Steinbach exchanged a glance and both were thinking the same thing—this was too damn easy.

Keough was surprised when Miss Henry showed them into Dexter Shepp's office. Anson was there, and a second man whom he recognized from the portrait in the office.

"Detective," Shepp said, advancing on them with outstretched hand, "I am Dexter Shepp. I understand from my partner that you very much wanted to speak with us about poor Mark Drucker?"

"Yes, sir," Keough said, wondering what was going on. Was Anson simply going to forget about what happened last night in the bathroom of the restaurant? For the moment the man seemed content to sit behind his desk with a stony expression on his face and let his partner carry the ball.

Keough directed his attention to Shepp, who, though shorter than his partner and rather stout, projected his personality much more forcefully. Of the five people in the room, four of them seemed to be orbiting Dexter Shepp.

"Detective Keough, is it?" Shepp asked.

"That's right," Keough said, "and this is my partner, Detective Steinbach."

"Please, gentlemen," Shepp said, "have a seat. Can we get you some coffee?"

"If you don't mind, Mr. Shepp," Keough said, "we came here for some answers, not refreshments." He felt his ears beginning to burn. He resented the attitude being projected by the attorneys.

"Of course," Shepp said, seating himself in a chair next to his partner's desk. "We'll help in any way we can."

"I'd like to know why the sudden turnaround?"

"Sudden?"

"You've been avoiding us like the plague ever since the murder."

"Oh, I don't think that's true," Shepp said. "I've been in Kansas City, and Franklin. . . ." He looked at his partner, who still hadn't spoken. "Well, I know Franklin has been busy, but we certainly never meant to avoid you."

Keough looked at Steinbach.

"Well," Steinbach said, and it sounded lame even to Keough, "it sure seemed that way."

Shepp stared at Steinbach, then looked at Keough, and said, "Ah, I see."

"You do?"

Shepp nodded. "This is why you chose to humiliate my partner last night? Because you felt we were avoiding you?"

At the mention of last night, Franklin Anson shifted in his chair, and Eileen Henry looked out the window.

"That's right."

"Detective," Shepp said, "I must tell you that I've persuaded my partner not to file charges against you in this matter."

"And why would you do that, Mr. Shepp?"

"It's my understanding that Mark Drucker was a friend of yours. I take that into account when viewing your actions."

"Well, that's very big of you, Mr. Shepp," Keough said. "Could we talk about Mark Drucker now?"

"Surely."

Keough closed his eyes. He hated people who said "Surely," when they could have said "Yes," or just "Sure."

"What kind of business was he in?"

"Mark had interests in many fields," Shepp said. "However, our dealings with him involved real estate."

"Not politics?"

"Oh, no," Shepp said. "No, we try to stay away from politics, Detective. Neither one of us is very good at it."

"And yet you go to political functions, parties, fund-raisers, that sort of thing?" Steinbach asked.

"Why, yes," Shepp said. "We try to give back to the community whenever we can."

Keough was studying Franklin Anson's face while Shepp answered Steinbach's question. It looked to him that the only thing Anson wanted to give to the community was Keough's liver. When Anson saw Keough looking at him, he averted his eyes—more out of hatred than fear, Keough was sure.

Steinbach was telling Shepp how he and his partner were attacked by two men when they went to Mark Drucker's office in the next building.

"How horrible."

"Of course, you knew Drucker had an office there?"

"Of course."

"And do you have a set of keys?"

"Why would we have a set of keys to his office?" Shepp asked.

"Well, if you were partners—"

"I never said we were partners, Detective," Shepp replied. "We had business dealings. In point of fact, Mark was a client—and a friend—but never a partner."

"I see," Steinbach said. "Well, as his friend would you have any idea who would want to kill him?"

Instead of answering, Shepp looked at Keough.

"It was my understanding you were the lead man on this case, Detective Keough."

That was interesting. Shepp must have made some calls.

"Detective Steinbach and I are partners," Keough said. "It doesn't matter to us which one asks the questions."

"I see."

"Could you answer my question, Mr. Shepp?" Steinbach asked.

"I *could*, Detective," Shepp said, "but I'm afraid anything I could come up with would be pure speculation."

"That's what I'm asking you to do, sir," Steinbach said. "Speculate."

"Well, then, I'd speculate that his wife might have a reason to kill him."

"What reason would that be?"

"I understood Mark was taking steps to break their pre-nuptial agreement."

"Could he have done it?"

Shepp spread pudgy hands that were so pale they looked like Mickey Mouse gloves and said, "There are always loop-holes, Detective."

"Especially in your business, huh, Counselor?" Keough asked.

"Life would be very uninteresting without them."

"Mr. Anson?" Keough said. "You haven't said very much. Would you care to speculate on who might have wanted Mark Drucker dead?"

Anson seemed to consider the question carefully before saying, "Motives for murder are so varied, aren't they, Detective? I mean, the smallest thing could cause one person to want another person dead."

Keough got Anson's message, loud and clear.

"Detective Keough," Shepp said, "I want to apologize if you thought we were trying to avoid you, and I assure you that we will be available to you at a moment's notice until you've caught this killer."

It sounded like a dismissal to Keough, and he wasn't ready to be dismissed.

"Do either of you gentlemen—and you, too, Miss Henry— know a man named Harry Brooks?"

"I don't believe I do," Shepp said. "Franklin?"

"Doesn't ring a bell."

"Miss Henry?" Shepp asked. "Is this someone we have done business with?"

"I don't believe so, sir."

"I don't think he would have been," Keough said. "You see, Harry Brooks was a security guard at the Arch."

"Was?" Shepp asked.

"He was murdered yesterday."

"And because of his job, and where Mark's body was found, you suspect a connection?"

"We're looking into it."

"Well, I'm afraid we can't help you there, Detective."

"What kind of businessman was Mark Drucker?" Keough asked.

"Rather ruthless, I'm afraid."

"And what kind of friend?"

"Loyal," Shepp said, "but I'm sure you know that."

Keough didn't comment.

"Was he involved in any big real-estate deals?" Steinbach asked.

"Many," Shepp said.

"I mean, the kind someone might kill him over?"

"I wouldn't want to make that kind of speculation, Detective," Shepp said. "Since you have found Mark's office, I would think you could get that kind of information from his files."

Keough and Steinbach exchanged a glance. This was not going as they'd hoped. It was too controlled, as if their questions had been anticipated, and the answers rehearsed.

"All right," Keough said, "we'd like to thank you all for

your cooperation . . . and Mr. Shepp, we probably will be calling on you again."

"As I said, Detectives," Shepp replied, "we'll be available."

As they started from the room, Keough turned and asked Anson, "How is Miss Morgan doing today? I hope I didn't make too bad an impression on her last night." Before Anson could react, Keough added, "Oh, never mind. I'll just ask her myself, next time I see her. Good-bye, gentlemen . . . Miss Henry."

The two detectives left, and Eileen Henry looked from boss to boss, wondering which one would explode. Her money was on Franklin Anson. She had no idea what had happened the night before, but she knew him well enough to recognize the fact that he was incensed about something.

"That'll be all, Miss Henry," Dexter Shepp told her.

Twenty-eight

"WHAT DO YOU think?" Steinbach asked, when they got outside.

"Something stinks," Keough said.

"You said it."

"They're holding something back," Keough said. "I just don't know if it adds up to murder."

"And what about Anson?" Steinbach asked. "After what you told me you did to him, he was pretty damn calm."

"It's Shepp," Keough said. "It's very obvious who the controlling partner is in this firm."

"What are they trying to pull, though?" Steinbach asked. "First they avoid us, and now they'll be available to us whenever we want."

"And what about that line about not being involved in politics?" Keough asked.

"They can't really expect us to buy that," Steinbach said. "They knew Drucker as more than just a real-estate client."

"That's for sure," Keough said, "and we know that they know Goddard, in the mayor's office."

Keough looked up at the windows of Shepp, Anson, and Associates.

"Al, we still got men on Drucker's office?"

"Men we borrowed from the locals, yeah," Steinbach said. "Don't know how long we can keep them there, though."

"Did you take anything home with you to check out?"

"Yeah, but it didn't show me a whole heck of a lot."

"Why don't we go up and have a look around now," Keough said, "since we're right here, anyway."

"That's fine with me," Steinbach said.

They walked from the first building to the second and encountered a uniformed officer in the lobby who nodded to them, recognizing one or both of the men.

In the elevator Steinbach said, "You think they sent those two guys who shot at you?"

"I'd bet on it," Keough said. "If it was them, and they didn't find anything, it must be killing them that they can't get into his office."

They got out of the elevator and walked down the hall to Mark Drucker's office.

"You know, Joe," Steinbach said, "a law firm like theirs probably has a lot of skeletons in its closet that they wouldn't want us to find during the course of this investigation."

"I know," Keough said, "but that doesn't necessarily make them murderers."

"It could still be anybody," Steinbach said, as they reached the door. "We can't afford to get fixated on them."

"I agree," Keough said. "We'll have to talk to the ex-wife again. Maybe she's had some ideas about people with personal grudges."

They opened the door and went inside and met up with a second uniformed officer. They displayed their shields for his benefit, and Keough said, "Why don't you and your partner go and get some coffee? We'll be here awhile."

"Thanks," the cop said. "We'll be back inside an hour."

"Fine."

As the man left, Keough walked to the window and looked

out. He could see the other building and the windows of Shepp, Anson.

"Try this, Al."

"Shoot."

Keough turned and looked at his partner.

"Drucker had something on Shepp, Anson, both, or the firm. He takes this office right across from them to rub it in their faces."

"They get fed up and kill him?" Steinbach asked. "And now they're desperate to find the info?"

"How's it fit?"

"Depends on how long the blackmail was going on, I guess," Steinbach said.

"Long enough for them to *get* fed up and decide to do something about it."

"Can't see either one of them doing it," Steinbach said. "They would have had to hire it done."

"Let's put the word out that we're looking for a professional hitter in town," Keough said. "He does Drucker and then the guard to cover up."

"And he's gone by now," Steinbach said.

"Maybe," Keough said, "or maybe he's not finished."

"You mean there's still somebody else who could be a weak link?"

"Maybe."

"Who do you have in mind?"

"Who was with Anson at the restaurant last night?"

"You mean the woman from the Arch?"

"Why not? She could be the one who found them the right guard to bribe," Keough offered.

"Well," Steinbach said, "if we could convince her that she might be in danger, maybe she'd talk."

"After we're done here," Keough said, "you take her, and I'll take the ex-wife. Let's see what we can get out of them."

"Okay," Steinbach said, "but for now let's see what we can get out of this place."

After Keough and Steinbach left Shepp, Anson, Dexter Shepp looked at Eileen Henry and said, "That'll be all."

"Yes, sir."

The two men waited until she left, and then Franklin Anson exploded.

"That sonofabitch!" he roared. "I should have killed him—"

"Calm down, Franklin," Shepp said. He didn't shout, but his tone sat his partner down, still fuming.

"Did you hear the comment about Morgan? See the arrogant look—"

"There's no arrogance in the man, Franklin," Dexter Shepp said, "but he is dangerous. I think that's fairly obvious. I don't think he's going to back away from this thing."

"Maybe for money?" Anson suggested, although he would much rather have broken Keough than paid him.

Shepp rubbed his jaw and tapped his index finger against his lips.

"No, I don't think he'd take money."

"Then what do we do?"

"Well," Shepp said, looking at his irate partner, "killing him is just not an option, but—"

"But what?"

"There are ways we could keep him otherwise occupied."

"Like what?"

"Let's make a few calls," Shepp said, "and find out, shall we?"

"Dexter," Anson said, "you're a devious sonofabitch, and you've got that look in your eye."

"Go back to your office and wait for me," Shepp said. "This shouldn't take very long."

Anson stood up and walked to the door.

"Make it something good, Dexter," he said before he left. "Make it something very good."

After a couple of hours of neatly ransacking Drucker's office, they still didn't find anything suspicious. Keough called the office and picked up a message left for him by Hannah Morgan.

"What's that about?" Steinbach asked.

"She says she has to see me about something urgent."

"Think she's going to give her boyfriend up?"

"I don't know," Keough said, "but whatever she wants to talk about she doesn't want to discuss it at work. The message says she's at home, and she left her address."

"Where does she live?"

"On Prague Street, near the intersection of Chippewa and Hampton? Do you know where that is?"

"I do," Steinbach said. "There's a big shopping center right across from there. Come on, I'll drive."

"I think we should split up, Al," Keough said. "One of us has to talk to Harry Brooks's wife and see what she knows."

"Okay, so change of plans," Steinbach said. "You take the Arch lady instead of me."

"And I can stop in on Mrs. Drucker again," Keough said. "Maybe she's come up with an idea about where her husband might have been living."

"I also wanted to play with the computer some, see if I can locate another address for Mark Drucker, either business or residence. Maybe whatever those two were looking for yesterday will be there."

"Okay," Keough said, "so you'll take me back to the office so I can get my car and then we'll meet up there again later, at the end of the day, before either one of us goes home."

"All right."

"And maybe I'll get my ass reamed by the boss about what happened last night."

"You think Anson and Shepp will report you?"

"If they don't," Keough said, "I'm really going to be waiting for the other shoe to drop."

They looked around the office, and Steinbach said, "I can't even think of anything here we should take with us."

"Why don't we come up with somebody of our own to watch this place and let the locals go?"

"Who'd you have in mind?"

"It's your town," Keough said. "Don't you know somebody who needs the work?"

"You mean . . . like a PI?"

"Unless you can think of somebody who owes you a favor."

"You know," Steinbach said, "I think I just might be able to do that."

"Okay, then let's get moving," Keough said. "We'll tell these two uniforms they can stay until the end of their shift, then go back to their boss, and tell him we don't need them anymore."

Twenty-nine

KEOUGH FOLLOWED HIS partner's directions, taking Highway 44 to Hampton and then Hampton to Chippewa. From
that point he was on his own, but managed to find Prague
with just a couple of turns. He followed the numbers and
found easy parking in front of Hannah Morgan's building.

They were what was called in Brooklyn "semiattached"
homes, which meant they were joined in the middle, but free-
standing on either side. It also looked like there were two
floors, so that each structure apparently housed four apartments.

He went up the steps and found the name MORGAN on a
doorbell. When he pressed it, he didn't hear anything from
inside, but within moments the door was open, and she was
standing there. She was wearing a pair of tight jeans and a T-
shirt with enough of a V-neck to show off some cleavage. This
was very different from the business attire he'd seen her in at
the Arch and the dinner attire she'd worn last night at the
restaurant.

Nothing he'd seen her in to date hinted at this kind of
showy dress in her private life. Not provocative, exactly, just
slightly revealing.

"Miss Morgan," he said.

"Thank you for coming, Detective. Please, come in."

He entered and found himself in a common hall. There was a stairway leading up and a door to his left which was open.

"I live right in there," she said, indicating the open door.

He entered, and she came in behind him, closing both doors. He turned and looked at her, and she almost jumped. She had her hands together in front of her, working them nervously.

"All right, Miss Morgan," he said. "I'm here. What was it that's so urgent?"

"W-would you like something to drink? Coffee? Iced tea? A-anything?"

"No, thank you. Maybe we could sit?" That might put her more at ease.

"All right."

The living room they were in was furnished very simply and serviceably. Nothing elaborate or fancy. A sofa, two chairs, an end table, a coffee table, a TV. They each chose a chair, which kept the sofa between them.

"All right, Miss Morgan," he said, giving her the okay.

"I'm, uh, sorry," she said, still wringing her hands. "I was frightened last night."

"By me? I'm sorry for that, but—"

"By you, but also by Franklin," she said. "He was furious after you left."

"Did he take it out on you? Physically, I mean?"

"Oh, no," she said. "We left right after you did, and he drove me home, but he was ranting all the way about what . . . what he was going to do to you."

"I see," Keough said. "Is that what you wanted to tell me?"

Nervously, she looked at her watch.

"Uh, no, that wasn't it."

She fell silent and had to be prompted.

"What was it, then?"

"I just . . . I didn't want you to think I was, uh, involved. . . ."

"In what?"

"In whatever you think Franklin was involved in."

"Did he tell you what it was?"

"No, he didn't."

"Can't you guess?"

She blinked at him, her eyes very wide and liquid, and said, "Um . . ."

"I'm still investigating the murder of Mark Drucker, Miss Morgan," he said.

"And you think Franklin was involved in that?"

"He knew Drucker," Keough said. "Right now everybody who knew him is a suspect."

"Oh, I see. . . ."

"Did you know him?"

"Well, I'd met him once or twice, but I wouldn't say I knew him."

"And how do you know Mr. Anson?"

"Um, he knows my boss, and we met at a party once. . . ."

"What kind of party?"

"Oh, it was business, something I had to attend for work."

"Was this the kind of party you might have met Mark Drucker at?" Keough asked.

"Well, actually, yes . . ."

"I don't mean to pry into your private affairs, Miss Morgan, but was last night your first date with Mr. Anson?"

"Date?" she repeated. "I don't think—I guess I don't think of them as . . . dates, exactly."

"What are they, then?"

"Dinners."

"And what happens after?"

"He drives me home."

"And that's it?"

"Yes."

"No movies, no holding hands, nothing . . . romantic?"

"I—n-no, nothing romantic. I just think he likes having . . . dinner companions."

"Attractive dinner companions, you mean?"

"Well . . . yes."

"So it wasn't the first time?"

"No."

"How many times before?"

"Three, maybe four."

"And yet you call him by his first name?"

"H-he asked me to," she said, and looked at her watch.

"Do you have an appointment, Miss Morgan?"

"What? No, I don't."

"You keep looking at your watch."

"I'm . . . nervous. I've never had a policeman in my home before."

"I see. Well, we don't bite."

She smiled wanly and said, "I know."

"Was there anything else?"

"Uh, n-no," she said, "I guess I just didn't want you thinking I was . . . involved in anything."

"Then I guess I'll be going."

"All right," she said, and stood up. Her hands were clasped together, and he had the feeling she wanted to look at her watch again.

"Miss Morgan."

"Yes?"

"Do you know a man named Kenneth Goddard?"

"I—well, yes, I do. He's one of the mayor's assistants."

"Is that the only way you know him?"

She frowned. "What do you mean?"

"I mean, did you meet him at the same parties you met Mark Drucker and Franklin Anson at?"

"I suppose so."

"Did you ever go out with Drucker or Goddard?"

"Go out? . . ."

"Date? Did you ever date them? Or go to dinner with them?"

"No, I didn't."

"Just Mr. Anson?"

"Yes."

"Why?"

"Because he asked me," she said, lifting her chin, "and they didn't."

He thought that was a good reason.

"Well," he said, "I guess I'll be going, if there's nothing else."

"N-no," she said, "nothing."

She walked him to the door but did not enter the common hall with him. She stood just inside her doorway, arms folded, hugging herself as if she were cold.

"Thank you for coming," she said.

"Not at all," he replied. "If you can think of anything else you'd like to talk to me about, please don't hesitate to call." He handed her one of his business cards, which she accepted. He couldn't remember if he'd given her one the first time they met, but he didn't think so.

He opened the door to outside, then turned and said, "Miss Morgan."

"Yes?"

"Did you ever go to dinner with Mr. Anson because your boss asked you, or told you, to?"

"What? No, of course not. Why would you ask that?"

He smiled and said, "Just routine."

He loved when he was able to use that line.

Hannah Morgan watched from her front window as Detective Joe Keough got into his car, sat for a moment, and then pulled away. She was unable to see what he had been doing for the few moments that he sat there.

Once he was gone, she went to the phone and dialed a number she knew by heart.

"He's gone," she said.

"How long did he stay?" the voice on the other end asked.

"About fifteen minutes."

"Exactly how long?"

She looked at her watch and said, "Seventeen—seventeen minutes. I couldn't keep him here any longer without him getting suspicious."

"That's fine, my dear," the voice said. "You did just fine. Now make the other call."

"Do I really have to—?"

"You'll be fine," he said, his tone at once soothing and threatening. "Make the call." And he broke the connection.

She hung up and hugged her arms because, suddenly, she *was* cold.

When Keough got behind the wheel of his car, he didn't leave right away. He thought a moment, wondering what it could have been that had been making Hannah Morgan so suspicious. He wondered about her clothes. They looked brand new. Then for no reason other than a sense of self-preservation, perhaps, he took out his notebook and made a note of how long he had been inside her apartment, and what they talked about. That done, he put the notebook back in his pocket and drove away.

Thirty

KEOUGH DROVE FROM Hannah Morgan's apartment to the home of Marcy Drucker. By the time he arrived, he'd forgotten about the interview with Hannah Morgan. All it had added to the mix for him was that Kenneth Goddard, Franklin Anson, and Mark Drucker attended the same parties—undoubtedly political functions. It cemented a connection among the three, but that had already been established.

He drove up the curving driveway and parked the car facing out, as if for a fast getaway. There were no other cars in the driveway. He knew it was possible she wasn't home, but he hadn't wanted to warn Marcy Drucker that he was coming. The element of surprise was rarely appreciated by those it surprised, but more often than not it yielded something interesting.

He rang the doorbell and waited. He was about to ring it again when it opened and Marcy Drucker appeared in the doorway. She looked very attractive in a pair of Capri pants— Val had told him they had come back—and a silk, button-down blouse that showed off her nipples. He could feel the air-conditioning from inside the house, which might have explained her appearance.

"Detective Keough," she said, with a welcoming smile. "Is this a social call, I hope?"

"I'm afraid not, Mrs. Drucker."

"I thought we'd gotten past that the last time you were here," she said, with a pout. "You were going to call me Marcy."

Keough was a man who didn't appreciate a pout on a grown woman. In fact, he hated all kinds of kittenish, so-called sexy mannerisms on women who were over twenty-one.

"All right, Marcy," he said, "but I'm afraid I'm here on business."

"Still looking for Mark's killer?"

"Yes," Keough said, "and his residence. May I come in?"

"Of course."

He entered, and she closed the door. It was like a refrigerator in the house.

"I'm sorry if it's cold," she said. "Mark would never let me keep it cold in the house, and since he left, I crank it up every so often."

"I see."

"I'll adjust it."

"That's all right," he said. "I doubt I'll be here long enough to feel the difference."

"Well," she said, "that doesn't make me happy." At least she'd done away with the pout. "What can we do that won't take long?"

"You can answer a few questions for me, and then I'll be on my way."

"Well," she said, "I get the feeling we won't even have to sit down for this. All right, fire away."

"I'm concerned with finding out where your husband was living when he died. Apparently, it wasn't anyplace he was getting utility bills, or we'd be able to find it in the computer. Can you think of anyone he'd be staying with?"

"No one," she said. "Mark did too much business at home

to be staying with anyone else. Hmm, were you thinking of a woman? A girlfriend?"

"Possibly."

"That would definitely be out," she said. "He wouldn't have been able to operate in that environment. I mean, even here in this big house he had a problem with me possibly knowing his business. Have a specific woman in mind?"

"Did your husband cheat on you, Marcy?"

"All men cheat, don't they?" she asked. "I mean, you have a woman in your life, don't you?"

"Yes."

"And yet if I asked you to come upstairs and fuck me, you would, wouldn't you?" He assumed this was all hypothetical, but suddenly it was warmer in the house.

"That would be different," he said. "I'm not married."

"Cheating is cheating."

"So I assume, then, that the answer would be yes?"

"I never caught him," she said, "but I always assumed he was—either that or he just wasn't interested in sex . . . not with me, anyway."

"Do you know a woman named Eileen Henry?"

"No," she said. "Was she sleeping with my husband?"

"I don't know," he said. "She works for Anson and Shepp, and I had the feeling there was something personal, but I don't know for sure."

"Cold, business type?"

"Yes, but attractive."

"Probably his type," she said. "Mark had a habit of pointing out women to me that he liked or disliked the look of. He preferred the high-button, straight-laced business type, and didn't like what he called 'slutty.' The odd thing was," she added, pensively, "the ones he always called 'slutty' sort of looked like me."

"High-buttoned, straight-laced business type" also described Hannah Morgan. Keough once again thought about his recent visit to her and her more "casual" attire.

"But to answer your question, I don't know where he would have been living now, but it wouldn't have been with a woman. Also, I wouldn't be surprised if he had all the bills listed under a different name."

"Was he hiding out from anyone?"

"Maybe," she said, "or maybe it was just a tax dodge. Mark was very good at finding tax dodges."

"Did he do it for other people? Recommend tax shelters?"

"You're confusing the two," she said. "Tax shelters are legal, while tax dodges are not. He was not in the business of supplying other people with tax shelters, and tax dodges he figured out for his own benefit."

"I see." He was finding out more and more about Drucker as the case went on. Unfortunately, a lot of it involved things he didn't feel he needed to know—not as a friend, anyway.

Keough wasn't finding out what he wanted to, either, so apparently this trip had been a waste of time.

"All right, then," he said, "I guess I'll be going."

"That's it?" she asked, coyly. "That's all you wanted?"

"That's it," he said. "Apparently your husband sort of disappeared when he left here. I don't know how anyone managed to contact him."

"At his office, I suspect. Did you find that?"

"Yes, we did."

"And you didn't find anything there?"

"Nothing helpful."

"I suppose I'll end up having to go through it myself," she said.

"As his ex-wife I wouldn't think you would."

"Oh, didn't you know?" she asked. "His lawyer, Ryn, called and told me Mark made me executrix of his will."

"That's odd," Keough said. "I'd never have expected him to put his ex-wife in control."

"Who then?" she asked. "A close friend? A business associate? There was really no one else he trusted enough."

"Maybe it's not odd," he said, with a shrug. What did he know? He'd always found people with money strange.

"Thanks for your time, Marcy."

She walked to the door and opened it for him and leaned against it seductively.

"What I said before still goes," she said. "Come back anytime."

"Thanks," he said, and left.

He always found it uncomfortable and comical when a woman came on to him during a case. It made him feel as if he were walking around inside a bad novel or a TV show.

Thirty-one

When Keough got back to the office, Steinbach was not in the squad room. He thought about checking on his partner's computer honey but decided he didn't want to take a chance of intruding on anything. He sat down at his desk, took out his notebook, and recorded what he'd found out from Marcy Drucker.

So far they knew that Mark Drucker was dead, that Harry Brooks was dead, apparently killed by the same man. They had found Drucker's office, but it told them nothing. They also knew that someone had been there looking for something. It seemed fairly obvious that Shepp, Anson, and Associates were running scared, maybe even Kenneth Goddard in the mayor's office, at the prospect of *something* that Mark Drucker had—the all-elusive McGuffin of Hitchcock fame— was going to turn up. Also, there seemed to be a fair number of women involved in the case—Marcy Drucker, Eileen Henry, and Hannah Morgan. Being the dirty business it was, Keough was sure that politics was behind the murder—not real estate, not tax "dodges" or "shelters."

And, if he'd found out nothing else, he'd discovered that his St. Louis benefactor—or "rabbi," as they called them in the NYPD—was some sort of power broker among the St. Louis and Missouri politicos. Something he would never have suspected of the man.

He was pondering the notes he'd made on Hannah Morgan when Steinbach came walking in.

"I had to see two women, and you had to see one, and yet I got back before you," Keough said.

Steinbach grinned and said, "Mine wanted my body. Who was I to say no?"

"Right."

Steinbach sat behind his desk. He was sweating and out of breath.

"Getting warmer," he said.

"Maybe you're getting fatter."

Steinbach looked at Keough, hesitated, then said, "Maybe."

"You've just been rushing around, Al," Keough said. "What did you get from Mrs. Brooks?"

"She's in total shock. She has no idea who would want to kill her husband. She said he used to be a guard with Brinks, and she worried about him then, but since he started working at the Arch, she thought he was safe. Plus it's freaking her out that he got killed in their garage. She and the kids are moving in with her mother until she can sell the house."

"Can't say I can blame her for that."

"I bounced some names off of her—Anson, Shepp, even Goddard—but she didn't know any of them. The only names she knew were the ones from the Arch."

"Hannah Morgan?"

"Right, her and the superintendent, what's his name, George Eastmont. She didn't like him at all."

"Why not?"

"Apparently he gave Brooks a hard time."

"Did she ever meet Eastmont?"

"No, just heard about him from hubby."

"And Miss Morgan? Ever meet her?"

"No," Steinbach said, "all she heard from her husband was what a bitch she was."

"Hannah Morgan?"

"That's her."

"I don't see her as bitchy at all."

"How'd you do with her?" Steinbach asked, wriggling his eyebrows.

"She was nervous and didn't have much to say."

"What was so urgent?"

"I don't know. She said she didn't want me to think she was involved in anything just because I saw her with Anson."

"How long have they been dating?"

"She said she's been to dinner with him three or four times, but they haven't been dates. Nothing romantic going on. He just wants a dinner companion."

"Why doesn't he call an escort service?"

"Because they *do* expect something romantic—or, at least, sexual."

Steinbach made a face. "I don't see Anson as very sexual, or the mousy little Miss Morgan, for that matter."

"She didn't look so mousy today," Keough said. "Tight jeans and a low-cut top, showing off a nice little body you don't see when she's dressed for work, or dinner."

"Think she dresses like that all the time when she's home, or was it for you?" Steinbach asked.

"The clothes looked new," Keough said. "She seemed nervous and uncomfortable and kept looking at her watch."

"What about the merry widow?"

"Wait until you hear this. She's the executrix of Drucker's will."

"Why would he do that?"

"She said he didn't trust anyone else."

"He trusts his ex-wife? How do you figure that?"

"The only thing I can think of," Keough said, "was that she was totally ignorant of his business dealings, and so didn't have her own agenda. We're not finding friends of his, only business associates."

"That's true."

"So maybe it makes sense."

"Yeah," Steinbach said, "in Bizzaro world!"

"She also says he wouldn't have been staying with anyone. That would cramp his style. She thinks it's more likely he had a place under a different name."

"Great," Steinbach said, "how do we find that in a computer?"

"What, your computer honey is not that good?"

"She can't find something that isn't there."

Keough checked his watch. Five minutes to end of shift—and that reminded him.

"Did you find someone to watch Drucker's office?"

"Yeah," Steinbach said, "I found a PI in town who thinks he owes me, so he's doing it pro bono."

"What's his name?"

"Bumper."

"Bumper?"

"Hey, what can I tell you? That's his name."

"And he's working free?"

"Well," Steinbach said, "he might want a few donuts, but that's it."

"So he'll call us if something happens?"

"When he can," Steinbach said. "I told him if anybody walks out of there with something to tail them and then call us."

"Okay," Keough said, "so we've got that covered."

Over the next few minutes he told his partner everything he'd been thinking while he sat there waiting for him to return.

"So somebody in politics in this town—Goddard, maybe Anson or Shepp, maybe some other politician we haven't met yet—had Drucker killed? That's what you figure?" Steinbach asked.

"They're scrambling to find something," Keough said. "They were avoiding us; Goddard called me down for a little talk. . . . You got another idea?"

"Well, maybe . . ."

"Let's hear it."

"What if it was only *after* Drucker was killed that these guys started to scramble?" Steinbach said.

"You mean, somebody else killed him, but they're afraid something will turn up that will incriminate them in some other way? They're not involved in either murder at all?"

"You asked me for another scenario."

"So I did," Keough said, and this one was very possible— but it also sent them back to square one without a murder suspect.

At that point Captain McGwire came walking in with two other people in tow, a man and a woman. They were dressed in simple suits and barely looked at Steinbach and Keough. They had the look of cops, but they also had a smell that was unmistakable to both men—Internal Affairs.

"You can wait in my office," McGwire said to them.

"Thank you, Captain," the woman said, and she and her partner went in and closed the door behind them.

"Who's IA after this time, Cap?" Steinbach asked.

"Joe," McGwire said, ignoring the question, "I need you in my office."

"We're a little busy right now, Cap—"

"Now!" McGwire said. "This is no joke."

"Me, too, Cap?" Steinbach asked.

"Nope," McGwire said, "for now just Detective Keough." He looked at Keough. "Let's go, Joe."

"Sure, Cap," Keough said, standing up and exchanging a glance with his partner, "I'm right behind you."

Thirty-two

As KEOUGH ENTERED the captain's office, the two Internal Affairs detectives were still standing. They turned to face him, but said nothing. They left the introductions to Captain McGwire.

"Detective Keough," McGwire said, "these are Detectives Angela Mason and Jack Gail."

They looked Keough over, so he returned the favor. Mason looked like the older of the two, probably the senior detective in the partnership. Gail looked like he was in his early thirties, a fast tracker who somehow ended up in the Internal Affairs Division. Maybe in his rise to detective at an early age he'd pissed somebody off. Keough knew that detectives who eventually transferred out of Internal Affairs were rarely welcome or trusted elsewhere. At least, that's how it was in New York when you'd done time as a "shoefly."

"Have a seat, Detective," Angela Mason said.

"Are we going to be here that long?" Keough asked.

"Who knows?" Mason asked.

Keough was amused to see Detective Gail start around the captain's desk to sit behind it only to bump into McGwire, who'd begun coming around the other side. McGwire glared Gail away from his chair.

"Captain," Mason said, "perhaps you'd better wait outside."

"My office, my man, Detective," McGwire said simply. "I'm staying."

Mason and Gail exchanged glances. Apparently, they didn't want to waste the time it would take to make a call forcing McGwire out of the room.

"Fine," she said, and turned her attention to Keough.

"Do I need counsel?" he asked.

"I don't know, Detective," Mason said. "Do you?" She was holding a file, which he hadn't noticed when they first entered.

Keough decided to remain calm. He thought he knew what this was about. Franklin Anson had obviously gone ahead and made a complaint against him for what had happened in the restaurant the other night. There was nothing about to happen here that was worth getting worked up over.

"I don't think I'm going to play this game, Detective," he said "so why don't you just tell me what you want to know?"

Mason opened the file and made a show of reading it. Keough was sure she already knew what was inside.

"You have quite an interesting record from your days in New York," she said.

"It was an interesting time."

"Yes, I know." She closed the file. "I read your book."

"It wasn't my book," he said. "It was Mike O'Donnell's."

"But it was about you."

"It was about two serial killers."

"Both of whom you caught."

"I didn't get any medals for it."

"And you caught one here last year, didn't you?"

"The FBI and we did, yes."

"You're modest," Mason said. "The fact is all three of these killers might still be at large if not for you."

"If you say so."

"Do you think this record puts you above the law, Detective?" Jack Gail asked.

Keough looked at him. "I didn't hear her give you permission to speak."

"I don't need permiss—"

"Jack," Mason said, cutting him off, "I'm conducting this interview."

Gail shut his mouth, worked his jaw until Keough thought the muscles would come popping through, and then said, "Go ahead, Mace."

This duo reminded Keough of the FBI pair last year. Were male and female partnerships becoming more prevalent? Was there a Mulder-Scully influence on law enforcement?

"My partner asked a good question, Detective Keough," Mason said. "Do you feel above the law?"

"No."

"You had some problems in New York before you caught those serial killers, didn't you?"

"Some."

"Got shifted around, dumped out of Vice into a precinct?"

"You've got the file."

"Temper problems?"

"That was then."

"And this is now? No temper?"

"No," he said, even though his temper had gotten the better of him last night.

"How do you get along with women, Detective?" Mason asked.

"What?" That question had come out of left field.

"Do you have a woman in your life? A girlfriend?"

"That's personal."

"Nothing's personal here, Detective," Mason said. "Not in this kind of case."

"What kind of case?"

Now she regarded him with an amused look on her face. It was a face of wide, flat planes—flat forehead, cheekbones, a decent-sized jaw. She had bags under her eyes that looked to be the result of fatigue, not age. He figured her for a hard worker, a digger. What had she dug up on him?

"You thought you knew what this was about, didn't you?" she asked. "When we walked in here, you thought you had it figured out."

He didn't answer. He looked past her at McGwire, who was watching with a dour look on his face.

"Okay," he said finally, "I'll bite. What is this about?"

"You thought it was about pushing some self-important lawyer—some *man*—around in a men's room, didn't you?"

"Isn't it?"

"Do you admit to that?"

"Of course."

"Well," she said, "it's about more than that."

"That's odd," Keough said, "because I didn't do more than that."

"That's not what a Miss Hannah Morgan and a Mrs. Marcia Drucker have to say," she said, without consulting her file.

He got a bad feeling in his stomach. *Now* he thought he knew what was coming, and if he did, he had played right into it.

"You're going to have to fill me in, Detective Mason," he said. "I'm not a mind reader."

"No, you're not," she said. "Maybe you thought you were, though. Maybe you thought you were reading the minds of these two women. Maybe you thought they were coming on to you? That they *wanted* you to put your hands on them—"

"Whoa!" Keough said, coming out of his chair. "Cap, do you know what's going on here?"

"I'm an observer, Joe," McGwire said. "Answer their questions."

"No, sir," Keough said, "no more questions until I find out what I'm being accused of."

"I'll lay it out it for you, Detective," Mason said. "Hannah

Morgan and Marcia Drucker have both accused you of sexual assault."

That was it. That was the bad feeling he'd had; *that's* why Hannah Morgan had been so nervous. She knew she was setting him up.

"Sit back down, Detective," Mason said. "We have a lot to go through."

He sat down.

Thirty-three

"THIS IS A setup."

"That's what they all say," Gail commented.

"Two clichés in a row," Mason said. "That's not going to get us anywhere."

"Cap," Keough said, "can we talk?"

"We're talking now, Detective Keough," Mason said. "You can talk to your captain later, when we finish."

"I want to talk to my captain now to determine whether or not I need counsel," Keough said.

"Later, Detective—"

"Detective Mason," McGwire said suddenly, "I think you and your partner should wait outside for a few minutes."

"Captain," Mason said, "this is an Internal Affairs investigation—"

"And this is still my office," McGwire said, "and the last time I looked I was still a captain. Outside, please."

"I'll have to call my captain—" Mason started.

"That's fine," McGwire said. "Do it from the squad room. In fact, I'm sure Detective Keough won't mind if you use his desk."

Mason faced off with McGwire for a few moments, but she didn't have the rank to pull it off.

"Let's go," she said to her partner.

"But Mac—"

"Out, Jack."

She went out the door, and Gail followed slowly. Before he left, though, he muttered, "It won't be his desk for long."

Once they were gone McGwire said, "What the hell, Joe! What the *fuck?*"

"Now, Cap—"

"You roughed up Franklin Anson?"

"Okay, I lost my temper," Keough said. "I admit it, but the rest—"

"The rest is crap!" McGwire said, his face red. "I know you didn't sexually assault anyone."

"But they've got two women—"

"I don't care if they've got twenty," McGwire said. "I know you well enough to know that's not your style."

"Thanks, Cap."

"Why didn't you come to me? We could have headed this off."

"It happened last night," Keough said, "and we've been on the go today."

"You saw those women today?"

"Yes, sir."

"Were you alone with them?"

"Yes, sir," Keough said, "one of them for seventeen minutes, and one for about twenty."

"You made notes?"

"Yes, sir."

"That's good. Are they both involved in this Drucker case?"

"Up to their necks," Keough said. "Marcy Drucker, obviously, because she's the ex-wife, and Hannah Morgan because she works at the Arch, and she was in the restaurant last night when I, uh . . ."

"Hauled Franklin Anson, an important attorney in this town, off into the men's room and humiliated him."

"Uh, well, yes, sir."

"Why did you do that, Joe?"

"He's been avoiding us," Keough said, "giving us the run-around. We had to talk to him about this case. I took him into the men's room to talk."

"Did you hit him?"

"No," Keough said, "he slipped on some water."

"Slipped on some water."

"Yes, sir."

"What else did you do today?"

"We saw Anson and his partner, Dexter Shepp, early this morning at their offices."

"That's interesting. They spoke with you?"

"Yes, sir."

"Calmly?"

"Shepp did most of the talking," Keough said. "Anson just looked like he was going to explode."

"What time was that?"

"Around nine-thirty, I guess."

"Anson's complaint came in around two," McGwire said.

"And the women?"

"From what I understand, the Morgan woman reported you this afternoon around three, and the Drucker woman around four-thirty. They called their local precincts and then Internal Affairs was called in. They then came to me, and we came to you."

"Why didn't you come to me first?"

"That's what I'm asking you."

"Sorry."

"Besides," McGwire said, "I couldn't. They've been up my ass since they first got here. This is the first chance I've had to talk to you, and who knows how long this will last? They'll call their captain, he'll call the chief. . . . I can't protect you, Joe. You'll have to answer their questions."

"I know."

"Do you want a department lawyer?"

Keough hesitated.

"I think you'll need one."

"It will look like I'm guilty of something."

"You are," McGwire said. "You've admitted to the Anson thing."

"Oh, yeah . . ."

There was a knock on the door just then, and Detective Angela Mason stuck her head in.

"There's a phone call for you, Captain," she said, smugly. "It's the chief."

McGwire looked at Keough, then said, "Thank you, Detective Mason. I'll take it here. You can close the door now."

She hesitated, then said, "Yes, sir."

"I'll take this call, Joe, and then we'll get you a lawyer."

"Yes, sir," Keough said. "Thanks, boss."

Thirty-four

STEINBACH WAITED FOR Keough to finish with the Internal Affairs detectives, which took awhile because they all had to wait for a department lawyer to arrive. His name was Jerry Calder; he conferred with Keough in private. Keough admitted to roughing up Franklin Anson, and then told the man everything that had happened while he was alone with the women.

The IA detectives wanted to question Steinbach, but the attorney advised him he didn't have to subject himself to that since he was not anywhere near Keough during any of the "alleged" incidents.

"I can testify to Joe's character—" Steinbach said at one point, but Calder cut him off and said, "This isn't a court of law. We'll save you for that."

"You think this will go to court?" Steinbach asked.

"We'll wait and see."

Finally, Calder and Keough went back into McGwire's office, and Steinbach waited in the squad room for them to come out—which they did, three hours later.

"Jesus, Al," Keough said, "you didn't have to wait."

"I figured we'd get a cup of coffee after," Steinbach said, "before either of us goes home."

"Good idea."

The lawyer came out behind Keough, followed by Mason and Gail, and finally McGwire.

"Well be in touch, Captain," Mason said, and she and her partner left without a word to Keough. Keough, Steinbach, Calder, and McGwire were alone in the squad room. The detectives working the shift were out on a call.

"What do you think, Jerry?" McGwire asked Calder.

"I think we have to find out what these women's stories are," Calder said. "Those IA detectives were not very forthcoming."

"You don't know the charges?" Steinbach asked.

"That's the problem," Calder said. "There are no charges yet. We're not sure if we're talking about sexual harassment, sexual abuse, or even attempted rape."

"Rape?" Steinbach said.

"Nobody said anything about rape," Calder said, "but then nobody said much of anything."

"In three hours?" Steinbach asked.

"We'll know more if and when they bring formal charges," Calder said. "I'm willing to bet they haven't even talked to the district attorney yet."

"Jerry," Keough said, putting out his hand, "thanks for coming so quickly."

"That's my job, Joe," Calder said. He shook hands with Steinbach and McGwire as well. "Now you fellas do yours. If what you tell me is true, this can all be cleared up by finding out who killed Mark Drucker, or who had him killed."

"We'll do our best," Steinbach said.

"I'll be in touch," Calder said, and left.

"Dapper little guy," Steinbach said. "Snappy dresser. I couldn't pull off wearing a lime-green shirt under a pale-yellow sport jacket."

"He's a good lawyer," McGwire said. "It doesn't matter what he wears."

"Cap," Keough said, "I'm sorry about this."

"All you have to be sorry about, Joe, is being a jackass about Franklin Anson," McGwire said, "and in a public place."

"You're right."

"The rest is not your fault," McGwire said. "I'm inclined to agree with you that somebody is putting these women up to this, and it probably is Anson and his partner."

"They're trying to distract us from the Drucker murder," Steinbach said.

McGwire rubbed his jaw.

"Maybe I should take you off this case, Joe," he said. "Team somebody else up with Al."

"I think that would be a mistake, Cap," Keough said. "That's what they want, and if you leave me on the case, they might make a mistake."

"Al?" McGwire asked.

"I agree."

"All right, then," McGwire said, "I'll keep you working it as long I can—but catch the sonofabitch responsible."

"We will, Cap," Steinbach said. "We will."

Keough and Steinbach decided to go to the Eat Rite Diner downtown. Keough had coffee while Steinbach had a slinger, a concoction consisting of a mound of home fries smothered with eggs, bacon, and chili.

"You know," Steinbach said, as they were served, "I forgot about the diabetes. Does it bother you if I eat this?"

"If it doesn't kill you," Keough said, "it won't bother me."

Keough couldn't eat. He'd lost his appetite.

"Are you okay, Joe?"

"I walked into this frame, Al," Keough said, "like a rookie. Hannah Morgan was so nervous she was about to jump out

of her skin. She didn't want to set me up, but she did. Whoever coached her even told her how to dress."

"And what about Marcy Drucker?" Steinbach asked. "She
wasn't expecting you."

"She probably had her instructions to report me whenever
I spoke to her again," Keough said. "The thing is, I think she
would have gone all the way. She was enjoying it."

"You know," Steinbach said, "this could have nothing to
do with the murder."

"What?"

"This could just be Anson trying to get back at you."

"If one of them is behind this, it's Shepp, not Anson,"
Keough said. "He probably decided to go ahead with it after
our meeting this morning. That was why he kept Anson from
reporting me earlier. He wanted to see me in person, feel me
out, and then decide what to do. And this is too much coincidence for it not to be connected with the murder. Either
they had Drucker killed, or they're scrambling—like you
said—to find something he had on them before we do."

"Okay," Steinbach said, "I agree."

"We've got to find it first, Al," Keough said, "whatever it
is. It's the key to this whole case."

"And maybe the key to your future."

"They can have my future," Keough said. "I want these
sonsofbitches. They just made this real personal."

"Hey," Steinbach said, "maybe your buddy O'Donnell can
write a book about this."

"Don't even mention that," Keough said. "He's still trying
to get me to let him write one about catching that Mall Rat."

Keough had two more cups of coffee while his partner de-
stroyed the slinger on his plate.

"That Mason is pretty good, Al."

"How do you mean?"

"She knew about the diabetes."

"What?"

Keough nodded. "That's right. She gave me an out. She asked if I was so upset about having a *disease* that it's affected my judgment."

"Jesus," Steinbach said, "what did you say?"

"I said that diabetes affected my sugar," Keough answered, "not my mind."

"If you'd jumped on that as a defense," Steinbach said, "she would have thought you were guilty for sure."

"I know, Al," Keough said. "I know."

When they left the Eat Rite Diner, they split up, each going home.

"When are you going to tell Valerie?" Steinbach asked, as they stood between their cars.

"Tonight," Keough said. "She deserves to hear it from me before it leaks out."

"You think it'll leak out?"

"What do you think?" Keough asked. "What happens when Shepp and Anson find out I haven't been suspended yet? What would you do?"

"I'd leak it to the press."

"If I'm not in tomorrow's paper, I'll be surprised as hell."

"Maybe you can knock Mark McGwire off the front page."

"Maybe."

"Take it easy, pal," Steinbach said. "You've got a few good people in your corner."

"And you."

"Right," Steinbach said with a smile, "and me."

"Why haven't they arrested you?" Valerie asked. "I mean, if these women are saying you raped them, or tried to rape them, why aren't you under arrest?"

When he got home, the red light on his phone was blinking. The message was from Valerie. He called her immediately and asked her if she'd come over because he had something to tell her. She'd demanded he tell her right there and then.

Now her voice was coming at him from the phone, sounding puzzled and a little hurt.

"Because," Keough said, "they're obviously not saying I raped them. Even if they said I tried to rape them, I'd be under arrest."

"So what are they saying?"

"I don't know for sure, but rape or attempted rape is not in the picture . . . yet."

"What do you mean, yet?"

"Well," he said, "since they're lying, they could always change the lie."

"Would they?"

"My theory, Val," Keough said, "is that they're being told what to say. If I'm right, they can always be told to change their story."

"Jesus," she said, "this is a nightmare."

"Not yet," he said, "but it could turn into one."

She was silent, and he wondered what she was thinking. After all, they had not been together that long. Was there even the slightest chance that she'd think he was guilty of what these women were accusing him of?

"Do you want me to come over?" she asked.

It was a nice offer, but the tone of her voice was telling him that's all it was. He could tell she was hoping he'd say no.

"That's okay," he said. "I'm pretty tired."

"Well, I'm not surprised," she said, "after being interrogated for three hours. It's not so nice when the shoe is on the other foot, is it?"

"What's that supposed to mean?" he demanded, stung.

"Oh, I'm sorry, Joe," she said, quickly. "I . . . I don't know why I said that. Forgive me."

"It's okay," he said. "It's late; I'm going to turn in."

"Will I see you tomorrow?" she asked.

"I don't know," he said. "I guess that depends on whether or not I'm still walking around free tomorrow."

"Could they . . . really arrest you, Joe?"

"Yes, Valerie," he said. "I'm afraid they could."

And he was afraid, he admitted, as he hung up. After all, this job was probably his last in law enforcement. If this got messed up, like the one in New York, who would hire him? He didn't have another Mark Drucker out there to get him a job and a place to live. It was all on the line here, his whole life, and the only way to save it was to find not only the killer, but who hired the killer. And then he had to beat the sexual-abuse charges. He knew he was going to have to take a hit for what he did to Franklin Anson, but he expected that. It was the least of his worries right now.

Jesus, he thought, diabetes, the possible loss of his job and his home, maybe even his freedom if the DA decided to file charges—a few days ago he was flying a kite with no worries beyond deciding which kid to give it to.

It had all turned to shit so quickly!

Thirty-five

THE NEXT MORNING Keough did not dress quickly and hurry into work. He rose and made a pot of coffee, then walked through the house carrying the cup. In all the months he'd lived there, he didn't think he'd ever properly appreciated the place. His windows were situated in such a way as to allow daylight to stream in the front early, but the sunlight never shone directly until midday, when it started to set in the west and light up the side windows. He walked to the front windows and looked out, saw his neighbor, Jack Roswell, using a hose on the bushes in front of his house. He felt bad about avoiding Jack since the whole diabetes thing. Maybe, when he was suspended, he could spend more time playing chess with the older man.

He walked to the kitchen and looked out the door at the backyard. Although it was overgrown, there were still slated areas and paths to walk on, which he had never taken advantage of. His life in St. Louis seemed to have exploded since day one. Even with the occasional morning or afternoon taken off for kite flying, it still kept rocketing along. It almost seemed like yesterday he had been living and working in Brooklyn, and yet in an odd way it felt a lifetime away. Even then, how often had he taken time like this over a cup of coffee to look out the window?

It was a foregone conclusion to him that he would be suspended; the question was for how long? And would he be able to solve this case before it happened? Even if he did solve the case and prove that Anson and Shepp were involved, he was going to have to pay the price for putting his hands on a "important" political figure. A suspension for that offense would be the shortest. If, however, he were suspended for the sexual charges, *and* charges were filed by the DA, that could last a hell of a long time.

Lots and lots of coffee and lots of staring out windows.

He looked at his watch. He'd managed to while away half an hour. Had that been with one cup of coffee or two? He couldn't remember. He felt kind of dizzy and frowned. Shit. He was supposed to eat something, or his sugar would be too low in the morning. And he was supposed to take a pill with it.

He rinsed out the cup, left it in the sink, and ran upstairs to dress for work.

Another man was taking his time dressing that morning. He was staring out the window of his hotel room, looking down over the city, drinking tea instead of coffee, listening to the sound of the shower from the bathroom. Behind him was a cart with a full room-service breakfast, which he intended to eat in a leisurely fashion. Today was the day he'd find out if his services were needed any further. If not, he was off to the airport. If, however, they were needed, there was the price to be discussed.

The tea cup looking incredibly small in his large hand, and the robe the hotel supplied for its guests was much too small on him.

He turned, put the tea cup down on the tray, removed the robe, tossed it on the bed, then sat down and proceeded to eat his breakfast naked. He didn't think the whore in the shower would mind when she came out.

Keough walked into the squad room wondering if he still had a job and a desk. Steinbach was already there.

"How you doin', buddy?" he asked.

"Okay," Keough said. "Sorry I'm late. I sort of took my time this morning."

"No problem."

"Boss in?"

"Yeah, he's inside."

"Looking for me?"

"Nobody's looking for you."

"Yet."

"Want to catch bad guys today?"

"Sure, why not?"

"We got some info back from the lab."

"On what?"

"The bloody handprints at the scene of the Brooks murder."

"What about them?"

"From the size of the hand, they're estimating the killer must be well over six feet or a little guy with incredibly big hands."

"That little actor on *The Wild, Wild West*," Keough said. "Michael Dunn. He had big hands."

"He had regular-sized hands; they just looked big on him," Steinbach said. "Besides, I don't think we're looking for a dwarf. The handprints were too high up."

"Okay, then," Keough said, "the actual killer is well over six feet."

"Right."

"That leaves out all the male suspects we interviewed so far," Keough said, "and we've already agreed that this guy is probably for hire."

"Right again."

"Anything else?"

"I ran an NCIC check to see if there was anybody in the system with this hand fetish, or even with big hands. Came back a no-show."

"So he's never been popped," Keough said. "Makes it harder. Anything else?"

"No, that's it. We might as well hit it. Where do you want to start?"

"The Arch." Keough replied without thinking, so the answer surprised him, too.

"What?"

"Yeah," Keough said, "let's go to the Arch."

"Joe."

"I just want to look around again, get the feel of it," Keough said. "Maybe go to the top."

"Maybe talk to Hannah Morgan?"

"Oh, that's right," Keough said, "she works there, doesn't she?"

"Joe—"

"I won't go near her, Al."

"No?"

"No," Keough said, "but you can."

"If I get caught interfering in an IA investigation, they'll have my ass, too," Steinbach said.

"You won't be interfering," Keough said. "You have every right to see her in conjunction with this case. And while you're there, you can talk to some of the other security guys. See what they can tell you about Harry Brooks."

Steinbach thought this over and then said, "Okay, I'll make you a deal."

"What?"

"I'll go to the Arch, and you stay away."

"So what do I do?"

"Work another aspect of the case."

"Like wha—oh, wait," Keough said. "I know somebody we haven't talked to."

"Good. Go and talk to them."

"I will," Keough said. "This is a good idea. You go to the Arch, and I'll go and talk to—"

"You'll stay away from Marcy Drucker, right?"

"Never intended to go near her."

"Then who's this other person you're going to see?"

"Somebody I know who won't accuse me of anything sexual."

"And who's that?"

Keough smiled and said, "The mayor."

Steinbach covered his face with his hand.

Thirty-six

KEOUGH DROVE HIS own car down to City Hall and parked legally, in a nearby parking lot. He doubted many people got in to see the mayor without an appointment, but he was going to try.

As expected, he was told, "I'm sorry, sir, but the mayor sees no one without an appointment."

He showed her his badge again and said, "Take a good look at this. I'm investigating a murder, and the word I got from the mayor was that he wanted me to be very thorough. Why don't you just try telling him I'm here, and let's see what happens?"

"Sir," she said, "I can have one of the mayor's aides—"

"I don't want an aide," Keough said. "I've talked with an aide. Ma'am, the mayor has let it be known he wants this case handled thoroughly. How do you think he would react if he knew you wouldn't let me see him? That, instead, you had made that decision for him?"

She thought about that for a moment and then said, "Just a minute, please, Detective."

"Not an aide," Keough said. "I've been that route."

"I'm calling the mayor's secretary."

"Fine."

"Would you have a seat, please?"

Keough sat across from her and watched it all play out. She made a call, hung up, got a call, spoke for a few moments, hung up, made a call, spoke briefly, got a call, and finally waved him over.

"The mayor will see you."

"There," he said, "was that so hard?"

"Please wait a moment, and someone will be out to take you back," she said, without responding to his remark.

He waited several minutes, hoping the person who was going to escort him would not be Kenneth Goddard. At last a woman appeared, dressed in a business suit with a knee-length skirt and sensible shoes.

"Detective Keough?" she asked.

"That's right."

"May I see your badge?"

He showed it to her.

"Follow me, please," she said, without introducing herself.

He followed her down several corridors until they reached an unmarked door.

"Is this the mayor's office?" he asked doubtfully.

"If you will wait inside, the mayor will be right with you."

"Thank you."

Keough entered the room and found it to be fairly large but devoid of furniture save for a long board table surrounded by chairs. In fact, it resembled the room in which he'd had his last meeting with Shepp and Anson. There was one other door in the back wall, and he didn't know if it led in or out.

There was one window, and when he looked out, he found himself staring down at Market Street. He knew he was taking a chance trying to get in to see the mayor without clearing it with his own superiors first, but he felt his career—hell, his life—was worth the risk.

Of course, there was still the possibility that he was waiting there for a mayor's aide, maybe even Kenneth Goddard.

Finally, however, the other door opened, and a black man entered. Keough had seen the mayor only once in person—he and Valerie had attended the implosion demolition of a large building at which the "switch" had been thrown by the mayor—but he had seen him many times on television. As the man closed the door and turned to face him, he was afraid he was staring.

"Detective Keough?"

"Yes, sir."

Keough hurried forward and took hold of the mayor's outstretched hand.

"I understand you felt a need to see me?"

"Yes, sir," Keough said, "I certainly did. Ah, you'll have to excuse me, sir, but I guess I didn't really expect to make it."

The mayor smiled and said, "You're in here for two reasons. One, my own background in law enforcement, and two, no one ever walks in here and asks to see me without an appointment—that is, unless they're homeless, or a little crazy, or both."

"Well, sir," Keough said, "I might be a little crazy, and there's a distinct possibility I'll be homeless before this is all over—homeless and jobless."

"I see," the mayor said. "And by 'all this' I assume you mean the Mark Drucker case?"

"Yes, sir."

The mayor looked at his watch.

"I've got about ten minutes, Detective," the man said. "We'll be in good shape if you can hit the high notes in that time, otherwise, we're going to have to go through channels and make an appointment."

"I'll take the chance, sir, and use the ten minutes," Keough said. "The last time I tried to go through channels I met your Mr. Goddard, who I didn't like much."

"Oh? Why?"

"With all due respect, sir," Keough said, "I don't think I want to use any of my ten minutes answering that question."

"All right, then," the mayor said. He turned, pulled a chair away from the board table, and sat down.

"The clock starts now," he said.

Keough had to pick out the high points carefully, as he did not want to waste his ten minutes. The mayor listened intently, never interrupting, simply regarding Keough steadily with intelligent eyes until he was finished.

"Let me get this straight," the mayor said, then. "You believe that a person in the political system of this state hired someone to kill Mark Drucker?"

"Yes, sir."

"And you think it's either Franklin Anson or Dexter Shepp?"

"They are suspects, sir," Keough said, "but what I mostly think is that they're looking for something Drucker had on them. Which is something I strongly suspect."

"And Kenneth Goddard called you down here several days ago, leading you to believe I had asked for you?"

"Yes."

"Well, I can assure you, I did not."

"I didn't think so, sir. I think Goddard was just looking to keep me away from Shepp and Anson."

The mayor stood and walked to the window so he could look down on Market Street.

"As I'm sure you know, Detective," he said, with his back still turned and his hands clasped behind his back, "politics has always been a dirty business."

"Yes, sir."

"I'm sure that over the years, murder has been used more than once to further a political career or goal."

Keough didn't feel the need to respond this time.

The mayor turned.

"I must admit to being distressed," he said, "even more so than when I heard Mark had been killed."

"Did you know him well, Mayor?"

"Not extremely well," the mayor said, "but we had some common goals which brought us together once or twice at the same functions."

"And did you also share those goals with Franklin Anson and Dexter Shepp?" Keough asked.

The door by which the mayor had entered opened, and the woman who had escorted Keough to the room stuck her head in.

"Mr. Mayor, you're going to be late."

"Shut the door, Beatrice," the mayor said.

"Yes, sir." And she did.

Keough realized he was being given an extension on his ten minutes.

"The law firm of Shepp, Anson, and Associates and I do not see eye to eye on many things," the mayor admitted.

"I have been given to understand that Mark Drucker was a client of theirs."

"I'd be surprised if that were true," the mayor said. "Who told you such a thing?"

"Well, they did, and Drucker's ex-wife."

"I'd be more inclined to believe he had something they wanted," the man said, "and that they're looking for it now that he's dead."

"Yes, sir, but would you be inclined to believe they had reason to have him killed?"

"Reason, perhaps," the mayor said. "But would they do it? That I can't answer."

The mayor looked at his watch.

"Sir, do you know of anyone else who might have had reason to have him killed?" Keough asked quickly.

"I'm afraid I don't, Detective," the mayor said. "And now I really am going to be late."

"I appreciate the time you've given me, sir."

"Detective Keough," the mayor said, "I'm aware of the

service you did to this city last year, catching that maniac."

"I had a lot of help, sir."

"You were the lead man on the case, were you not?"

"Yes, sir."

"And you are lead man on this one?"

"Yes, sir."

The mayor walked toward Keough until he was about two feet away.

"I'm going to leave word with my secretary that any calls from you be put through to me immediately, even if they have to be forwarded to my home."

"I appreciate that, sir."

"I want to help in any way I can," the man said. "And I will be having a talk myself with Mr. Goddard."

"Yes, sir."

The mayor extended his hand and shook Keough's firmly, as he had the first time.

"Good luck, Detective."

"Thank you, sir."

"Can you find your own way out, or shall I have someone show you?"

"I can find my way, sir," Keough said, "I have a good sense of direction."

"Yes," the mayor said, "I rather suspect you do."

He walked back to the door he had used to enter, then turned with his hand on the doorknob.

"I have some advice for you."

"I'll take it."

"Franklin Anson is the front man for that law firm, tall, handsome—he is the *perfect* front man, but it is Dexter Shepp who is the brains. Don't underestimate that man."

"I sort of had that part figured out already, sir."

"Good for you," the mayor said, and Keough felt oddly satisfied with the man's apparent seal of approval.

With that he went through one door while Joe Keough

went through the other. While he negotiated the corridors, going back the way he came, he wondered why he had not told the mayor about the phony sex charges that had been made against him.

Thirty-seven

"YOU SPOKE TO him?" Steinbach asked, astounded. "You actually walked in off the street and got to see the mayor?"

"Yes." Keough said.

"I thought you were going to call and make an appointment."

Since they were both downtown, they had agreed to meet at Mike Shannon's for lunch or a drink, whichever they needed the most after their respective interviews. As it turned out, they were having both. Shannon, a former third baseman for the St. Louis Cardinals, was now a play-by-play man for the club. The restaurant sported tons of sports memorabilia, but also served great steaks and seafood.

"Are you all right?" Steinbach asked.

"A little dizzy," Keough said. "I forgot to take my pill this morning, and I didn't have any breakfast."

"Neither of those things sounds like they can be any good for you."

Keough took out one of the pills and swallowed it with some water.

"Order something good for you, will you?" Steinbach said.

"I can't have you . . . doing whatever it is you do when your sugar goes . . . high? Low?"

"In this case, low, I think."

"Well, whatever," Steinbach said. "Jesus, that's all you need is to make yourself sick."

Keough thought that was amusing, since technically speaking what he had was a disease. Can you get much sicker than having a disease?

"I'll be okay," he said, looking at the menu. "I'll order a salad with some chicken in it."

"Whatever works."

A waitress came over and took their orders, the salad and iced tea for Keough and a steak sandwich and beer for Steinbach.

"What kind of dressing, sir?" the waitress asked Keough.

That stumped him for a moment.

"What's good for diabetics?" Steinbach asked her,

"Well . . . we have a low-cal Italian?"

"That'll do it," Steinbach said. "Bring him that."

"Yes, sir," she said. "I'll be right out with your drinks."

"Thanks," Keough said.

"You better start learning about this stuff."

"I know," Keough said. "As soon as this case is over."

"So what did the mayor tell you?"

"Apparently, he and Drucker were on one side of the political fence while Anson and Shepp are on the other."

"And Drucker was a client of theirs?"

"The mayor doubts it."

"But his ex-wife confirmed it."

"Yes, she did," Keough said. "Somebody should ask her about that."

"Not you!"

"No, not me."

"What else did he say?"

"He's cleared the way so that my calls to him will go right through, no matter what."

"Wow. A direct pipeline to the mayor. Maybe he can get you out from under these phony charges. Did you ask him?"

"I didn't mention anything about it."

"Why not?"

"Because I had ten minutes," Keough said.

"And you spent them talking about the case and not the phony charges?"

"Yes."

Steinbach sat back.

"I don't know if I could have been that selfless in your place, Joe," he said, staring at his partner in . . . what? Wonder? Admiration?

"Cut it out," Keough said. "The solution to all this is solving this case, not crying to the mayor because somebody's accused me of something I did not do."

"I hope you're right."

"I am," Keough said. "You'll see."

"By the way, we didn't discuss how Valerie reacted to the news."

"About the way you'd expect."

"Supportive?"

"I guess."

"Stunned?"

"Definitely."

"I haven't seen a newspaper today, have you?" Steinbach asked.

"No," Keough said, "but if something were in there, you'd think the mayor would have mentioned it, wouldn't you?"

"If he saw it."

"He runs the city, Al," Keough said. "I think he probably reads the paper first thing every day."

"Who knows what mayors do behind closed doors?"

"Hey," Keough said, "that's my new buddy you're talking about."

The waitress came with their drinks at that moment.

"Would you like me to bring your salad out at the same time as his lunch, sir?" she asked Keough.

"That'd be fine."

She smiled and left.

"What did you find out at the Arch?"

"Talked to a few security guards," Steinbach said. "None of them noticed Brooks spending more money than usual, and he wasn't bragging to anybody about anything. If he took a payoff, he kept quiet about it."

"And Hannah Morgan? Did you see her?"

"I did."

"And?"

"I don't think she recognized me as your partner," Steinbach said. "I think she thought I was investigating her . . . allegation."

"And?"

"And I let her think it."

"You dog," Keough said. "You pretended to be from Internal Affairs."

"I confess."

"What did she say?"

"She's alleging that you put your hands on her and made suggestive, uh, suggestions."

"That's all?"

"Well, she indicated that you threatened her if she didn't succumb to your advances."

"Is that what she said? 'Succumb' to my 'advances.'?"

"Her exact words."

"Did you get the feeling she'd been coached on what to say, Al?"

"Oh, yeah. She was real nervous and seemed to be reciting. I don't think she'd stand up in court, Joe."

"Maybe she wouldn't," Keough said, "but I bet Marcy Drucker would."

"She does seem to be a more together lady."

"Maybe somebody should talk to her and see if her allegations are the same," Keough suggested.

"Now you're doing it to me," Steinbach said.

"Doing what?"

"Being suggestive."

"At least I'm not pressuring you to sleep with me."

"In your dreams, pal."

Thirty-eight

KEN GODDARD SAT down behind his desk and mopped the sweat from his brow, face, and the back of his neck with his handkerchief. He dropped the now grimy, damp cloth on his desk and picked up the phone. He dialed, waited one . . . two . . . three rings before beginning to mutter, "Pick up . . . pick up . . ." and then it was finally answered by a man.

"We got trouble."

"What kind?"

"I just got my ass reamed by the mayor," Goddard said.

"Do you still have your job?"

"Just barely," Goddard said, "but he's going to be keeping an eye on me now. He says he can't have aides or assistants making decisions for him."

"How did this happen?"

"Keough, that's how. He came to see the mayor."

"And you didn't intercept him?"

"He didn't have an appointment!" Goddard hissed. "He walked in off the goddamned street and told the mayor everything."

"Everything?"

"Well, enough."

"Then you're useless to me now."

"No!" Goddard said, before realizing this sounded like a plea. "No, I can still maneuver. It'll just be harder."

There was silence at the other end of the line, and then the man said, "We'll see," and hung up.

Goddard hung up, picked up his handkerchief, then dropped it, and headed for the men's room to wash his face.

The whore was in the shower again when the phone rang. She took a damn shower every time they had sex. He smiled, then, at the thought of her body getting all wrinkled by the time he was done with her.

The breakfast tray was long gone, and the lunch tray, as well. He was starting to think about dinner. The whore said all he seemed to do was eat and fuck. Little did she know. . . .

He reached for the phone and picked it up. He put it to his ear but didn't speak, just listened.

"You're not checking out," a voice said.

"Right," the man in the room said, and hung up.

He walked to the window, placed his right hand flat against it, fingers splayed. Even as a child he'd always had the biggest hands of anyone in school. Then they were a curse, giving rise to many hurtful nicknames, but in the end it had all turned out well. He'd grown into his hands in high school and began meting out vengeance for the years of taunts. Later, the large hands were perfect for his chosen profession. When he removed his hand from the cold window, his print mark was still there. He was glad he wasn't leaving, yet. He liked this hotel. It had twenty-four-hour room service, and every room had a view of the Arch and the Mississippi.

The shower stopped, and the whore came back out, ready for more.

* * *

District Attorney Jeff Peters stared across his desk at Detectives Angela Mason and Jack Gail. Between them, on the desk, was the file they had prepared on Detective Joseph Keough.

"This man was a hero last year," Peters said.

"Nobody remembers," Mason said. "There was no splash in the papers, no parade down Market Street."

"Nevertheless . . ."

"What does that mean?" Gail asked.

"What?"

"I've never understood what that word means," the younger detective said. " 'Nevertheless.' Is it the same as 'Nonetheless'?"

Peters looked at Angela Mason, who simply shrugged. Nobody liked her partner and, if anything, she disliked him more than anyone.

"Are you gonna charge him?" she asked.

Peters touched the file on his desk. He was a youthful-looking man, very tall and slender, with pale blue eyes everyone said worked to his advantage. He was supposed to have a future in politics in this town.

"Leave it," he said. "I'll go over it again."

"You've got two complainants," Mason said, holding up two fingers. "Two, Mr. Peters."

"I can count, Detective," Peters said. "Leave it. I'll read it again and let your superior know my decision."

Mason and Gail exchanged a glance, then Mason stood and the younger detective followed.

"Detective Mason."

She turned at the door.

"You put this together fairly quickly, didn't you?"

"Yes, we did."

"How?"

"Hard work," Gail said, but neither of the other parties in the room paid any attention to him.

"I don't like male cops who force their attention on women."

"I see."

"No," Mason said, "you don't," and left.

Jack Gail looked at Jeff Peters and said, "Just between you and me, she don't like male cops . . . period."

"That must make it very hard for you."

Gail shrugged and left the office also.

District Attorney Jeff Peters sat back in his chair and thought about Detective Joseph Keough. Hero one minute, sexual predator the next? Maybe his heroism didn't make the papers or rate a ticker-tape parade, but people would remember, and if he filed against the man and didn't get a conviction, his name would be shit come election time.

He opened the file and started to read it again, then picked up the phone and dialed a number he knew by heart.

Outside the office, in the hall, Gail asked Morgan, "What do you think he's going to do?"

"I don't know."

"You really think we've got enough on Keough?"

"We've got two women who say he came on to them, touched them, tried to use his authority to solicit sex from them," she said savagely. "I think we've got enough on him, yeah. I think we've got an airtight case."

"What if they're lying?"

"You would think that."

"What, you mean because I'm a man? Angela, you don't hate all men, do you?" her partner asked.

"No," she said, "just the ones that are still walking around."

She started for the elevator, and he followed. They rode down in silence and didn't speak again until they were out on the street.

"A woman DA would file," she said, then. "No problem."

"You're probably right," he said, blowing off the remark. "What do you want to do now? Get something to eat?"

She bit her lip, then said, "No. I want to talk to those women again."

"Why?"

"Just to make sure."

She started away, and he watched her back and wondered how, between the tenth floor and the street, her airtight case had suddenly developed a leak.

Thirty-nine

KEOUGH FELT BETTER after the salad and the pill. He was going to have to go to the doctor and find out what to do when he felt dizzy, how to tell when he was suffering from high sugar or low.

They split up in front of Mike Shannon's and walked to their respective parking lots. Steinbach was going to drop in on Marcy Drucker. It was doubtful she would make another complaint of a sexual nature so soon after the first, especially if she—like Hannah Morgan—thought Steinbach was investigating her allegation. They both had the same opinion about her, though. She was not as unsteady as Hannah Morgan. Keough thought that whoever had put the two women up to lying might have made a wrong choice with her, and soon come to regret it.

Keough considered going back to the office but was afraid of what might be waiting for him there. As long as he stayed out in the field, moving around, keeping his cell phone turned off, nobody could suspend him or, worse, arrest him. He felt badly about shutting Captain McGwire out this way, but there really was no one to depend on but himself and—to a lesser extent—his partner.

By the time he reached his car, he still had not decided what to do. He pulled out of the parking lot and drove down Chestnut past the Adam's Mark hotel, the Arch rising majestically in front of him. He turned right and got on Highway 44. He was still not sure where he was headed, but by using 44 he had plenty of options.

Detective Al Steinbach spent about twenty minutes talking with Marcy Drucker. He could tell when she suddenly thought he was investigating her allegation. Her body language changed from naturally flirtatious—overtly "sexual" actually described it better—to something more sedate. She even buttoned the top two buttons of her blouse while they talked. By the end of the conversation, she had all the sexual demeanor of a nun.

She maintained that Keough had come on to her, touched her, rubbed up against her, and made lewd suggestions. She was a good actress, if Steinbach was any judge. She would bury Keough if this went to court.

So far he'd gotten away with interrogating both the women who had accused his partner of sexual misconduct without them catching on, but he knew his luck had run out when he exited the house and saw Detective Angela Mason getting out of her car. She had been staring at his car with a frown, and the frown deepened when she turned her head and saw him. He squared his shoulders and kept walking.

"Detective Steinbach, isn't it?" she asked. She pronounced it Stein "beck" instead of "bach," but he didn't correct her.

"That's right," he said. "Detective . . ."

"Mason."

"That's right," he said, "Detective Mason."

"What are you doing here?" Mason asked. "Interrogating my complainant in an effort to get your partner off?"

"I'm conducting a homicide investigation, Detective," Steinbach explained. "In fact, we both are, my partner and I, but you've made it impossible for him to talk with the ex-wife of the victim. Therefore, I have to do it."

"*I've* made it impossible?" she asked. "Maybe if he was able to control his animal urges—"

"Animal urges?" he asked, interrupting her. "Do you really talk like that?"

"When I'm discussing animals," she said tightly, "yes."

"I think I've got you figured, Detective."

"Let me guess," she said, pugnaciously sticking out her jaw. "You think I'm a ball-busting, man-hating dyke."

"Ball-busting and man-hating, yes," Steinbach replied, "but it never occurred to me that you were a lesbian. See, I don't happen to think that hating men naturally makes you a lesbian. Excuse me, Detective."

He moved passed her and walked to his car. He could feel her gaze on his back. As he got into his car and drove away, he could see her in his rearview mirror, still standing in the driveway staring after him.

He knew he was going to hear about this later.

When Keough came to the Kingshighway exit, he got off and headed home. Why not? If the red message light were flashing on his machine, it didn't mean he had to pick it up. Later, he could go into the office and hook up with Steinbach, find out what happened with Marcy Drucker, and take his suspension or arrest—if one were waiting for him—like a man.

He pulled up in front of the house and saw Jack Roswell watering his bushes across the street again. He crossed over, figuring he could at least mend some fences here.

"Hello, Jack!"

Roswell looked up from what he was doing, then smiled, turned off the hose, and waved. "Hi, Joe. How are ya?"

"Good," Keough said, moving inside Roswell's gate until he was standing close to him. "Well, not so good."

"Oh? What's wrong?"

Then he did something he didn't know he was going to do. His only intention in crossing the street had been to make contact with the old man again. He hadn't really spoken to him since reporting that the doctor he was going to seemed legit. He hadn't even told him, then, of his own feelings that the doctor had his own agenda. And he certainly had not yet told the man that he, himself, was diabetic.

"Do you have some time, Jack?" he asked. "Maybe we could sit on your porch and talk a bit?"

"Sure," Roswell said, dropping the hose, "I got nothing but time, Joe. Wanna play some chess?"

"No," Keough said, "I just want to talk."

Keough ended up telling Jack Roswell *everything*—the case, the diabetes, the charges of sexual misconduct, even doubts he now had about himself and Valerie—doubts he didn't even know he had until they came out of his mouth.

At one point Jack had gone inside to get them some iced tea, which they both drank without sugar. In the end Keough sat back and heaved a huge sigh. He felt better than he had in days. Just getting it all off his chest made a world of difference.

"Well," Jack said, "first off I got to say I'm sorry."

"About what?"

"Well, if you hadn't gone to that doctor to check him out for me, you wouldn't know you had diabetes."

"Jack, I should thank you for that."

"Naw, you don't understand," Roswell said. "See, now you *know*. Now you're startin' to feel dizzy at certain times of day, or you're confused about what to eat or drink. . . . See, if you didn't know, you'd be doing everything you used to do and this . . . this *thing* woulda come up much later."

"You mean, like with you?"

"No," Jack said, "even at my age I wish I didn't know yet. It's only since I found I'm diabetic that I'm havin' trouble with my damn feet. It's like goin' ta the damn hospital, ya know? If you're not sick, they make you sick. Believe me, Joe, you'd be better off right now if you didn't know you were diabetic. For one thing, you don't need the extra pressure."

"You got that right."

"I can't help ya with the other stuff," Jack said, shaking his head. "Seems to me you coulda told the mayor about the sex stuff."

"Not his problem," Keough said.

"I gotta admire you for that."

"For what?"

"There you were in a room with the most powerful man in St. Louis—'cept maybe for Mark McGwire—and you didn't go cryin' on his shoulder about your troubles. You're a man, Joe. I don't know what else ta call ya."

"I'm here crying on your shoulder instead."

"Yeah, but like I said, I can't help ya none."

"It helped just to talk about it, Jack," Keough said, "and to apologize."

"Ya don't have to apologize to me about nothin'," Jack said. "Ya find out somethin' like that, that ya got a *disease*, it plays with yer head awhile. Jeez, don't worry about apologizin' ta me. You got enough troubles."

"Speaking of which," Keough said, checking his watch, "I've got to meet my partner."

Both men stood up and shook hands.

"You wanna play some chess sometime you let me know," Jack said.

"You're on."

Keough crossed back to his car, got in, and drove away. Never even made it into his own place.

Forty

WHEN KEOUGH WALKED into his office, nobody slapped handcuffs on him. He took that as a good sign. There were no other detectives in the squad room, as he and Steinbach were "on." He peeked into the captain's office, and no one was there, either. Maybe just talking it all out with Jack Roswell had made things better.

When he checked his desk, there were no messages. However, when he looked at Steinbach's desk, there was an envelope with his partner's name on it. Before he could open it, the phone on his desk rang. He walked over and answered it.

"There you are." McGwire said. "I've been trying to get you for a couple of hours."

"I haven't been home, and I think my cell phone is on the blink."

"I didn't want to leave this for you in a message," McGwire said.

"What is it, Cap? The DA?"

"No, it's not that," McGwire said. "It's Al Steinbach."

"What about him?"

"He's at St. John's," McGwire said. "He had a heart attack, Joe."

It had been Angela Mason who discovered something was wrong. She'd been watching Steinbach drive away from the Drucker house in his car when suddenly the vehicle veered off into some shrubbery. She ran after it and found Steinbach slumped over the steering wheel, clutching his chest. She used his radio to call for an ambulance. The doctor said her quickness in getting him help had saved his life.

When Keough got to St. John's, Steinbach was in intensive care, and his wife was with him. McGwire was in the hallway, and so was Angela Mason. After McGwire explained everything to him, he looked at Mason and said, "Thanks for saving my partner's life."

"No problem," she said. "We'd all do that for each other."

"Yeah, we would," Keough said.

"But that doesn't mean I'm backing off your case, Keough."

"Why would it?"

"I'm just letting you know," she said. She looked at McGwire. "Captain, I'll be in touch."

"Thanks again, Detective."

"You're welcome."

"She called me right away," McGwire said, as she walked to the elevator and got in. "You want to tell me what Al was doing at the Drucker house?"

"Do we have to talk about that now, Cap? I'd like to see him."

"The doctor says he's going to be okay. His wife is with him now," McGwire said. "Let's go someplace and talk."

They found a lounge with leather furniture and a coffee machine. They each got a cup and sat down.

"What was he doing there?"

"Hannah Morgan and Marcy Drucker are still part of a homicide investigation, Cap," Keough said, "but we figured I couldn't go and talk to them now, so Al had to."

"He saw the Morgan woman today, too?"

"Yes, this morning."

"Detective Mason didn't bitch about that," McGwire said. "I guess she doesn't know yet."

"Have you heard from the DA?"

"No," McGwire said. "Morgan saw him today and thinks he's dragging his feet because of that case last year."

"Maybe that'll keep me on the streets a little longer," Keough said.

"I'm taking you off the Drucker murder."

"Why? You can't do that."

"You said it yourself," McGwire replied. "There are people involved in the case you can't go near. You're handicapped, and you have no partner. I'll put someone else on it."

"Assign someone to partner with me, then," Keough said. "You can't take me off."

"I can, and I have. We have other detectives, Joe."

"But you assigned me," Keough reminded him. "You brought me in on my day off and gave it to me."

"And I didn't make a lot of friends doing that," his superior officer told him. "Hell, if I partner you with someone else, I have to break up another team to do it, and that won't make them any happier."

"Give me someone from uniform," Keough said. "I just need a body to do legwork."

"Another team would have the advantage of having worked together," McGwire said. "You'll have to fill them in on what you have."

"I bring something to the table they don't, Cap."

"And what's that?"

"A direct pipeline to City Hall."

"What the hell are you talking about?" McGwire demanded.

Very calmly Keough told him what he had done that morning and how it had turned out.

"You just waltzed in there and got to see the mayor?" McGwire asked.

"That's right."

"I don't believe it."

"It's true."

"No, no, I believe you talked to him," McGwire said. "I just don't believe that you did it. Why did you do it?"

"Because this case involves politics, and he's the biggest politician of all," Keough said. "He had to be interviewed."

"You didn't tell him about what you did to Anson?"

"No, sir."

"And you didn't tell him about the complaints that have been made against you by the two women?"

"No, sir."

"Why not?"

"They don't have any direct bearing on Mark Drucker's death," Keough said. "Those things are about me. That's not what I was there to talk to him about."

"You know," McGwire said, staring at him, "most of the time I'm glad you're on my side."

Keough held up his hands. "Don't explain what you mean by that," he said. "I'd rather take it as a compliment."

McGwire got up.

"So," Keough asked, also rising, "am I on or off the case?"

"I'll answer that in the morning," McGwire said, "after I've slept on it."

"So for tonight I'm still on?"

McGwire nodded and said, "For tonight."

"Thanks, Cap."

"Don't thank me, Joe," McGwire said. "I'm probably not doing you any favors by leaving you on this thing, even for tonight."

Forty-one

KEOUGH HAD TO introduce himself to Steinbach's wife. Prior to this they had never met. She said she had to go home and tell their kids what had happened, and she'd be back in the morning. He waited until she was gone, then used his badge to get in to see Steinbach. It impressed a nurse enough to give him five minutes.

"Hey, buddy," he said, as he approached the bed, not knowing if his partner could hear him or not.

Steinbach lay there a moment without reacting, then opened his eyes. He looked pale and drawn.

"Ain't this a knock in the head?" Steinbach asked. "I've been after you lately to eat right and take care of yourself and look what happens."

"Take it easy," Keough said.

"I can talk," Steinbach said. "I'm just really . . . tired, you know?"

"I know."

"That Mason . . . she saved my bacon, didn't she?"

"She did that."

"And after I called her . . . a ball buster."

Keough laughed. "You did?"

"She got me mad . . . talking about you."

"Well, I appreciate that, partner."

"Don't mention it."

"I'm going to leave," Keough said. "I just wanted to see for myself that you were . . . well, you know, still with us."

"I'm sorry about this, partner."

"About what?"

"You don't need . . . the extra pressure."

"Don't worry about me, partner," Keough said. "Pressure is my middle name."

"That Marcy Drucker . . ." Steinbach said in a barely audible tone, ". . . she'll bury you in court."

"I'll try not to get to court."

"Joe . . ."

"That's enough, Al," Keough said. "Get some sleep. I'll check on you tomorrow."

Steinbach's eyes closed, and he said, "Not gonna argue . . ." and then he was asleep. At least Keough hoped he was asleep. He checked the heart monitor Steinbach was hooked up to—along with an IV and some oxygen—and saw that the line and the heartbeat were nice and steady.

"You take it easy, partner," he said, almost to himself. "You handle this part; I'll take care of the rest."

When Keough left the hospital, he was feeling wide awake but uneasy as to what to do with himself. The only thing he knew for sure was that he was still on the case, at least until tomorrow morning. It was only eight P.M., early enough to pay a visit to people involved with the case—but who?

Keough wondered if he should use tonight to rattle a few cages, to see if he couldn't get somebody to make a mistake.

Like the mayor's assistant, Kenneth Goddard. Keough believed the mayor that morning when he said he was going to "talk" to his assistant. Maybe Goddard was shaken up enough to say something he wasn't supposed to say. All he had to do was find out where the man lived. He thought he knew how to do that.

He got in his car and drove back to the office.

Kenneth Goddard didn't usually drink hard liquor when he was home alone, but tonight he was making an exception. He fixed himself a gin and tonic then took it out onto the balcony. From there he was able to look over Forest Park, serene at this time of the evening, when the nearby Science Center and Botanical Gardens were closed, and the Zoo in the park was also closed. There were some people jogging as well as the red taillights and white headlights of cars driving through. Goddard's apartment was in the old, renovated Chase Park Plaza Hotel on Kingshighway, which now housed apartments and condos.

The mayor had torn him a new asshole, chastizing him for making "mayoral" decisions on his own. His instructions for the future were not to do anything without checking with the mayor first. Thinking he was going to be fired, Goddard readily agreed. There was too much at stake not to. After a while, when all this furor died down, he could get back to what he had been doing, but now it was time to lay low. It was all that goddamned Detective Keough's fault anyway. How dare he bypass Goddard and go directly to the mayor. Who did he think he was?

The ice moved in Goddard's glass, reminding him that the drink was in his hand, and he sipped it. He hadn't yet swallowed when the arm came across his neck from behind and jerked him back so that his feet were dangling. The glass crashed to the floor of the balcony, and the breath gurgled in Goddard's throat. Pressure across his throat was tremendous, and he kicked his legs in an attempt to get away, but they flailed uselessly. Suddenly, the arm became a hand that pulled up on his chin, and then something swept across his neck and chest, and he felt a hot wetness. He couldn't breathe, couldn't speak, even after the arm released him, dropping him to the floor where he flopped about like a fish that had been reeled in and dropped onto the deck of a boat.

Forty-two

KEOUGH WENT DIRECTLY to Steinbach's desk and searched it until he found what he was looking for—the lists supplied by Kenneth Goddard's secretary. As he had hoped, the woman had included even Goddard's home address.

"How's Al doing?" Detective Hawthorne asked. He and his partner, Ellis, were sitting at their desks, drinking coffee when Keough came in.

"He's going to be okay."

"That's good," Ellis said. "Tough break for you, though. You don't have a partner now."

"We heard the boss might take the Drucker case from you," Hawthorne said, "and drop it in our laps."

Keough grinned at both men and said, "You heard wrong."

"Your partner know you were gonna search his desk?" Ellis asked.

"He insisted on it," Keough said, and left. He had nothing more to say to the two men.

Keough was surprised to find that Goddard lived so close to him, on the edge of the Central West End. He drove to the building on Kingshighway and parked right in front. He went into the foyer, where the mailboxes and doorbells were, found Goddard's name, and rang his bell. There was no answer. He wondered whether he should just press all the buttons and see if someone buzzed him in, or simply wait for someone to come home, or leave. He tried the door, but it was locked tight. He pressed all the buttons but apparently people were not as gullible as they used to be. No one buzzed him in. On a whim, he played "shave and a haircut" on one of the buttons, and suddenly the door buzzed and clicked open. People and their "codes."

He made his way to the elevator and took it to Goddard's floor, the tenth. He didn't know why, but he had a feeling Goddard was in. If he'd been yelled at by the mayor that day, he probably didn't feel like having company.

Keough got off at the tenth floor without running into anyone and walked to number 1013. Odd, he thought. Those were the call letters in New York for an officer in need of assistance, or "officer down."

He knocked on the door, waited, then knocked again. When there was no answer, he looked both ways, then squatted down in front of the door to inspect the lock. If he needed lockpicks, he was out of business, but if a credit card would open the door, he was okay. Like most buildings that had a system where people had to be buzzed in, the doors to the actual apartments were not difficult to force. In fact, this one might have been forced already.

It was unlocked.

Keough drew his gun and entered.

Forty minutes later, the apartment and the hallway outside of it were a flurry of activity. Uniformed cops, lab men, ME's men—not to mention the ME—several local detectives, and a uniformed major were all scurrying about, doing their jobs.

Upon entering the apartment, Keough found himself in a

poshly furnished living room. He also noticed that the balcony door was open. He found Kenneth Goddard on the floor of the balcony, which was tile and therefore slippery with blood. Keeping his gun ready, Keough avoided as much of the blood as he could and got close enough to ascertain that the man was dead. He also saw, on the low wall of the balcony, two bloody handprints, as if the killer had stopped to look out over the park after slitting Goddard's throat.

Keough could not immediately prove to the locals that this homicide was connected to his, so he stood aside and allowed them to do their jobs after identifying himself as having made the call to 911. There would be time enough tomorrow—if he was still on the case—to draft a report that would get this case assigned to him.

Even before he called 911, however, he had made a quick search of the apartment to determine whether or not the killer was still there. But, of course, the man was a pro and was long gone.

Keough made one other call before he dialed 911.

He called the mayor.

"Have much experience with homicides?" Keough asked the local detective, whose name was Calhoun.

The man was older than Keough, but there was a deference to experience in the way he spoke.

"To tell you the truth, no," he said. He looked around, as if checking if anyone could hear them. "In fact, if you can take this over, I wouldn't mind."

"I'm not sure it will be me," Keough said, "but I know somebody from my squad will end up with it."

"I thought you were top homicide man in the city?"

"I may have my hands full," Keough said, but didn't elaborate.

"Well, since you're here, is there anything you'd like me to put in this report?" Calhoun asked.

"Yes, now that you mention it," Keough said. "The apartment was neat as a pin, so all the activity took place on the balcony. Also, the door was opened slick as you please, so this was a pro job right from the beginning."

"Not a break-in?"

"Not at all," Keough said.

"So now your killer's struck three times," Calhoun said. "Serial?"

"I don't think so," Keough said. "Connected, yeah, but methodically so. A serial killer kills in the same way, but the victims don't usually know each other or have any connection. These three are all connected. We wouldn't even need the bloody handprints to do it, but they seal the deal."

Calhoun finished writing and said, "Well, just between you and me I hope this ends up on your desk."

"So do I," Keough said. "Thanks."

"Are you through here?" the major asked, approaching them. This was the one rank Keough had a hard time reconciling himself to. There were no majors in the New York City Police Department. Here the major ran the local cop shop, not a captain. Keough assumed the top man had been called out on this one because of the identity of the dead man.

Calhoun said, "Yes, sir."

"So the ME can have the body?"

"Yes, sir," Calhoun said again, "he can."

"You done with him?" The captain indicated Keough.

"Oh, uh, yes, sir. He can go."

"You're free to go, Detective Keough. Don't get me wrong, but until this case is transferred to you, my guys are in charge."

"I understand, sir," Keough said.

"Thanks for the ID on the victim, though," the major said. "I'll have to notify the mayor."

"Yes, sir." Keough did not tell the man that he had already called the mayor.

"You can go," the major said, "with my thanks."

"Yes, sir, Major," Keough said, and to Detective Calhoun he said, "Good luck," and left.

Down in his car, Keough paused before starting the motor. He'd walked through the entire apartment before all the others had arrived, which is what he would have done if he'd been called in. The killer did not seem to have gone into any of the other rooms, including the bathroom. He'd checked there first, to see if any bloody handprints had been left on the mirror, as in the Brooks house. There were none. Apparently, the killer left one pair of prints behind, and at this scene they were on the balcony.

His conversation with the mayor had been brief, once he got connected to the man at his home and told him what had happened. . . .

"Jesus Christ," the mayor said, "I just bawled him out today!"

"Just between you and me, Mayor," Keough said, "I think we got him killed, you and I."

"How's that?"

"He obviously had his own agenda—or somebody's agenda—and once you caught on he wasn't going to be very effective."

"So you think he was planted inside my administration from the beginning?" the mayor asked.

"Either that or somebody recruited him shortly after."

"And now he's dead because you exposed him to me."

"Right."

"Well, Detective Keough, I don't think you or I are responsible for his death," the mayor said. "I believe men have to take responsibility for their own actions, and this is the result of his. He got himself killed."

"Yes, sir," Keough said, "that's another way of looking at it."

"I could come out there—"

"I'd prefer you didn't, sir," Keough said. "I'm the sure the locals will notify you. I wouldn't want anyone to know that I called."

"Why not?"

"I'd just like to keep this under my hat for a while, sir," Keough said. "Only my captain knows that I can get you on the phone when I need to."

"All right, Detective," the mayor said. "I'll play it your way for now."

"I appreciate that, sir."

"Will you end up with this investigation, as well?"

"It's possible, sir."

The mayor apparently sensed something in his tone.

"Why would you not?"

"There are other factors being considered, sir," Keough said. "I . . . might be taken off the case completely."

"That seems foolish to me."

"As I said, sir," Keough repeated, "there are other factors being considered."

"Like what?"

"I'd really rather not say at this time, sir, if you don't mind."

"Detective Keough," the mayor said, "I want these murders solved, and it seems to me you're the person who is in position to do that."

"Thank you, sir," Keough said. "I'll certainly put my best foot forward."

"Do that," the mayor said, "and keep in touch."

"Yes, sir."

Now was the first time he'd replayed in his mind the conversation he'd had with the mayor, and it seemed to him he'd let the cat out of the bag. The mayor was sure to make some calls tomorrow and would find out about the Internal Affairs investigation. What his reaction would be only time would tell.

Keough had parked far enough away from the hotel entrance that he was not blocked in by the phalanx of official vehicles that had formed there. He started his car and pulled away. He'd be in front of his residence in five minutes, but he wasn't sure he wanted to go home just yet. His option, however, were extremely limited. He'd made no close friends since arriving in St. Louis, his relationship with Valerie had not yet progressed to the point where he would just drop in on her, and the only other person he might have called was in the hospital.

In the end, he drove home and parked in front. He paused a moment, considered walking across the street and ringing Jack Roswell's bell, but all the lights were out, and Jack was probably asleep.

Looking toward tomorrow morning, he decided that would be a good time to fly a kite.

Forty-three

SIX A.M. found Keough in Forest Park trying to get a kite into the air. There wasn't a lot of wind available—that day in the park with Valerie, just before this had all started, had been better—but he finally managed to coax it up. He didn't need it to fly long, just enough to collect his thoughts.

His thoughts, however, were not of his own plight, but of the sequence of events that had begun with Mark Drucker's murder. In seemingly quick order Harry Brooks was dead—no doubt to hide the identity of the killer, who had used Brooks to gain access to the Arch—and then Kenneth Goddard—probably to hide the identity of the man who was "running" him in the mayor's administration and, in Keough's estimation, the man who had hired Drucker's killer.

Everything was connected. For it not to be was to put too much credence in coincidence, which Keough never did. That meant that the murders were politically motivated. They had to be. Someone with a personal grudge against Drucker probably would have killed him outright, and not hired it done. Also, the killer had to be high-priced because he had a flair. Using the Arch, leaving the handprints, the use of gloves—probably the thinnest of rubber ones—to keep his fingerprints hidden . . . the man had an ego that could only come from a long string of successes.

His own problems—except for the diabetes and Steinbach's heart attack—were also a result of Drucker's murder. Whoever was pulling the string had set him up for the sexual misconduct charges in order to get him off the case. But why? They must have known that somebody else would be assigned. That there would still be someone looking for the murderer, and looking for whatever it was Drucker had left behind that was not much interest to both Shepp and Anson.

Shepp and Anson. Keough was convinced that they were behind the whole thing. Maybe—as the mayor had pointed out—even Anson was dancing to a tune that Dexter Shepp was playing.

Sure, Shepp ran Anson; he'd been running Goddard—probably through Anson—and how he was doing the same with the women, Hannah Morgan and Marcy Drucker—Morgan unwillingly and Marcy Drucker very willingly. Marcy was, after all, executrix of Drucker's estate, and Shepp probably needed her. She, knowing that, would cooperate but probably for a very high price.

After a while, flying the kite became second nature. Without thinking, Keough would make the necessary adjustments to keep it in the air while his mind worked on the case. Kite flying always seemed to do this for him, it separated his mind from his body. There was a freedom that came from knowing his body could do without his mind for a while, leaving it the time to work on other things.

Like murder.

Keough wrapped one hand in the string, held the spool with the other, and snapped it. Released, the kite flew off, swooping and rising, eventually coming to rest somewhere in the park. He didn't need it anymore. He knew what had to be done—if this was still his case.

* * *

While Keough was flying his kite in Forest Park, the phone rang in the home of Captain Mark McGwire. McGwire, sleeping on the couch for the third night in a row, rolled over and answered the phone groggily.

"Hello—yeah, what?"

"Is this Captain McGwire?"

"Yes, it is."

"I've awakened you, I know, Captain," the voice said, "but do you know who this is?"

Suddenly, McGwire did, and he sat up.

"Yes, sir, I do," he said respectfully. "What can I do for you, sir?"

"You can tell me about Detective Joe Keough, Captain."

"Uh, what do you want me to tell you, sir?"

"Everything, Captain," the man said, "everything."

District Attorney Jeff Peters had come into work that morning with his mind made up. He was filing charges against Detective Joseph Keough for sexual misconduct and sexual abuse based on the complaints of Hannah Morgan and Marcy Drucker. What he had to decide was if he had enough for an additional charge of attempted rape. In behalf of both women and Franklin Anson he was also charging Keough with assault, harassment, and misapplication of authority. All he needed was for his secretary to draw up the proper paperwork, and Joe Keough's career as a police officer was all but finished.

"Mr. Peters?"

He looked up and saw his secretary with her head stuck in the door.

"I'm glad you came in, Rhonda," he said, "I have some paperwork—"

"Sir, there's a call for you on line one."

"Rhonda, I don't want to take any calls this morning," Peters said. "I've made a difficult decision, and we need to get the papers drawn up and filed before I change my mind."

"Sir, I think you'll want to take this call."

He frowned at her and asked, "Why? Who is it?"

"It's the mayor, sir."

"The mayor?"

"Yes, sir," she said. "On line one."

"All right, Rhonda," he said, "I'll take it."

She backed out and closed the door as he picked up the telephone and spoke into it.

"Good morning, Your Honor," he said, "what can I do for you?"

Forty-four

BEFORE GOING IN TO work, Keough stopped at "The Palace on Ballas," which was what everyone in St. Louis called St. John's Hospital on Ballas Road. He wanted to check on Steinbach's condition before he did anything else.

The nurse got the doctor for him after he showed her his badge. His partner was asleep, but his condition had not changed. His wife was in with him; his children had been to see him. The doctor said that if Keough wanted to get in, he would arrange it, but Keough didn't want to intrude. It would have been different if he'd known the family at all, if he'd even been over their house for dinner or a barbecue, but he hadn't. He always kept his relationships with his partners separate from his private life. Unlike other cops he'd known, he didn't become close friends with his partners. It was just the way he chose to do things.

Satisfied that Steinbach's condition had not worsened, he left the hospital and drove to work.

Time to face the music.

*   *   *

When he entered, he immediately became aware that Mc-Gwire was in his office. He looked at Hawthorne and Ellis and pointed at the office.

"He came in early today," Hawthorne said, with a shrug, "and he didn't seem happy about it."

"He's sleeping on the couch at home," Ellis said.

"How do you know?" Keough asked.

"That's how I looked after a night on the couch when I was sleeping there—just before my divorce."

Keough remembered a snatch of telephone conversation he'd heard between McGwire and his wife earlier in the week and figured Ellis was right.

"Keough! Is that you?" McGwire shouted from his office.

Keough went to the door and said, "Yeah, it's me, Cap."

"Come in and close the door," McGwire said. "We have to talk."

Keough entered and pulled the door closed behind him. McGwire's hair was sticking up in the back, and he was rubbing his eyes, which were red-rimmed.

"Bad night, Cap?"

"Early morning," McGwire said. "Phone kept ringing."

"Okay, Cap, give it to me straight," Keough said, sitting down. "What's the bad news?"

"The news," McGwire said, "is that you don't work here anymore, Joe."

"The DA filed charges, huh?" Keough asked. "I'm suspended?" He'd been expecting it, and yet now that the time had come he felt a coldness in the pit of his stomach.

"No," McGwire said, "you haven't been charged, and you're not suspended, Joe. You've been transferred."

"Transferred? To where?"

"From now on," McGwire said, "you report directly to the mayor."

Keough was stunned. "What?"

"You heard me."

"How—when did that happen?"

"This morning," McGwire said. "The mayor called the chief, then he called me at home, and then the chief called me. Then—from what I understand—the mayor called the DA."

"All of that this morning?"

"Yeah, and all to make sure that you're still working on the Drucker case."

"But I thought you said I was transferred?"

"You're still working the Drucker case," McGwire said, "but you report to the mayor."

"What about Internal Affairs? And the DA?"

"There's no more Internal Affairs investigation," McGwire said. "The mayor pulled the plug on that."

"But . . . why? How?"

"When he called me this morning, he had me tell him everything I knew about you and this case. In the end, he agreed with me that you were being set up in order to get you off the case."

"What about the allegations?"

"We're having them investigated to determine if they were false or not," McGwire said. "Meanwhile, you're free to work the Drucker murder, which includes the guard from the Arch and the mayor's assistant. I understand you were on the scene last night?"

"That's right," Keough said. "I went there to talk to Goddard and found his body. I called it in."

"And apparently you called your new friend, the mayor, as well."

"Yes, I did."

"It would have been nice if you'd called me, too."

Keough wondered why he hadn't thought of that himself while he was sitting in the car lamenting the fact that he had no one to talk to.

"Sorry, Cap," he said. "I didn't think of it."

"Well, you're free now to work the case and not worry about those criminal charges."

"I appreciate that, Cap," Keough said. "I realize you had a lot to do with that. Apparently the mayor puts a lot of credence in your word."

"More in your actions than in my words."

"What do you mean?"

"He's impressed with you and the fact that you never once told him about the allegations and asked for his help."

"I just didn't think it had anything to do with him."

"Well, that's what you say," McGwire said. "The mayor feels you have a tremendous sense of duty and can't imagine that a man like you would sexually harass anyone, especially while you were working on a case. Besides that, he's apparently acquainted with Marcy Drucker. He says he doesn't find it hard to believe that she'd pull something like this."

"What about what I did to Franklin Anson?"

"Well, there you're lucky that the mayor and Anson don't get along. When I told His Honor what you did to Anson, he thought it was funny."

"I—I don't know what to say," Keough said. "I'm still trying to take all this in."

McGwire stood up.

"Yesterday your life may have looked like it was going to shit," the captain said, "but it looks like it's coming up roses now. You can continue to work out of this office until you've solved the Drucker case."

"What happens after that?"

"I don't know."

"Well . . . is this a permanent appointment?" Keough asked.

"You'll have to take that up with your new boss, Joe," McGwire said. "He wants to see you this morning, as soon as we're done here. Right now I'm gonna go out and get some coffee. I'll see you later."

"Listen, Cap," Keough said, standing up, "I don't know how to thank you."

"Just don't make me look like a jerk in front of the mayor, Joe," McGwire said. "That would piss me off."

"Don't worry, sir," Keough said. "I won't."

Forty-five

DRIVING DOWNTOWN TO see the mayor, Keough was thinking that, in spite of the fact he still had diabetes and Al Steinbach's heart attack to deal with, he couldn't help feeling a
sense of relief now that criminal charges and possible suspension—or worse—had been removed from the equation.

This time, when he presented himself at the mayor's office,
his reception was entirely different.

"Oh, yes, Detective Keough," the woman at reception said,
"the mayor is waiting for you. Just one moment."

It seemed only seconds later that the same woman who had
led him back last time appeared again and, this time, introduced herself.

"Detective Keough, I'm Beatrice, the mayor's secretary.
Come this way, please? His Honor is waiting for you."

He followed her down corridors again, but this time, instead of being taken to some impersonal meeting room, she
escorted him directly to the mayor's office.

"You may go right in," she said, holding the door open.

The mayor was seated behind a large desk as Keough entered, talking on the phone. He waved Keough forward and
indicated that he should sit. Keough did so, looking around

the office while the mayor finished his conversation. There were the usual collection of flags you found in political offices and photos of the mayor with other dignitaries on the wall. Other than that, the office was actually quite tastefully furnished. One wall was lined with bookshelves that seemed to hold everything from reference books to popular novels.

The mayor hung up and said, "Welcome to my staff, Detective Keough—or may I call you Joe?"

"Well, sir," Keough said, still shaken by the morning's turn of events, "since I apparently work for you, I guess you can call me whatever you like."

"I'll call you Joe," the mayor said, "for now. How do you feel?"

"Stunned," Keough said, shaking his head. "Quite frankly I'm stunned, sir."

"Only natural, I expect," the man said. "Joe, I have to tell you that I admire you a great deal. That's the main reason I wanted you on my staff."

"Sir, I'm just a cop—"

"No false modestly here, Detective," the mayor said. "You had my ear yesterday, and you never once asked me to intervene on your behalf. You spoke only of the case you were working on."

"Sir, that's all I thought of talking to you about," Keough said. "There was nothing noble in my not bringing up my own problems. They were just that, my problems."

"Well, they're not problems anymore," the mayor said.

"With all due respect, sir," Keough said, "how can you make criminal charges simply go away?"

"The obvious answer to that, Joe, would be to say that I'm the mayor; that's how I can do it. But I'm not going to tell you that. Let's just say that these charges have been put on hold until they can be more closely investigated."

"By whom?"

"That's not your concern," the mayor said. "I'll assign a special investigator to ascertain whether or not those charges were false. If they were, then the people bringing them against you will be charged. For the time being you have only one thing to worry about, and that is your investigation of Mark Drucker's murder, and the murders that have followed it."

"Yes, sir," Keough said. "I appreciate that."

"I have also learned from your captain that you have diabetes. This is a recent development in your life?"

"Yes, sir."

"I'm going to have you examined by my personal physician, Joe," the mayor said, "and he will help you deal with this."

"I—I don't know what to say."

"I'm not done," the mayor said, with a smile. "I've also sent my man over to St. John's to take care of your partner. You see, I truly don't want you to be concerned with anything but this case."

"I appreciate that, sir."

"You can continue to work out of your present location, or I can offer you an office here."

"Um, sir. Is this a permanent position or a temporary one?"

"That's something we can discuss after you've taken care of this case, Joe," the mayor said.

"I think I'll just stay where I am and work from my, uh, present desk."

"Suit yourself," the mayor said. "I want you to be comfortable. You'll need this, though."

The mayor took out what looked like a black billfold and tossed it across to Keough. He picked it up and saw that it was an ID holder.

"That identifies you as a member of my staff," the mayor said. "Doors will be open to you now that were closed to you before."

"Thank you, sir," Keough said, putting the ID away. He'd take a closer look at it later on.

"If there's anything else I can do for you, just let me know."

"I think you've done plenty, sir," Keough said, standing up.

"Seems to me I better get to work and start showing I deserve all this."

"You've got nothing to prove to me, Joe," the mayor said. "Just do your job. I suspect that will always be good enough."

Keough wasn't sure what he'd done to deserve such respect from the mayor of St. Louis, and he wasn't at all sure how to react to it. He certainly couldn't keep saying "thank you" all the time.

"I'll be in touch, sir," he finally said.

"Good," the mayor said.

"Before I go," he said, "I'd like to ask some questions about Goddard."

"All right, go ahead."

"How did you come to hire him?"

"He applied for the job," the mayor said. "I needed an assistant with some ideas, and the balls to back them up. He fit the bill."

"Was he recommended?"

"No," the mayor said, "but he sure knew that I was looking for someone." The man sat back in his chair. "I guess I should have thought of that then. Somebody who knew what I needed sent him to me, knowing he'd fit the bill."

"And then they'd have someone inside your administration."

Shaking his head, the mayor said, "It's going to take me a while to even figure out how much damage he might have done."

"Seems to me your head of security would have checked him out," Keough said.

"You'd think, wouldn't you?" the mayor said. "I guess I'm going to have to reexamine the man I have in that job as well."

"Well, sir," Keough said, "I'll leave you to your work and get to mine."

"Oh," the mayor said, "before you go leave me your cellphone number."

Keough took out a business card and wrote the number on the back.

"Oh, and your captain told me you have a habit of turning it off?"

"Um, sometimes it just doesn't, uh, work right—"

"Make sure it works right from now on, Detective," the mayor said. "I like to be able to reach the members of my staff when I have to."

"Yes, sir," Keough said. "I'll remember that."

Forty-six

KEOUGH WAITED UNTIL he was in his car before pulling out his new ID. It did, indeed, identify him as a member of the City Hall staff, and he began to wonder what doors it would open. He decided to try it right away. As he pulled his car up to the parking booth to get out of the lot, he showed the ID to the parking attendant.

"Pass," the man said, and raised the arm so Keough could drive out without paying.

Well, he thought, that was worth the price of admission right there. He never liked using his badge to get special privileges, but he felt like he'd suddenly been given the key to the city.

He went over the meeting with the mayor in his mind as he pulled his car onto Highway 44. The mayor had gotten a handle on just about everything but Keough's relationship with Valerie. He supposed he was going to have to work on that one himself.

He took 44 to Highway 270 and drove back to St. John's Hospital again. This time, when he inquired about Al Steinbach's condition, he was told there had been improvement and that Detective Steinbach was no longer critical and was, in fact, no longer in the intensive care ward. The doctor told Keough where Steinbach had been moved to, and he took the elevator to that floor and found the room. It was semiprivate, just Steinbach and one other bed, which was now empty. When Keough walked in, Steinbach was propped up in bed and smiled when he saw him.

"Hey, partner!" he greeted. "Looks like I'm going to be around for a little while longer."

"Shit," Keough said, "and I already had your desk rented out."

He approached the bed and shook hands with his partner. Steinbach was still hooked up to a heart monitor, but he looked much better. Some color had crept back into his face.

"What are you doing here all alone?"

"If you're talking about my wife and kids, I chased them out," Steinbach said. "They were starting to suffocate me. If you're talking about the other bed, it's unoccupied right now. Interested?"

"It's tempting," Keough said, "but I've got a lot of work to do."

"Fill me in," Steinbach said. "What happened with the DA? They filing charges?"

"Nope."

"Really? What happened?"

Shaking his head, Keough said, "You're not going to believe any of this, Al. . . ."

Steinbach listened in rapt attention as Keough told him everything that had occurred since his heart attack, and the thing that most interested his partner was his new ID.

"Let me see it!" he said.

Keough took it out and handed it over. Steinbach ran his fingers over it.

"That's the City Seal," he said.

"I know."

"You know how many doors this could open for you?"

"That's what His Honor said."

"That what you call him?" Steinbach asked, handing the ID back. "His Honor?"

"Hell, I don't know what to call him," Keough said. "I'm not used to this yet."

"What's he call you?"

"Right now, Joe."

"Jesus," Steinbach said, chuckling, "you came out of this on a first name basis with the mayor. Only you."

They talked awhile longer about the new position, about the charges basically just "going away," about Goddard's murder and what it meant, even about Keough's own health.

"The mayor's going to take care of that, too, it seems," Keough said. "He even sent his own doctor over here to look after you."

"That's who that was," Steinbach said, snapping his fingers. "I thought I saw somebody in here this morning, but I was groggy. I thought I was dreaming. The mayor's doctor?"

"Yup."

"Ain't that a kick in the head. Wait'll I tell my wife."

Keough noticed a get-well card on the stand next to Steinbach's bed. It had a computer screen on the front, and it said "Getwell.com" on it.

"Is that from who I think it is?" he asked.

"Sure is."

"Is that smart, Al?"

"Come on, Joe," Steinbach said. "We're just friends."

The card was from Steinbach's "computer sweetie," and it was signed with "Love."

"If you say so, partner."

"Look," Steinbach said, "I'm happy for you and all, but what's going to happen when I get out of here?"

"What do you mean?"

"I mean you and I won't be partners anymore when I get

back to work. What am I supposed to do, break in somebody new—again?"

"Are you coming back to work, Al?"

"Well, sure," Steinbach said. "Doctor says I'll be okay; he says there's no permanent damage. . . ."

"Did he tell you you'd be coming back to work?"

"Well, no," Steinbach said, "not in so many words."

"Why don't we wait and see what happens before we start talking about it?" Keough asked. "I don't even know if my assignment to City Hall is permanent. Nothing's going to happen until after this Drucker case gets closed."

"And how are you going to do that?"

"I got some ideas this morning, while I was flying a kite."

"That really help you think?" Steinbach asked. "Flying those kites of yours?"

"It clears my head. Sometimes I feel like my brain is up there floating around with the kite."

"I'll have to try that some time," Steinbach said. "Maybe before I get back to work—you know, while I'm convalescing."

"It'd be good for you, I'm sure," Keough said.

Suddenly, it seemed to be very awkward between them. Both of their futures were literally up in the air. There was no guarantee there would be room for each of them in the other's life.

"I've got to get to work, Al," Keough said.

"Yeah, right," Steinbach said. "I've got to get some rest. The troops'll be back in a little while."

They shook hands again.

"I'm glad those bogus charges aren't hanging over your head anymore, partner," Steinbach said.

"I'm glad you're going to be okay. Anything I can do, or get for you, before I go?"

"Naw, I'm good," Steinbach said. "I'll just relax until the family gets back."

"Okay," Keough said. "I'll get going, then."

He walked to the door, then turned around and looked at his partner once more.

"Hey, keep me informed, okay?" Steinbach asked. "I got a vested interest in this case."

"You got it," Keough said. "I'll see you."

"Yeah," Steinbach said, "see ya, partner."

Forty-seven

SUDDENLY, HE FELT very odd walking into the office and sitting at his desk. At least Hawthorne and Ellis were gone. The team working days was Sykes and Freedman.

"No room at City Hall?" Sykes asked. He was the younger of the two, a detective for only two years, while Freedman was an old-timer, on the job almost twenty years, eleven of them as a detective.

"Shut up, Jerry," Freedman said. "Joe, how's Al?"

"He's doing good," Keough said. "They took him out of intensive care. He's anxious to get back to work."

"Are they gonna let him come back?" Freedman asked. He had a basset-hound face that was enhanced by the fact that his cheeks were always red and shiny.

"Don't know yet, Ben," Keough said. "He has to talk to his doctor." Or the mayor's doctor, but he decided not to bring that up while Sykes was feeling testy.

Keough went to his desk and checked for messages, but there were none. As an afterthought he checked Steinbach's desk, and there was a message from the PI they were using to watch Drucker's office, Bumper. The message was dated the previous morning. He sat at Steinbach's desk and dialed the number.

"Bumper Investigations," the man answered. Keough wondered how much work he got with a name like that.

"Yeah, this is Detective Keough from the St. Louis—"

"Steinbach's partner, right?"

"That's right."

"I was wonderin' what happened to you guys. Al didn't tell me how long he wanted me to stay on that place, but I think I got you what you wanted."

"What did you get?"

"Fella came along that first night, went into the building after all the offices were closed. So I go in after him and watched the indicator for the elevator. He stops at your guy's floor. So when he comes out I follow him."

"Was he carrying anything?"

"A folder, under his arm. Musta been important because he had like both hands on it. Didn't even wanna turn it loose to unlock his car."

"You followed him?"

"Yeah, and I got his plate."

"Let me have it, and I'll run it."

"I already ran it," Bumper said. "I got connections."

"So who's the car registered to?"

"You know a George Eastmont?"

"Oh, yeah, I know him."

"Well, it was his car, and I followed the guy to his house, so I'm guessing this was Eastmont."

"What's the address?"

Bumper read it off, and Keough recognized it as a Ladue address. That was money, much like Clayton.

"You want me to go back on the office and watch it some more?"

"No," Keough said, "that's fine. You got us what we wanted."

"Good," Bumper said.

"Do we owe you some money?"

"Hey, Al took care of that," Bumper said. "Where is he, anyway?"

"Listen, I'm sorry, but Al's in the hospital. He had a heart attack yesterday."

"Jesus. Is he bad?"

"No, he was in intensive care for a while, but he's out today."

"What hospital?"

"St. John's."

"Ah, the Palace . . ." Keough gave him the room number, and he could hear Bumper writing it down. "I'll send 'im somethin'. "

"Good, he'll appreciate it—and thanks for this, Bumper."

"Forget it. I owe Al."

Keough hung up. So George Eastmont, the superintendent of the Arch, was connected to Drucker in such a way that he knew where to go and what to look for. The fact that he'd left Drucker's office with something in hand meant that there'd been something there that Keough and Steinbach didn't understand, and the two gunmen Steinbach had interrupted hadn't had time to find.

"Hey, Ben, tell the boss I'll check in with him at the end of the day. I may have something on this Drucker killing."

"Sure, Joe."

As he left he heard Sykes saying to his partner, "McGwire ain't his boss no more. . . ." and he realized that was true. Still, old habits were hard to break.

George Eastmont watched as Hannah Morgan got dressed. He enjoyed watching her put on her bra. She had lovely breasts, and she would bend over so that they dangled a bit and then fit the lace bra to them. His wife had huge, doughy breasts, and it didn't matter what kind of bra she wore; they overflowed like rising bread.

She straightened and caught him watching her. He looked away, embarrassed.

"You're so sweet to be embarrassed, George."

"I'm sorry I'm not a more . . . worldly man, Hannah."

"You're worldly enough for me, George," she said, putting her hand beneath his chin, "and very sweet." She leaned over and kissed him gently. The touch of her soft lips made him instantly hard again. This young woman was a revelation to him in his middle age. Sex had been something he and his wife hadn't talked about for years, and something he tried so hard not to think about. However, over the past three months it had become a very important part of his life—not just sex, but sex with Hannah Morgan.

It amazed him that she had worked for him for two years without his really knowing her. Suddenly she had seemed to become more of a presence in his life and then, three months ago, *she* had made advances toward *him*. Initially he had thought she was simply sleeping with her boss to get ahead, but then he realized he could not even do himself any good—at least, not in his job. It was only when Mark Drucker had come to him with his deal that things seemed to change for George financially as well as personally.

"We'd better get back," she said, putting on her jacket. "I'll see you back at work."

"All right." He would follow about a half hour later, which was their usual pattern when they had an afternoon tryst during work hours. "Maybe we can do something after work?"

"We'll see, George," she said.

This Hannah Morgan was not only different from the one he had hired two years ago, but she was totally different from the one Joe Keough knew. She certainly wasn't the nervous young woman whose apartment he had visited. This woman was more self-assured, and certainly more sexually attractive.

As she went to the door and opened it, she looked back at Eastmont to say good-bye.

"I love you, Hannah," he blurted.

She blew him a kiss and left. Eastmont did not notice that she had left the hotel room door unlocked. As she walked down the corridor to the elevator, she reached into her large purse to touch the folder he had given her, the same one he had gotten out of Mark Drucker's office.

In the lobby of the hotel she turned right and went out the Fourth Street exit, nodding to a man who was standing in the foyer. Without nodding back to her, he went inside and took one of the elevators to the floor she had just left. There was a woman in the elevator with him who got off at the fourth floor, thinking that this man had the largest hands she had ever seen. When he reached the floor he desired, he walked down the hall until he reached the unlocked hotel room door.

As he entered silently, he heard George Eastmont talking on the phone.

". . . my dear, yes, I might have to work late tonight. I just didn't want you to worry."

Eastmont was listening to his wife's reply as the man closed the door quietly behind him and waited for the conversation to end. . . .

Forty-eight

KEOUGH DROVE DOWN to the Arch, thinking he could have walked there from City Hall earlier. This made the mayor's offer of an office in the building more attractive, but then he wouldn't have gotten the message from Steinbach's PI, Bumper.

He parked in the municipal lot and walked to the Arch, where it had all started, and entered, moving past the lines of people waiting to go up to the top. After finding his way back to the offices, he showed his badge to the security guard there, who let him pass. Keough was almost sorry the man hadn't made it necessary for him to pull out his new ID as well. He went down a hallway and saw Hannah Morgan sitting at her desk.

Since he was one of probably three people—including her and the man who put her up to it—who knew the women had lied about him, he thought that this might be fun.

"Hello, Hannah."

She glanced up and, when she saw him, a look passed over her face that he hadn't expected. It was annoyance, he thought, and she did not resemble at all the Hannah Morgan he'd seen in the past—and then the look passed, and she seemed frightened. Suddenly, he was sure that even her nervous act in her apartment had been an act. He was wondering if *this* might not be even more dangerous than Marcy Drucker.

"I'll call security," she said, reaching for the phone.

"Go ahead," Keough said. "They already let me pass."

Her hand stopped on the phone.

"Come on, Hannah," he said, "it's just you and me here, and we both know I never touched you or came on to you, so let's drop the act. Where's George Eastmont?"

"I don't know," she said. She didn't drop the act, as he suggested, but she did take her hand off the phone. "He hasn't come back from lunch. Frankly, I was getting worried."

"Why?"

"He's never late."

Hannah did not look as neat and tidy as she had the last time he'd seen her at work. Also, there was a mark on the side of her neck that looked like a hickey.

"When did he leave?"

"Around noon."

"When did you leave for lunch?"

"I left—why do you want to know that?"

"You seem to have dressed a little quickly before coming back," he said, causing her to look down at herself. The movement of her head made the love bite more noticeable.

"And your lover left a little mark on your neck."

Her hand flew to the left side of her neck.

"Other side," he said, and she glared at him. "Why do I get the feeling, Miss Morgan, that you're not the little mouse you make yourself out to be?"

"I don't know what you mean."

"Sure you do," he said. "That whole nervous act you put on in your apartment for me. It was very good."

She compressed her lips and looked annoyed again.

"Tell me," he said, "how often do you and your boss sneak away for these little nooners?"

"I find you rude and insulting."

"Then report me," he said. "Have me brought up on charges."

"Apparently," she said, "that does little good."

Keough's mind was jumping hurdles. If someone had planted a man in the mayor's administration, why not plant someone here in the Arch? After all, the Arch was the scene of the first murder, and George Eastmont was seen coming out of the building where Mark Drucker had an office. Politics and the Arch seemed to be strange bedfellows in this little drama. If Goddard was a plant, why not Miss Morgan? And if he were alive, it meant things were going bad. Why was she still alive?

And where was George Eastmont.

"Which one of these hotels do you use, Miss Morgan?" he asked. "Something fancy like the Adam's Mark or the Regal Riverfront? Or do you walk over to the Doubletree so you can have their chocolate chip cookies with your sex? Or maybe you take a longer walk to the Drury Inn?"

She didn't answer.

"Did you hear about Kenneth Goddard?" he asked suddenly.

"The mayor's aide? What about him?"

"He was killed yesterday," Keough said, "murdered."

"I haven't seen the paper today. That's terrible."

It occurred to Keough that he hadn't seen a paper in three days. He needed to catch up.

"Doesn't that worry you?"

"What?"

"That Goddard was killed?"

"Why should it?"

"Or maybe you already knew?"

"How would I?"

"I'll tell you how, Miss Morgan," he said. "In fact, I'm going to tell you exactly what I think so you can pass it on. I think you, just like Kenneth Goddard, were planted here for some reason—or maybe you were both bought and paid for after you arrived. Either way, you're both involved in whatever is causing bodies to pile up. Now, either you should be worried that you'll be next, or you already know who will be."

"You're talking nonsense."

"I don't think so," Keough said. "See, the more people who die, the less suspects there are. Eventually, the only ones left will be the guilty parties. One more murder is probably all it would take for me to find out who's behind the whole thing."

He stood there staring at her for a few moments until she started to fidget beneath his gaze.

"Do you know if someone is next, Miss Morgan? And who it will be?"

She looked up at him, then stared him straight in the eyes and said, "Perhaps it will be you, Detective Keough. Have you ever thought of that?"

"Actually, no, Hannah," he said, "but you know what?" He put both hands flat on her desk and leaned over her so close that she pulled back to get away from him. "I think that's the only way anybody is going to stop me from putting this whole thing together."

With that he straightened up and said, "Have a good day," and left.

Outside the Arch he stopped and looked toward the city. The two most noticeable hotels from there were the Regal Riverfront and the Adam's Mark. George Eastmont seemed like a fussy little man who would want to have his trysts in expensive hotels. He was also not the kind of man a girl like Hannah Morgan would sleep with unless she had to.

Of course, he could have it all wrong, but if he didn't, then he probably just painted a great big bull's-eye on his own back.

* * *

Inside, after she felt she had given Keough enough time to leave the Arch, Hannah Morgan picked up her phone and dialed a number.

"We have to talk," she said, when her call was answered, "now!"

Forty-nine

IT WAS TIMES like these when he really needed a partner.

If Steinbach were with him, one of them would stay and wait for Hannah Morgan to leave, and then follow her. Or, at least, remain behind and wait for George Eastmont to show up.

Suddenly, Keough thought of a way to test his new City Hall ID, and maybe even sharpen that bull's-eye on his back.

He reentered the Arch an hour later with the easiest search warrant he'd ever applied for in his jacket pocket. He was also accompanied by the officer who had delivered it to him after he made a call on his cell phone. He waved at the security guard, who recognized him, and then went back down the hall to Hannah Morgan's desk. She was still there, but she looked harried rather than annoyed or frightened.

"What now?" she asked, looking up at him and the uniformed officer.

He handed her the document, which she accepted as if it were contaminated.

"That's a search warrant giving me the authority to search anywhere on these premises."

"For what?" she demanded.

"I'll know that when I find it, Hannah," he said, "but it's something George took out of Mark Drucker's office, something only he knew the location of, after Drucker's death. And it's something a lot of people are looking for. So, if you don't mind. . . ."

"I do mind," she said.

"Tough," he said. "Move away from your desk—in fact, go out onto the museum floor and stay there until I call you back."

"You can't do this," she said.

"Watch me." He turned to the cop behind him. "Officer, go with her and make sure she doesn't leave the premises."

"Yes, sir. Ma'am?"

"This is ridiculous," she snapped, but stood up and started to leave. Suddenly, she stopped, turned, grabbed her oversized straw purse, slung it over her shoulder, and preceded the officer out.

It took Keough forty-five minutes to go through George Eastmont's office and Hannah Morgan's desk. He came up empty-handed. During that time, Eastmont had not yet returned from lunch. With the number of bodies that were turning up, Keough started to worry.

He went out into the museum where Hannah Morgan was waiting with the uniformed policeman, who had gotten into a conversation with the security guard. They all looked at him.

"You can come back in, Hannah," he said. "Officer, you can go."

"Thank you, sir."

Keough went back inside with Hannah, who stood by her desk, looking around.

"Don't worry," he said, "I'm good at this. I don't leave a mess."

"I'll be the judge of that."

She walked to Eastmont's office and went inside, still holding her bag. She went to a couple of cabinets that he had left ajar and shut them emphatically.

"Come on, Hannah," he said, standing in the doorway.

"What?"

"Who do you work for? How much do you know? How deeply involved are you in all this?"

"I don't know what you mean."

"Where's George, Hannah?" he asked. "Is he dead, too?"

"Aren't you finished here?" she asked. "I have work to do."

"I don't think I am finished yet," he said. "You see, I've suddenly got this feeling that you're the weak link in this chain of events."

"Weak link?" Suddenly, the look on her face was one of complete disdain. "If I were involved in . . . in whatever it is you think I'm involved in, Detective Keough, I certainly wouldn't think that I had anything to fear from you. After all, you've been on this case since the very beginning, since Mark Drucker was murdered, and all you've got to show for it are some sexual misconduct charges against you and three more dead bodies."

"Three?"

"What?"

"You said three more dead bodies," Keough said. He ticked them off on his fingers. "There's Harry Brooks, Kenneth Goddard and. . . . and who, Hannah? George Eastmont?"

"I . . . was mistaken," she said. "I told you, I haven't been reading the papers. I don't know how many bodies—how many people you've allowed to be killed."

"I'm right, aren't I?" he asked. "You are my weak link, aren't you, Hannah? You think you're on the inside here, but you're not. In fact, you might even be the next one they kill. Suddenly, whoever's running this little show is afraid of being found out and is trying to cover their tracks."

"Get out of here."

"If George Eastmont turns up dead, Hannah," Keough said, "I'm coming after you."

Her eyes flicked around the room, and he noticed she was holding her purse even tighter. Her big, oversized, straw purse, which did not go with her business suit at all.

In the past he had solved many cases with sudden leaps of logic. He had learned to go with these when they occurred. That had been what was happening here, since he entered the Arch, because he thought he saw a different Hannah Morgan than he had seen before.

"Hannah," he said, "give me your purse."

"What?"

"Your purse," he said. "I want to look inside."

"You can't," she said. "It's mine."

"Oh yes, I can," Keough said. "The search warrant covers you, and it covers your purse."

She clutched it even more tightly.

"I want a lawyer."

"You're not under arrest," he said. "I haven't read you your rights, you have no need for a lawyer, and you're not entitled to one."

He held his hand out.

"The purse."

Her eyes darted around the room, looking for an escape, but there was none.

"In fact," he said, walking across the small room to her, "you don't even have to give it to me. I just need to stick my hand inside."

When he reached her, she tried to turn away, but he plunged his hand into the purse. He knew what he was feeling for and when he felt the file folder, he grabbed it and pulled it out then held it aloft as if it were the Holy Grail.

"I want a lawyer," Hannah Morgan said.

Fifty

"I BLEW IT."

"Sit down and relax, Joe."

Keough was pacing in Captain McGwire's office.

"All I had was the file," he said. "I never should have taken her into custody."

"You thought she was going to crack," McGwire said. "She asked for a lawyer, didn't she?"

"Yes," Keough said, "but that was a momentary lapse. She soon realized I had nothing to connect her with the murders. She claims she doesn't know who the killer is."

"Do you believe her?" McGwire asked.

"No."

Keough felt he had two bosses, McGwire and the mayor, but after taking Hannah Morgan into custody, he felt McGwire was the man to talk it all over with.

It had taken all night to sort things out. First he took Hannah Morgan to Clayton to book her for impeding a homicide investigation. That was all he had on her now, even though he'd found the mysterious file in her purse, and she had initially said she wanted a lawyer. She regained her composure and realized he had nothing on her beyond possession of the file.

"My boss asked me to hold it," she said, once she was in custody.

"Which boss, Hannah?" Keough asked.

"George Eastmont."

Well, that much could have been true. According to Steinbach's PI, Bumper, Eastmont did take a file out of Drucker's office. Was it this file? They wouldn't know that until they found Eastmont, who was still among the missing.

"What's in this file?" McGwire asked.

Keough tossed the file on the desk in front of McGwire. It was a Xerox, as he had signed the original in as evidence.

"It's a file about 2004," he said. "That's about all I know, for now. We need someone who can interpret it, but my guess is it'll show that somebody stands to make a lot of money who probably shouldn't."

"Politics," McGwire said, "that's what that whole program is about. Make improvements in the city? Somebody makes money. Zoning changes? Somebody makes money. Build an office building or a mall? Somebody makes money. You think Drucker was killed for this file?"

"I can't say that," Keough said, "but I can say that once he was dead, people started looking for this file."

"People like Anson and Shepp."

"And George Eastmont," Keough said, "who apparently knew where to find it, but he had to wait until he thought we had left Drucker's office unguarded."

"How did he know that?" McGwire asked.

"Hmm?"

"How did he know you pulled the men off of Drucker's office?" McGwire asked. "Was he watching it?"

"No," Keough said, "but you can see the building from most of the windows in the Anson and Shepp offices."

"Eastmont was working with someone in that firm?"

"No," Keough said, thoughtfully, "not Eastmont, Drucker."

"But Drucker's dead."

"So maybe Eastmont and the contact inside the firm decided to get together," Keough said. "They wanted to find the file before Anson and/or Shepp did."

"So who's the girl working for?" McGwire asked. "Who'd she try to set you up for?"

"I don't know that for sure," Keough said, "but I can tell you who she called with her one phone call."

"Her lawyer," McGwire said, and then added, "Ohhhh, Franklin Anson?"

"Exactly."

"So she's working for him."

"Right now," Keough said, "it looks like he's working for her. He got her out on bail this morning."

"And where did she go?"

"I don't know," Keough said, "but she'll be around."

"How can you be so sure?"

"Because there's still the smell of money in the air."

"Which she's not going to give up all that easily."

"Right."

"Did she admit to sleeping with her boss?"

"Once she regained her composure," Keough said, "she admitted to nothing."

"So you both overreacted to the situation," McGwire said.

"I suppose," Keough said morosely. "Maybe I'm just not thinking straight these days."

"Don't second-guess yourself, Joe," McGwire said, "not after convincing me to leave you on the case. This thing is yours to close out now. You've got the mayor depending on you."

Keough looked across his former boss's desk and said, "Uh, about that, Cap. That wasn't something I went looking for. I was perfectly happy working for you here—"

McGwire held up his hand and said, "No need for this, Joe. I realize what happened. This is a big break for you, and I don't hold it against you."

"It may not be permanent," Keough said. "If, when this is

done, the mayor doesn't want me full time, or I don't want to work for him—"

"You're welcome back here anytime," McGwire said. "As far as I concerned, you went off the deep end once in this case."

"With Anson, in the men's room."

"Right, but it doesn't seem to have hurt you much."

"Thanks to the mayor."

"If you come back though," McGwire said, "I can't have that happening again. The mayor may not bail you out next time."

"I understand."

"You going to stop in and see Al today?"

"I've got to get some sleep," Keough said, "clear my head. I think I'll drop by this afternoon."

"Go home and get to bed, then," McGwire said, "but stay alert. If Hannah Morgan is what you think she is, the killer may be coming after you next."

Keough recalled Hannah's veiled threat and said, "Don't worry. I'll booby-trap the house."

"Maybe we should put a man on you—"

"No," Keough said, "you don't need to do that. I can handle it."

McGwire pointed a finger at Keough and said, "Don't do a Dirty Harry on me here, Joe. Set yourself up as a target for a professional hit man and think you're going to come out on top."

"Believe me, Cap," Keough said, "I don't want to be a target for anyone."

He got up and took the file folder from McGwire's desk.

"Why don't you leave that with me while you get some sleep?" McGwire asked.

"I have a real estate broker friend who can probably interpret it for us."

"Fine," Keough said, putting it back down. "If I were rested and alert, it would make me dizzy, so I'm sure as hell not going to be able to make any sense of it now."

Keough walked toward the door.

"You know, finding that folder on Hannah Morgan may not be the immediate break you thought it would be, but you did find it. And once we know for sure what's in it, it could be enough to bring this whole house of cards crashing down."

"I hope so, Cap," Keough said, rubbing his gritty eyes. "I sure hope so."

Keough went home, saw the red light flashing on his phone machine, and decided not to play the messages just yet. He needed to get some sleep first before he dealt with anything else. He went up to his bedroom, shed his clothes, and left them where they fell, dropping onto the bed. He was asleep in seconds.

When the phone rang, he jerked awake and grabbed for it. His brain wasn't working well enough to consider letting the machine answer it.

"Yeah, wha—" he said, then stopped to clear his throat.

"Joe? Sorry to wake you, but we've got a situation," Captain McGwire said.

"What's up, Cap? Is it Al?"

"No, no, Al's fine," McGwire said. "It's George Eastmont."

"Where is he?"

"He turned up in a room at the Adam's Mark," McGwire said. "He's dead, Joe."

Fifty-one

HE'D GOTTEN TWO hours of sleep, and by the time he got back to the Fourteenth Street office after overseeing the cleanup, his eyes were red-rimmed and gritty.

"What's the story?" McGwire asked, standing in the door-way of his office.

"Looks like Eastmont and Morgan did their business, then she left and went back to work. He stayed behind, probably for the sake of appearance, so they wouldn't get back to work at the same time."

"And?"

"Somebody got in without forcing the door and cut his throat."

"Handprints?"

"On the mirror in the bathroom."

"Same size?"

"Yup."

"Same killer," McGwire said, only this time it wasn't a question. "Do you think she fingered him?"

"It would seem likely, don't you think? I've sent a car to pick her up."

"Where?"

"Work and home," Keough said "but if she's as smart as I think she is, she won't be at either."

"Bodies are piling up way too quickly, Joe," McGwire said. "Somebody's in a panic."

"It's got to be Dexter Shepp," Keough said. "Who else is left?"

"Anson?"

"He's Shepp's front man," Keough said. "If the mayor knows it, everybody knows it."

"Then he's your weak link," McGwire said. "Squeeze him and maybe he'll crack."

"Squeeze him?" Keough asked. "Is this coming from the man who doesn't want me to go off the deep end again?"

"Squeeze him," McGwire said, "in a controlled, professional fashion."

"Okay," Keough said, "that I can do."

"What's going on, Dexter?" Franklin Anson demanded.

"What do you mean?" his partner asked.

They were in Shepp's office, Anson having just burst in.

"Mark Drucker, okay, I can see that," Anson said. "The security guard? I don't know about that. I can understand Goddard, but I just heard about George Eastmont. It's all over the radio. What the hell is going on?"

Dexter Shepp sat back in his chair and asked, "Why are you asking me?"

"Because you're in charge, aren't you?" Anson asked. "You're pulling the strings?"

"Franklin," Shepp said, "have a seat . . . now!"

Sullenly, Anson sat down.

"Franklin," Shepp said, "I don't know where you got the idea that I know anything about these murders. As far as I'm concerned, we haven't killed anyone."

"We?"

"Yes, we," Shepp said. "We're partners, remember? Besides, we have more pressing problems than the death of the Arch superintendent."

"Like what?"

"Before he died he found the file."

"What? How do you know?"

"Because Hannah got it from him."

Anson slammed his fist down on Shepp's desk and said, "Yes!"

"No," Shepp said, "it's not good news."

"Why not?"

"Because," Shepp said, "Detective Joe Keough got it from her."

All the color drained from Franklin Anson's face, and he seemed to shrink in his chair.

"Jesus . . ."

"As soon as he has someone read it, and as soon as they start backtracking through dummy corporations, they're going to find out that we've been playing both ends against the middle. They're going to realize that what we've been doing is *illegal*, Franklin, and we're going to be in a lot of trouble."

"I knew it," Anson said. "I knew it. I knew we shouldn't have gotten involved with Drucker and his schemes—"

"Too late for recriminations, Franklin," Shepp said. "We need to come up with a plan. Personally, I like Portugal."

"Leave the country?"

"Why not? What's left for us here?"

"Isn't there . . . a way out?" Anson swallowed. "Dexter, you always have a way out."

"Well," Shepp said, folding his hands across his belly, "I can give it some thought."

"Okay," Anson said, "okay, why don't you do that. I'll, uh, I'll—"

"Go home, Franklin."

"What?"

"Go home to your wife, or go to your mistress, but get out of here," Shepp said. "You're no good to us right now."

"Yes, yes," Anson said, "all right, yes, I can do that."

"Think about liquidating your assets, Franklin," Shepp said, "just in case."

Franklin Anson stood up slowly, as if in a trance, and turned to go to the door.

"Franklin?"

"Yes, Dexter?" he turned slowly, like a man with a bad back.

"Did you really think I had all these people killed?"

"I, well—yes, Dexter, I thought—"

"And you went along with me?" Shepp asked. "That's . . . extraordinarily loyal, Franklin."

"Well, Dexter," the other man said, "we are partners, after all."

"Yes," Shepp said, "yes, we are."

"Dexter?"

"Yes."

"If you—if *we* haven't been having these people killed, who has?"

"That's a good question, Franklin," Dexter Shepp said. "A damn good question."

The killer answered the phone, and the voice said, "More work."

"This is starting to get sloppy," he said. "I don't like it when it's sloppy."

"You're being paid."

"I'm going to be paid more," he replied. "I've been here too long, and there are too many bodies. I'm gonna raise my price per head."

"This'll be your last job," the other voice said, "but it might be more than one. Is that a problem?"

"Like I said," the killer answered, "not as long as you pay me my new price per head."

"Something can be arranged. . . ."

Sometimes just being in the right place at the right time solves a case. Keough didn't know if that would happen this time, but he was about to enter the building that housed Shepp, Anson, and Associates when the elevator opened, and he saw Franklin Anson stepping out. He backed off immediately and, in fact, ran back to his car.

He got behind the wheel of his car and watched Anson leave the building and walk to his car, a black Lexus. He decided to follow the man and see where he was going. Surely, by now, both Anson and his partner knew that the 2004 file was in the hands of the police. Dexter, Keough felt sure, would have some kind of plan which might or might not include his partner. When playing with the law, a prudent man makes sure he has an alternate plan for when things go wrong.

Anson, on the other hand, struck Keough as the type who would panic. Even now, his foot was heavy on the gas pedal as he followed the lawyer on I-270. The man had to constantly press on his break as he drove up on the bumpers of other cars. They were going south on 270, but did not stay there long as Anson got off on Highway 40 and drove east. He was heading toward Brentwood, or maybe Clayton or, if he kept on going, downtown. They were close to St. John's at this point, and Keough could easily have veered off onto Ballas to go and check on his partner. He didn't, though. He stayed on Franklin Anson's tail.

When Anson got off Highway 40 at Lindbergh, Keough thought he knew where the man was going. When he turned onto Clayton Road, he was sure of it, so it was no surprise when he turned into the driveway at Kenilworth Circle, the home of Marcy Drucker.

Keough pulled in far enough to be able to watch Franklin Anson use a key to enter the house. Apparently Marcy Drucker had not been very forthcoming when she told

Keough that she and Shepp, Anson were not on speaking terms.

He left his car where it was and approached the house. He was trying to decide whether to break in or not when he suddenly thought, why? Why not just knock on the door and surprise them together? He could call the locals for back-up but decided not to. He still wasn't sure that the people inside were killers—or even people who *hired* killers. Besides, he was pretty sure he could handle Franklin Anson, even with Marcy Drucker around.

He rang the doorbell and waited.

Fifty-two

WHEN MARCY DRUCKER answered the door, her eye flared, but she kept her composure.

"Well," she said, "you've got a lot of balls coming here alone. I'll give you that."

"Hey, why not?" he asked. "There's nobody here for you to lie to."

She leaned against the door and said, "You can't come in, you know. I'm busy."

"With Franklin Anson?"

She made a face and asked, "Why would I have that slime-b—"

"That lie won't fly, Marcy," Keough said. "That's his car, and I followed him here. In fact, the first time my partner and I were here there was a black Lexus in your garage. Son-ofabitch! He was in the house that day, wasn't he?"

"No comment."

"I'm coming in to talk to both of you, Marcy," Keough said. "It's time to wrap this up. Too many people have died."

She studied him for a few moments then backed away, saying, "I don't suppose I can stop you."

"No."

He entered, and she closed the door.

"We're in the living room having brandy," she said. "Would you like some?"

"No, thanks."

When he and Marcy entered the living room, the other two people there got to their feet. Franklin Anson looked slightly panicked, as if Keough had come to finish what he started in the men's room that night. The other person simply stared at him with a combination of annoyance and resignation on her face.

It was Hannah Morgan.

"I've got men out looking for you," Keough said to Hannah. "I told you if George Eastmont turned up dead I'd come for you."

"How did he get here?" she demanded.

"I followed him," Keough said, pointing at Anson.

"Damn you, Franklin," Hannah said.

"Relax, Hannah," Marcy said. She walked to an end table and picked up a glass of brandy. "He can't prove a thing."

"Maybe not against you ladies," Keough said, "although I don't know if that's true, but we've got Mark's 2004 file, and we're having it examined now. It's my guess Shepp, Anson, and Associates is not going to come out smelling too good."

"That's their problem," Marcy said, her arms folded in front of her, the brandy glass dangling from one hand. "Drink your brandy, Hannah. He can't touch us."

Hannah picked up her glass and emulated Marcy Drucker.

"They're throwing you to the wolves, Franklin," Keough said. "What do you think of that?"

"Look," Anson said, "I had a long talk with Dexter today. He swears we're not involved in the murders. Okay, we made some shady deals involving 2004, but that was business."

"These deals involved you, Mark, and George Eastmont?"

"It was all Mark's doing," Anson said. "He came to us with these deals. He could handle zoning laws and permits, he just needed some extra backing."

"So you and Shepp and Eastmont were just investors?"

"Partners."

"Where did the superindendent of the Arch get that kind of money?"

"He has a wealthy wife," Anson said.

"Fat," Hannah said, "but wealthy."

"This has all been in the works for two years, hasn't it?" Keough said. "Mark got you into the Arch, didn't he, Hannah? And Goddard onto the mayor's staff?"

"He had a lot of connections," Hannah said.

"And you, Marcy?" Keough asked. "What's your involvement?"

"I have my own money," she said. "I became a partner."

"Lots of partners, huh, Franklin?" Keough asked. "Except not so many left."

"We didn't kill Mark," Anson said.

"But you panicked when he died," Keough said. "You didn't want that file showing up in the wrong hands."

"We couldn't find the damn thing!"

"Hannah, how did George find it?"

"He and Mark were friends," she said. "The deal was cooked up by the two of them."

"Then why put you in the Arch?"

"Mark decided he didn't trust George," she said. "He wanted me to keep an eye on him."

"Okay, people," Keough said, "who killed Mark Drucker? Do we want to blame it on George Eastmont, since he's dead and can't defend himself?"

"George wouldn't have had the nerve," Hannah said.

"It doesn't take much nerve to hire a hit man."

"More than George had," Hannah said.

"Okay, so not George."

"And not us!" Anson said.

"Well, maybe not you, Franklin," Keough said, "but I'm not so sure about your partner."

"Why?"

"Because somebody tipped Eastmont off that the cops had left Drucker's office unguarded. That's when he went in to get the file. And Hannah, are you going to tell me it wasn't Dexter Shepp who told you to get the file from George?"

Hannah didn't answer. She just sipped her brandy.

"Because if it wasn't Dexter," Keough said, "it still had to be somebody who was in that building, who could just look out the window and see that the cops had left—wait a minute. There *is* somebody else, isn't there?"

Hannah and Marcy exchanged a look while Franklin Anson looked completely puzzled.

"If it wasn't Dexter," he asked, "who was it?"

Keough knew, but before he could say anything someone else joined the party.

"I'll ask all of you to stand very still, please," a man's voice said, "especially you, Detective. I'm going to need your gun."

Keough turned just a little, but it was enough to see the man standing in the doorway holding a gun on all of them. He was wearing white rubber gloves on both hands.

Fifty-three

HE HELD ONE hand out to Keough and said, "The gun. Take it out slow and put it on the floor, then kick it. . . . Come on, just like in the movies."

"If this were a movie," Keough said, doing as he was told, "I'd somersault across the room and kick you in the face." He kicked the gun across the room instead.

The man with the gun chuckled and said, "Jackie Chan. I love that guy."

"What now?" Keough asked.

"Well," the man said, "I can see two things right off."

"What's that?"

"I'm gonna get paid more, and it's gonna be messier than I thought, 'cause there's more of you than I was told. Oh, well, who wants to be first?"

"Wait a minute," Marcy said, exchanging a panicky glance with Hannah. "You can't kill *us*."

"You work for us," Hannah said.

"What?" Franklin Anson said.

"I do?" the man with the gun asked. He was young, black, in his twenties, and while he'd managed to get into the house, he didn't seem to Keough to be all that smooth at what he was doing. For one thing, the four of them were still pretty spread out in the room, and for another he was talking too much.

But all that would, hopefully, work to Keough's advantage.

"Well, yeah," Marcy said, "she's right. We're paying you."

"I don't remember talkin' to either one of you about this," the man with the gun said.

"Well, we'd be stupid to talk to you ourselves, wouldn't we?" Hannah asked.

"What's going on?' Anson demanded.

"Something you and I never envisioned, Franklin," Keough said. "It's been the ladies all along."

"What?"

"Sure, don't you see? Marcy's been sleeping with you, Hannah with George Eastmont—they've been running the show all along, using this guy—and probably others like him—to do the dirty work."

"I-is this true, Marcy?" Anson asked, looking wounded.

"Well, come on, Franklin," Marcy Drucker said. "Would I be sleeping with you otherwise?"

"Ooh," the man with the gun said, "that be a low blow."

"And there's one other member of this little equation," Keough said.

"Who?" Anson asked.

"Hello?" the man with the gun said. "Woo-hoo? I got the gun here? It don't matter who be in what equation."

"Wait, wait," Marcy said, "you don't understand. You're working for us." She indicated herself and Hannah.

"Sorry, sister," the man said, "but I got orders to waste everybody I find in the house."

"What?" Hannah said.

"Double cross, Hannah, Marcy," Keough said. "Apparently your partner has just gone way off the deep end and is taking everybody out."

"That bitch!" Marcy said.

Suddenly, they all fell silent as the sound of the hammer being cocked on a revolver filled the air.

"I shoot the old guy first," the black man announced.

"Jesus, no!" Franklin Anson said. He sank to his knees and started blubbering.

"Wait," Marcy said, "wait. Listen. Y-you can kill them, and then you, me, and my friend, we can go upstairs, huh? Wouldn't you like that? Two white women?"

The man looked at Keough, and his expression said, "Do you believe this?" Keough just shrugged, keeping his eyes on the man.

"Well, lady," the man said, "as temptin' as that offer is, you be just a little too old for me, and your friend be a little too mousy. 'Sides, I do like my women on the dark side."

He pointed the gun at Anson, and both women screamed as Anson put his forehead right down on the carpet and waited for the shot.

"I wouldn't," someone said from the hallway.

"Wha—?" the black man said, turning to look over his shoulder.

Keough didn't somersault across the room, but he damn near dived all the way. He buried his shoulder in the black man's midsection, and they tumbled to the floor together. Keough rolled away from him then, but the man had retained his hold on his gun.

"Son'abitch," he managed to gag, most of the wind knocked out of him. He tried to bring the gun around to point at Keough, but the PI, Bumper, stepped in and slapped him on the top of the head with a .45 the size of a cannon.

"Jesus," Keough said. For a minute there he didn't think he'd ever have to worry about having diabetes. "How long have you been here?"

"Long enough to hear everything they said," he replied, indicating the people in the living room. He bent over and picked up the fallen hit man's gun. "This guy sure was talkative."

"How did you get here?" Keough asked.

"Your partner called me from the hospital," Bumper said. "He said you were gonna get your nuts in a wringer, and I should stay on your tail to bail you out. Looks like he was right."

"Yeah, he was," Keough said, "and when I see him, I'll kiss him for it."

Keough got to his feet. Bumper bent and picked up Keough's gun and then handed the detective both his own and the hit man's.

"You wanna take all these people in our cars or call for transportation?" the PI asked.

Keough took out his cell phone and said, "No, I think I'll call for transportation. I've got another stop to make anyway."

While he waited for someone to answer the phone, he was staring down at the failed hit man, frowning.

"He's got really small hands," Bumper observed, "doesn't he?"

Fifty-four

KEOUGH ARRIVED AT the office of Shepp, Anson, and Associates a few hours later with uniforms in tow, startling the receptionist.

"Miss Eileen Henry, please," he said.

"She's in a meeting—" the receptionist started, but Keough cut her off and said, "That's okay. We'll find her."

He started down the hall with the uniformed cops behind him, wondering if they had beat Franklin Anson's phone call, or if he would have even called his partner with his one call. Anson had been arrested along with Marcy Drucker and Hannah Morgan, but Keough knew they wouldn't be able to hold him—not on what was said in the house. He'd probably be cut loose, but they could pick him up later when they learned what was in the 2004 file.

He found Eileen Henry's office, but she wasn't in it. That left Dexter Shepp's office. Keough—always able to retrace his steps once he learned a route—found Shepp's office and slammed the door open. Both Shepp and Henry looked startled.

"Eileen Henry," Keough said, "you're under arrest for conspiracy to commit murder."

"Wha—?" she said, jumping up from her seat. "Dexter!"

"Sorry, love," Shepp said, spreading his pudgy hands. "I've been retained by Franklin to get him out, but I'm afraid there's nothing I can do for you. Apparently, your partners are talking."

"My partners?" Eileen Henry said, looking at Keough.

"They're alive," he said. "Your hit man didn't get any of us, and now Marcy and Hannah are really pissed at you, and talking."

"Hit man?"

"The one you sent after Franklin, knowing he'd go to Marcy's? The one you told to kill everyone in the house? Well, I was there. By the way, he's talking, too."

Of course, the black hit man wasn't giving up any of the women, because he didn't know any of them. He had been hired by a man.

"Dexter—" Eileen said again.

"I can't help you, my love," Shepp said. "You took everything just a step too far, you know. Murder is something you can never walk away from."

"I learned from you!" she snapped.

"Not about murder, you didn't. Business, maybe . . . dirty business? Perhaps. But certainly not murder."

"Why you—you kept me here—" she started, but Keough cut her off by telling the uniformed men, "Take her out."

They hustled her out of the room, hands cuffed behind her.

"I'll be getting Franklin out in about an hour," Dexter Shepp said to Keough.

"I'll be back for both of you, Shepp," Keough said, "soon as we dot the I's and cross the T's on your dirty deals with Mark Drucker."

"Your friend," Shepp said, "only you didn't know him very well, did you, Detective?"

"Well enough to know he wouldn't stoop to murder."

"Well, neither have I," Shepp said.

"No," Keough said. "Dirty business and dirty politics, those are your games."

"His, too," Shepp said, "and he played them masterfully. If he were alive, we would have pocketed a lot of money by now, believe me."

"Oh, I do, Shepp," Keough said. "I really do."

"Amazing about these women, eh?" Shepp asked. "Franklin told me on the phone what happened. All three of them, working together? With Eileen directing them?" He shook his head. "I don't know what she expected to accomplish by killing Drucker. As far as I'm concerned he was the golden goose."

Keough wondered that, too, but right now Eileen Henry was the only one who knew the answer.

"Your protégé, I'll bet," Keough said. "A case of the student trying to outdo the master?"

"Like I told her," Shepp said, "she went one step too far. Now she'll pay for it."

"And you'll pay for your part, too."

"I will walk away, Detective," Shepp said, "but she never will, not from a murder charge. She thinks she learned very well, but she didn't learn enough—not nearly enough."

"I'll be back, Shepp," Keough said. "It'll go easier on you and your partner if you don't make me come looking for you."

"We'll be around, Detective," Shepp said.

"Think they will be?" McGwire asked later, in his office.

"With the money they have? They're probably on a plane right now to another country, and I say good riddance."

"Wouldn't they be surprised to find that Drucker didn't trust Eastmont any more than he did them?" the captain asked. "That there's really nothing in that file that can incriminate them? It would throw some dirt on them if it got to the newspapers, but it certainly doesn't have anything in it we can hold them for, even if they hired those two goons who shot at you that day."

"An error in judgment on their part. There is a file out there somewhere, though, that does incriminate them," Keough said, sitting across from the captain. "That's the one they'll be running from."

"And the three ladies? Are they still talking?"

"The DA is very happy. He's gotten enough from Marcy and Hannah to charge all three women, and he'll tell the court that they cooperated in the apprehension of Eileen, who was the brains behind the whole thing."

"She's the one who made the decisions about who to kill, and the one who hired it done?"

"That's right," Keough said. "Marcy might have set up her ex-husband for a meeting by the Arch, and I'm pretty sure Hannah set Eastmont up to be killed at the Adam's Mark, but neither of them have had any contact with the killer."

"So that's why he didn't know either of them at the house."

"He says he was never contacted by any woman," Keough said. "He says he was hired by a man, and only for this hit. He says he had nothing to do with Drucker, Brooks, or Eastmont."

"And you believe him?"

"Oh, yeah . . ."

"Why?"

Keough held up his hands.

"He's got these little hands, Cap," Keough said. "He sure didn't leave those prints behind."

"So what are you figurin', that Eileen Henry's hitman with the big hands hired this one?"

"That's what I'm thinking."

"But why?"

"Because he sensed the whole thing was coming apart. He wasn't about to walk into that house, and he was right."

"So he's still out there."

"I'll find him," Keough said. "Maybe Eileen will give him up, maybe not, but I'll find him."

"What are you going to do about the mayor's job?"

"I still have to talk to him about it," Keough said. "He's real happy that the murders have been solved. He doesn't seem to mind that the actual killer is still out there. He's satisfied that without Eileen Henry hiring the guy, he's finished killing in St. Louis and will go away."

"And what do you think?"

Keough drummed his fingers on his knee and said, "I'm not so sure he's finished, Cap."

Fifty-five

KEOUGH LEFT MCGWIRE'S office and headed for the hospital to check on Steinbach again, and to give him the news that the case was broken and everyone was accounted for except the trigger man.

He got in the elevator, and the doors were almost closed when a hand shot between them. It was a big hand, belonging to a rather average-sized man in green scrubs, apparently a doctor.

"Sorry," the man said.

"That's okay."

The door closed, and the man did not press a button, apparently going to the same floor as Keough. The only thing was, Keough knew that surgery was in a different wing of the hospital, which made it odd that this doctor was wearing scrubs.

One of the big hands shot out and caught Keough right in the face, only Keough had already been preparing. If he'd been caught flat-footed, the blow would have stunned him and might have knocked him out. As it was, he was moving his head back as he got hit, which absorbed some of the force of the blow.

The man's other hand punched the red emergency button, and the elevator lurched to a stop.

"Those hands," Keough said, blood trickling from his lower lip, "are a dead giveaway."

"Dead is the operative word here," the man said.

They were now standing at opposite ends of the elevator, their backs to the wall. Hospital elevators are large, in order to accommodate stretchers and gurneys, and this was no different. There was a decent amount of space separating them.

"I figured you'd be long gone by now," Keough said.

"I couldn't do that," the killer said. "You're a stubborn man. I read about you in the newspaper. Hero cop assigned to the mayor's staff," the killer said. "Real impressive stuff. Told how all you were gonna work on were these murders, which may or may not have been politically motivated. You were gonna solve them, it said, no matter what."

"And I did," Keough said. "Your employer is behind bars, friend. No more paid assassinations for you."

"This one's for me," the killer said, "because you don't seem like the kind of man who gives up."

"I can be persuaded."

The killer grinned and said, "Not today."

"You know," Keough said, "you're no bigger than me, a little broader in the shoulders, maybe. You must have gotten a lot of teasing about those hands when you were a kid."

"They were merciless," the man said, "and I learned from every one of them."

Suddenly, there was a knife in the man's hand, and Keough cursed himself for talking and not drawing his gun. He was guilty of the same folly he'd ascribed to the hit man at the Drucker house—talking too much. Maybe that man had been nervous, like Keough was now.

"What next?" he asked. "You've got a knife; I've got a gun."

"My knife is out," the killer said. "You a fast draw?"

"I guess we're going to find out."

Keough wanted to watch the man's eyes, but he couldn't take *his* eyes off those big hands.

"What was with those bloody handprints?" he asked. "A little showy, don't you think?"

"The first set was an accident," the killer said, with a shrug. "After that I kind of liked it."

They remained where they were, still staring.

"Well?" Keough asked.

"We can make a deal."

"What kind of deal?"

"We start the elevator," the killer said. "When it stops, we step out and go our separate ways."

"What changed your mind?"

"Not your gun, if that's what you're thinking."

"What then?"

"I kind of like you," the killer said. "We're both pros. You know there was nothing personal in what I did. I was just doing my job, what I'm paid to do, same as you."

"So?"

"So if I do you," he said, "then it becomes personal. I do you, I've got to change jobs."

"You're saying that killing me goes against your code of ethics?"

"I guess that's what I'm saying."

"I think you should have thought of that before you got into this elevator," Keough said.

"I should have done a lot of thinking before I took this job," the man said. "I hate working for amateurs. It always gets sloppy. I knew that, but . . ."

"But?"

The man shrugged. "The money was good."

"So this is your deal? I let you go, and I don't come looking for you?"

"I let *you* go—but that's about it," the man said, "or one of us doesn't leave this elevator."

"I've got to tell you," Keough said, "I give myself the best chance here. I mean, gun verses knife?"

"The knife is my weapon of choice," the man with the big hands said, "and like I said, my knife is out."

Keough felt a trickle of sweat running down the center of his back.

"How about it?"

"I can't do it."

"Why not?"

"Goes against my code of ethics."

"I thought it might."

"Yeah . . ."

Keough went for his gun as the man lunged forward with the knife. He sidestepped and lifted his left arm so that the knife would go by, but it sliced his side before he could pin the man's hand with his arm. The killer put his left hand beneath Keough's chin and tried to free his right. Meanwhile, Keough put the barrel of his gun beneath the killer's chin and cocked the hammer, and all movement stopped.

"Tell me the truth," Keough said.

"What?"

"Did you really think you could take me with the knife?"

"I really did."

Keough made a "tsk" sound with his tongue.

"Drop the knife," he said.

"Pull the trigger."

"Not if you drop the knife."

"Can't do it."

"Shit," Keough said.

"Yeah."

The killer slammed Keough back into the wall in an attempt to get his knife free, and Keough pulled the trigger, splattering the best part of the killer all over the ceiling of the elevator. . . .

* * *

When the elevator opened, Keough released the dead man's arm and stepped out as the man slumped to the floor. The knife fell and bounced out into the hall.

"Jesus," a passing young doctor said. "Are you all right?"

Keough looked down at himself and saw that he was spattered with the killer's blood.

"I'm fine," he said. "It's not my blood."

"Detective Keough?"

Keough turned his head and saw the doctor who had been treating Al Steinbach coming toward him. Not the mayor's doctor, but the regular doctor.

"I'm fine," Keough said, "but I need someone to call 911."

"I'll do it," the young doctor said.

"I'll also need this elevator closed-off."

"I'll take care of it," the doctor said. "You better let me see to that."

"What?"

"That," the doctor said, pointing.

Keough lifted his left arm and saw that he'd been cut. He hadn't felt it when it happened, but now it stung.

"Come on," the man said, "I'll take care of it. . . .

The doctor helped Keough remove his blood-soaked shirt, cleaned the wound and stitched it, then bandaged it.

"You can wash up over there," he said, pointing to a large sink in the corner.

Keough washed the blood from his hands, then looked in the mirror, and saw that he had it on his face and in his hair. The sink was large enough for him to lean into and wash himself off. There was a used towel nearby, which he thought was unsanitary for a hospital, but he used it to dry his hair as best he could.

"I think this'll fit."

He turned and saw the doctor holding a clean shirt out to him.

"It's mine," the doctor said—maybe so Keough would know it didn't come off some poor soul who didn't make it out of the emergency room.

"Thanks. Is the elevator sealed off?"

"It's closed, and one of our security force is in front of it. Also, we called 911."

"Good," Keough said, "very good. I came to see my partner, and I end up closing my case in the elevator."

"Detective," the doctor said, "I brought you in here to clean up but also to tell you something."

"Oh? What's that?"

"Well . . . it's about your partner."

"Al? What about him? I was told he was going to be fine."

The doctor didn't answer.

"He is going to be fine, isn't he?"

"I'm sorry, Detective," the doctor said. "Detective Steinbach suffered a second heart attack this afternoon, a *massive* cardiac arrest."

"Is he . . ."

"There was nothing we could do. We informed the family, but his wife didn't want us to call you on the phone. She wanted us to tell you when you got here." The doctor put his hand on Keough's shoulder and said again, "I'm so sorry."

Keough hesitated a moment. All kinds of thoughts were going through his mind. Was Al dying when he was at the Drucker house? Was Al Steinbach dying at the same moment he had saved his partner's life by sending Bumper after him?

"Detective?" He realized the doctor had spoken to him several times. "Detective Keough?"

"Doctor," Keough said, "when the officers responding to the 911 call arrive, will you see that they are brought right up here?"

"Of course."

"I'll be at the elevator, waiting."

"Yes, yes," the doctor said, "of course."

"I made a mess," Keough said to the doctor, "a big mess . . ."

Epilogue

THE KITE WAS a Chinese dragon with a long, trailing tail that enabled it to swoop and dive in the hands of someone who knew what they were doing. It was swooping and diving in Keough's hands, but he was doing it without really paying attention.

He'd been playing chess the same way with Jack Roswell that morning until the old man said, "You better give up, son. You ain't even concentratin' enough to give me a fight."

That was when he decided to go to Forest Park and try out the new Chinese dragon. There he figured he could put everything into perspective, come to terms with Al's death, decide what he wanted to do, stay where he was or take the permanent job the mayor had offered him. He'd still be a St. Louis Police Detective, but he'd be assigned to the mayor, reporting directly to him, working on cases that were most suited to his expertise.

"We can even make you a sergeant, if you want," the mayor had said.

"No," he'd replied, "that's fine, sir. If I take the job, I'd just want to be a detective."

Whatever he wanted, the mayor said. Take some time off,

mourn his dead partner, and come to a decision.

"That one's a beauty."

He turned at the sound of her voice and almost lost control of the kite. His hands automatically made the necessary adjustment to save it.

"Valerie."

"Hello, Joe. I stopped by the house, and your neighbor, Jack, told me you'd be here."

She looked lovely in a purple T-shirt and tight blue jeans. Her brown hair was pulled back from her forehead and tied into a ponytail. It was longer than he remembered, but then he hadn't seen her in a while.

"It's getting hotter," she said. "Going to be hard to fly kites pretty soon."

"I've got a pretty warm air stream up there right now," Keough said.

She put her hands in her pockets. Keough almost felt the same nervous awkwardness he'd felt in the hospital elevator three days ago.

"I've been reading about you in the paper for almost a week."

"Really? I still haven't caught up with the newspapers. What have they been saying?"

"Oh, all sorts of good and bad things I probably should have been hearing from you."

"Valerie—"

"I really think I should talk and you should listen, Joe."

"All right."

"Things haven't been going well for us, lately," she said. "Of course, we share the blame for that. I don't think I reacted very well to your diabetes."

"Val—"

"Please," she said. "I kind of have this all planned out. I don't think either one of us reacted well to the diabetes, but then as things started becoming difficult for you with your work—and I started reading about it in the newspaper—I realized you weren't coming to me to tell me about any of this. When two people are in a relationship, Joe, they're supposed to share, and you haven't done that. When Al went to the hospital, I wish you had called me . . . and when he died . . ."

She trailed off, and he looked at her and saw that she was watching the kite. He didn't bother with any kind of defense, didn't remind her that he had come to her about the sex charges, that she hadn't reacted very well to those either.

"Things started to happen so fast, Val," Keough said. "I felt . . . overcome by it all. I almost called you several times."

"You were *stabbed* three days ago," she said, her voice shaking. "I had to hear about it on TV, and you never called."

"I'm not good at this, Val," he said, shaking his head, "never have been . . ."

"You were getting good at it, Joe," she said. "Believe me, you were."

They stood there silently for a few moments, and then he said, "Do you still want to try?"

"That's not the question," she said. "The question is, do *you* still want to try? And you don't have to answer it now. I know you have a lot of decisions to make, professionally, and you're a man whose work takes precedence over his life, Joe. So you take your time, and make your decisions, and when you've decided what you want to do with your personal life, you let me know. But I want you to know something. . . . I'm not just going to be waiting. I'm going to be exploring other options, so if you're going to make up your mind, do it quickly . . . or I may not be available."

She put her hand on his arm and said, "I'm so sorry about your friend Al."

"He was my partner," he said, looking up at the kite. "Not my friend, my partner."

She shook her head. "See what I mean?"

She walked away.